The President's Head Is Missing!

Brendan Mallory

"The President's Head Is Missing!"

5th Edition, with the fucking typos fixed[1]

Cover Design by Jae Zander Kitinoja
https://linktr.ee/jzanderk

Contact me at: mallorywriter95@gmail.com

---

[1] Like, seriously… I'm not updating this thing again. If you find any more typos after this, they're in here forever.

…swear to Christ, I'm just going to pay a fucking editor to go over the next one of these…

Author's Note

Okay, we all know who this book is *really* about, right? I don't need to say it? I mean, come on… a buffoonishly incompetent, dictatorially corrupt United States President named Frank DONALD-son? It's not exactly subtle.

This book was written between 2016 and 2020, and was finally released in February 2020… RIGHT before the entire country shut down because of the Covid-19 pandemic. Which means that, because of timing issues, what was supposed to be my savage "brutal takedown" of everything that was wrong with the 2020 political landscape ended up completely missing the botched response to the pandemic, the authoritarian crackdown on peaceful Black Lives Matter protestors, and the attempted coup at the U.S. Capitol.

Oops…

Because of this, some of the edgelord bullshit in this book that seemed like the height of satire back in 2019 almost feels quaint now in retrospect. Hey, remember when watching Capitol authorities stand by and do nothing to prevent a violent power-grab seemed so ridiculous and impossible that we could all laugh about it? Remember when "the worst thing the President had ever done" was throwing a roll of paper towels at someone? What innocent times…

If I were writing this book today, I think I definitely would've changed the ending. The worse and worse Donaldson's avatar got in the real world, the more I felt like I went too *easy* on him in this book. He never *really* faces any consequences for his actions, his definitely-complicit wife and daughter both get the happiest endings possible given the circumstances, and the speech at the end about his mental illness almost sounds downright sympathetic. (To be honest, I mostly tacked that part on just to cover my ass in case the Secret Service ever came to question me about what is clearly self-insert fan-fiction about assassinating the then-sitting U.S. President.) And, not to put too fine a point on it, but even though this book was written as a comedy… I don't find anything about D****d T***p very funny anymore.

So, as you're reading this, just keep that little bit of context in the back of your mind. This book was first published at basically the last possible point in history it could've been, back when we knew the orange motherfucker was BAD, but he wasn't quite "the-blood-of-half-a-million-people-on-his-hands"-bad yet. Nowadays, in the wake of everything else he's done, I think I'd end the book with what was left of Donaldson's corpse being tied to the back of a jeep and dragged through the streets of D.C., Mussolini-style, surrounded by cheering civilians, followed by a confirmation that Hell exists in this universe and that Donaldson's putrid soul did, in fact, go there.

Ah, well. I'll save it for the sequel.

—Mallory, 2021

Author's Note II

It was supposed. To be. A SATIRE!!!

You want to know why I rushed this thing out as a self-published book in 2020 instead of trying to get it traditionally published? Because I was terrified that if I didn't get it out into the world ASAP, it would immediately become dated.

DATED.

Ha-ha. Ha-ha-ha. HA…

Ugh.

You know what, fuck it. Nothing matters anymore. Here's a list of jokes I came up with in the immediate aftermath of the actual, real-world assassination attempt:

This is the only time in human history that someone can genuinely say they missed Donald Trump.

A lot of people say Donald Trump is a bad listener, but if you show up at one of his rallies, he's happy to lend an ear!

Do you remember where you were when you idly glanced at your phone, muttered "Ah fuck, they missed," and then went on with your day?

I'm just sad that Stephen Sondheim didn't live to see this. He could've added an entire new song to Assassins*!*

This must've been an extremely harrowing experience for Trump, so I think we all owe it to him to extend the exact same grace and decorum that he extends to everyone else.

Looks like Pennsylvania just adopted a new early voting system…

Remember to vote in November, because Trump shouldn't be the only one who can dodge a bullet!

Look, I know he's desperate to appeal to the youth vote, but getting his ears pierced on live TV is just tacky!

Disney is no longer the first result that pops up when you Google, "Donald, duck!"

And, finally, here is the political cartoon I drew up and actually submitted to *The New Yorker* within 48 hours of Trump getting shot at:

"Okay, who ordered the shot, who ordered the silver bullet, and who ordered the old fashioned with blood orange?"

My name is *definitely* on a government watch list somewhere.

Try and stay safe, try and stay sane.

—Mallory, 2024

CHAPTER 1

Secretary Albertson was sitting at his desk, doing paperwork, when he heard his office door creak open and an unfamiliar voice say, "Uh, hello?"

Albertson instinctively flipped over the paper on his desk so no one could see what was printed on it and abruptly stood up in his chair.

"What? Who are you?" he said. "How did you get in here? What do you want?"

This was the first chance he got to take a good look at the person standing in his doorway. She was a short, chubby-ish Black girl dressed in a navy blue blazer and formal, businesslike dress that cut off just below the knee. She had straightened, shoulder-length hair dyed roughly the same color as her skin, and looked like she was approximately twenty years old.

"I'm sorry!" she stammered, stumbling back in surprise. "My name's Cassondra Warren, I'm supposed to be the new White House intern, they told me to show up today, but nobody came out to meet me, and the door was unlocked, so after waiting a while I just kinda came in, and… and there were two people *having sex* in the waiting room, so I didn't really want to hang around there, and… I'm sorry."

Albertson stared at her for a moment longer, then let out a long, beleaguered sigh and walked around to the front of his desk.

"No, no, that's okay," he muttered. "Your story scans. I'm just getting paranoid is all. Hell, everyone here is. I do have one question for you, though, and I need you to listen carefully, because your answer could be of the utmost importance."

Cassondra gulped.

"Yeah?" she said.

"The people screwing their brains out in the waiting room. Are they on the couch or the coffee table?"

Cassondra blinked once, wondering if she'd heard him correctly.

"Um. The coffee table."

"Oh, good," Albertson said. "The couch is a pain in the ass to clean." He shuffled back around his desk and returned to his seat, then gestured for Cassondra to sit in one of the chairs across from him. "Please," he said, then flipped his paperwork back over and resumed filling it out. Cassondra waited for a half-second before tentatively walking back into the room.

"It, um, looked like one of the bushes in the Rose Garden was on fire, too."

"Yeah, it's been on fire for a while," Albertson said, without looking up. "Don't worry, it's not hurting anything."

Cassondra carefully lowered herself into the chair Albertson had motioned to, without taking her eyes off of the man. He was an overweight Caucasian man in later middle-age, about six inches taller than her when he was standing at full height, with thinning dark gray hair. In other words, he looked like literally every other person working in the White House. She felt like she knew who he was in the back of her mind, but since she was still coming down from the craziness of her arrival, it took her another couple seconds of staring before it finally, fully registered.

"Oh my gosh," she finally said, her eyes going wide. "You're Jeff Albertson!"

"One and the same," he muttered, still not looking up from his work. He finished whatever paper he was working on, pushed it to the side, and immediately grabbed another one from the large pile next to him.

"But you're the Secretary of State!"

He let out a dry laugh.

"Yeah, this week," he said. "I was something else when I started—God, I don't even remember what—but President Donaldson fired his Secretary of State and replaced him with someone else from his cabinet, so I took *that* guy's old job, then when *he* got fired too, I got bumped up into this one, and—shit, why am I telling you all this? You must be a poly-sci major, right? You wouldn't have this job if you weren't. You already know all this crap."

"I mean, yes, I do," Cassondra said, offering her hand. "But it's still an honor to meet you, sir."

Albertson glanced up idly at her hand then returned his gaze downwards, without otherwise moving.

"Sorry," he said. "I don't do the whole 'hand shake' thing. It's nothing personal, I…" He hesitated for a moment. "I'm just kind of a germophobe, if you must know."

"A germophobe?"

"Yeah," Albertson said. "Ever since I was a kid. My father was a garbage collector. Which, I mean, is a perfectly respectable American job, of course. But one time I went to work with him when I was, like, seven, and I accidentally fell into one of the dumpsters. But he didn't see me, and almost fed me into the trash compactor in the back of the truck. So, you know, ever since then, trash and germs have been very, you know, traumatic for me."

"Oh," Cassondra said, slowly letting her arm go back down to her side. "Okay…"

Albertson lowered his head and sighed.

"I'm sorry," he said. "It's nice to meet you too, Cassondra. None of this is your fault, I'm just really busy, and kind of flustered, and wasn't expecting to have company right now."

"Oh," Cassondra said. "Well, I mean, I'm not really supposed to be here. Like, here-in-this-specific-room. I should probably go try and find he person I was actually *supposed* to meet with when I showed up this morning."

"I am almost one hundred percent certain that the person who was supposed to receive you is one of the people you saw banging on the coffee table earlier," Albertson said. "You're probably better off not interrupting them."

"Right," Cassondra muttered sheepishly. Her gaze returned to Albertson again. He was smoking. Had he always been smoking? She supposed he had been, she'd just been too keyed up to notice it when she'd first arrived. But now that the thing cigarette hanging from his mouth finally *had* registered, the smell was really starting to get to her. "Oh," she said quietly, trying to sound casual. "Are you really allowed to smoke in here?"

Albertson rolled his eyes.

"You just walked past two people doing the shag-nasty in public like it was nothing," he said, "but you're going to give me crap about a ciggie?"

"I guess not," she said. "It's just, like, if you're a health nut, I wouldn't think that you'd—"

"Germophobe, not a health nut," Albertson said. "Two totally different things."

"Oh," Cassondra said. There were a couple seconds of silence, except for the scratching of Albertson's pen on paper. "You know, now that you mention it," Cassondra finally said. "Why *were* those two on the coffee table? The couch seems a lot more comfortable."

"Probably because they're sick of me yelling at them about doing it on the couch," Albertson muttered. More silence. He finished another paper, pushed it to the side, then reached over for yet another unfinished one. As the seconds ticked on, Cassondra couldn't help herself from sneaking a peak over at what he was doing, but as soon as she saw she let out a quiet gasp.

"Oh my gosh," she said. "That's an Executive Order form! Are you *forging the President's signature?*"

"No one will know the difference," Albertson grumbled, still without looking up. "He's got the penmanship of a toddler. All I have to do is scrawl out some indecipherable scribble on the signature line, and everyone will think it was him. See?" He held up the one he was working on. Cassondra had to admit, it did look genuine. Albertson then slid it off into the "done" pile. "And since he's got the memory of a goldfish, he won't even remember what he did and didn't sign. Doing it this way is just easier on everybody."

"Jeez," Cassondra said. "I know he's not super popular, but, I mean, he *is* still the President. And he is still your boss. You sure you're okay talking about him like that?"

Albertson glared up at her and arched an eyebrow. His cigarette dropped a couple millimeters of ash onto his desk.

"You know what?" he said, abruptly standing up from his desk again. "You've never actually met President Donaldson in person, have you?"

Cassondra almost choked, and had to force herself to hide her excitement.

"I—I haven't—*no*," she said. "Do you think… Are you saying that I…?"

"Sure!" Albertson said, walking around his desk towards the office door. "His office is right down the hall! Why don't you drop in and say hi? I'll even introduce you!"

"Oh my gosh, I'm about to meet the *President!*" Cassondra giggled, scrambling up out of her chair. "Wait, are you sure he won't be too busy right now?"

Albertson rolled his eyes again.

"This is Frank Donaldson we're talking about," he said. "I promise you, that man is never busy."

Just as Albertson opened his office door, a small potbellied pig just barely past piglet-age ran by, squealing at the top of its lungs, and disappeared around a corner down the hallway. Cassondra froze in place halfway between her chair and the door, then stared at Albertson, wide-eyed.

"What the heck?"

"A bunch of the White House aides thought it would be fun to hold a luau-style barbecue a couple weeks back," Albertson grumbled, facepalming, "but there was a communication error, so the guy in charge of the meat brought a live pig instead of a dead one, and nobody had it in them to slaughter the pig, so now the pig just kinda lives here, and I'm the only one who remembers to feed the pig, because I'm the only one who remembers to do anything around here." Albertson sighed. "I don't mind the pig, really. The pig is less of an asshole than most of the humans I have to work with." Albertson paused for a moment, with an almost fond expression on his face. "I call him Squeally Dan."

"Oh," Cassondra said quietly. "Okay."

Albertson seemed to just kind of stare blankly into space for a second or two, without making a sound, then abruptly turned towards her with the warmest (clearly fake) smile he could muster.

"So!" he said, clasping his hands. "You wanted to meet the President?"

"Oh, yeah!" Cassondra said. "Of course!"

"Follow me," Albertson said, stepping out into the hallway and beckoning for her to join him. She stepped out as well and closed the door to Albertson's office behind her—or at least, the office he had been using; she wasn't sure if it was actually, officially "his" or just the most convenient room handy for his purposes—then shadowed him as he lead her down the hall, around several corners, and up to what she knew to be the entrance to the Oval Office.

Cassondra could feel her breath drawing short; she had been preparing herself for this moment ever since she'd applied to the White House internship, and as soon as she'd been accepted, she knew this was bound to happen eventually, but she still couldn't stop her heart from pounding in her chest. Albertson pushed the door open with one hand and waved for her to enter with the other. Cassondra swallowed hard, then proudly strode in for her first ever face-to-face encounter with the President of the United Sates.

"*Oh my God!*" she shrieked.

"What?" Albertson said. He had waited outside while she made her grand entrance, but now poked his head in and saw what she saw: President Donaldson was lying face-down on the floor in front of his desk, with his pants around his ankles and his pale, wrinkled ass hanging out for all to see.

"Oh," Albertson said flatly, stepping into the room and closing the door gently behind him. "Yeah, no, that's no biggie. We find him like this all the time." Cassondra just stood frozen in place while Albertson strode across the room and knelt down over the President. He's just drunk again. Or coming down from a cocaine binge. It could be any number of things, really." With a little effort, he slid his hands under President Donaldson's chest. "Here, come help me roll him over so he doesn't choke on his tongue or something."

Cassondra slowly crept over, one step at a time, until she was standing directly over the President's limp form. She hesitated.

"That smell," she said. "Did he *piss himself?*"

"Yeah, that's not super uncommon either," Albertson's grunted as he attempted to haul Donaldson up into a sitting position. "Come on, don't be squeamish! Trust me, if you keep this internship, you're gonna be doing this *a lot*."

Cassondra took in a deep, sharp breath, let it out slowly, then knelt down and grabbed the President's legs.

"*There* we go," Albertson said with a slight, self-conscious smile as they flipped Donaldson over. "Why do you think our turnover here is so fast? It's probably how you got this gig in the first place. There's no one left who even *wants* this internship."

"*His dick. Is on. My hand.*" Cassondra winced, scrunching her eyes shut.

"Well, if you'd gotten to him first, you would've been able to pick which end you wanted to carry," Albertson said, "but if I'm the one who has to get this shit started, I'm going to pick the chest."

"It… it's *wet,*" Cassondra whined, turning her head as far away as it could. "It's *cold.*"

"What?" Albertson said, abruptly snapping to attention. "Oh, that's not good. Come on, set him back down, let's prop him up against his desk."

Cassondra abruptly dropped the President's legs and backed away while Albertson pushed his limp torso up to the hard, flat mahogany. In this position, the bottom of Donaldson's trademark abnormally long red necktie draped low enough to obscure his genitals from sight, and Cassondra found herself quietly thanking the universe for small mercies.

"Oh, shit," Albertson breathed, pressing two fingers against the President's neck. He gestured towards Cassondra without looking at her. "Do you have, like, a makeup compact or something? Something with a mirror?"

"Y-y-yeah," she stammered. Cassondra could feel her eyes starting to glaze over as she mechanically reached down and started fishing around through her purse on autopilot. She didn't walk back over. When she found her compact, she just knelt down and slid it across the floor over to Albertson. He snatched it up off the ground and held the mirror under the President's nose. Cassondra could see Albertson's body language gradually stiffening as the seconds ticked by without any fog appearing on the mirror. She knew what he was going to say long before the arm holding the compact fell limply to his side, but she could still feel the lump forming in her throat as he stood up, closed his eyes, and let out a long, weary sigh.

"He's dead," Albertson said quietly, turning towards her. He opened his eyes, large and watery with barely-contained shock. "The President of the United States is dead."

CHAPTER 2

Cassondra sat on the floor of the Oval Office, opposite the President's desk, hugging her knees and slowly rocking back and forth, her eyes not focused on anything in particular.

"I touched a dead man's cum," she whispered quietly under her breath. "I touched a dead man's cum. I touched a dead man's cum. I touched a dead man's cum."

"Okay, this is bad," Albertson said, stroking his chin as he paced back and forth on the other side of the room. He was on his third cigarette since they'd entered the room. "I mean, *obviously* this is bad. President Frank Donaldson is dead. What does that mean, now? What do we need to do?"

"H-h-how?" Cassondra stammered. She tried to look up at Albertson, but kept her eyes unfocused so her brain didn't have to register the dead body in the room any more than was absolutely necessary. "How did he die?"

Albertson paced back over to where Donaldson's body was still propped up and gazed down at him with a detached, only *slightly* curious expression.

"You remember the position he was lying in when we found him?" Albertson said, kneeling down. "His pants down, with his hand kind of tucked under him at crotch-level?" Albertson stood back up. "My best guess, I think he had a heart attack while he was jacking off."

"What's that?" Cassondra said, pointing with a trembling hand to a piece of paper lying on the floor near where they'd found the body. (She could tell because it was near the stains on the carpet.) Albertson walked over and knelt down again.

"It's his professional headshot," Albertson said, picking up the paper off the floor and standing up again, "from back when he was an actor. President Donaldson had a heart attack while jacking off to a picture of himself." Albertson just stared off into space for a second, then sighed and lowered his head. "Yeah... that scans." Albertson stalked back over and laid the picture over the President's face, tastefully covering up the less-than-flattering expression his facial muscles had frozen into. "I mean, have you seen the fucker's eating habits? Nothing but fast food and pizza! Honestly, I'm kind of surprised it took *this* long for his heart to give out."

"The President is dead," Cassondra said slowly.

"Yes, we've gone over that part already," Albertson said. "Do try to keep up." He glanced over at her for a moment, then let out a long, slow sigh and massaged his forehead with one hand. "I'm sorry," he said. "I shouldn't be so snarky. It's how I deal with stress. This is your first dead body, isn't it?"

Cassondra nodded slowly, still without looking directly at him *or* the body.

"Yeah, popping your corpse cherry is always a little rough. Hell, I'd probably be worried about you if you *weren't* freaking out right now." He puffed on his cigarette a couple times. "So, you, like, want me to get you a water bottle or something?"

"What are we going to do?!" Cassondra blurted out, suddenly scrambling to her feet. "How is the country going to—we, we need to—" For the first time, her head turned to look at the body, but her eyes still didn't exactly seem to "see" it. She started staggering towards it. "I—I know CPR! We should try giving him mouth-to-mouth!"

"Whoa, whoa, whoa," Albertson said, sidestepping smoothly in between her and Donaldson. "He'd been dead for at least an hour before we showed up, he is way beyond that kind of help." He glanced back at the President over his shoulder. "Besides, even when he was alive, I promise you, you did not want to be putting your lips on *that*."

Albertson shuddered to himself for a moment, then turned his attention back to her. "Look, *you* don't need to do anything. You're the intern. I just called his daughter Luna, so she and her little weasel of a husband should be here any minute now. The three of us will figure out what the next steps are."

"I need to get out of here," Cassondra stammered, whipping around and stumbling towards the door. "I, I, I can't breathe, I need air, I'm in here with the *body* of the *President*, who's *dead*, and they're going to *find* me here, and they're going to start asking *questions*, and, and, and, and—"

She felt Albertson's hand clasp down on her shoulder, hard.

"*Hey*," he said. There wasn't a hint of the mildly amused humor or softness he'd occasionally addressed her with earlier. "You're right about how serious this is, but I can't just let you make a run for it. You *are* probably going to have to answer some questions, but you just walked in here, same as I did. All you need to do is tell the truth, tell them how we wandered in and found the fucker with his dick in his hands, and that's it."

"*No*," Cassondra gasped, wrapping her hand around Albertson's wrist. "Let *go* of me!" She wrenched his hand off of her shoulder and slammed it against the wall so hard she could hear the face of his wristwatch *crunch* on the impact. Albertson suddenly pulled his arm out of her grasp and stumbled back, staring down at his mangled watch with wide-eyed shock. That brought her back for a second. "Oh!" Cassondra gasped. "I'm sorry, I didn't mean to! Is it expensive, or…?"

Cassondra's words caught in her throat. Before her eyes, as Albertson fiddled with his watch, his entire appearance *flickered*. His face became pixelated for a moment, like the filter that cheap reality shows use to hide someone's identity, then came back into focus. He turned

African American for a second, then Asian, then back to Caucasian. The entire time, as Cassondra watched, sparks were coming out of Albertson's watch and he was stammering, "Shit, shit, shit, shit, shit," under his breath. Finally, with one last loud, electrical *pop* from the watch, Secretary of State Jeff Albertson disappeared from view.

The creature that stood in his place still had the same basic proportions—two arms, two legs, and a little bit of a beer gut. And it was still wearing Albertson's suit. But its skin… Albertson's skin was now a deep shade of blue-teal, slightly metallic, and covered in fine, reptilian scales. His eyes—all four of them—were solid yellow, sort of the color of snot, and his nose was smashed-in and surrounded by wrinkles kind of like the face of a pug or a bulldog. He didn't have ears or hair, but a ring of small black goat-like horns circling the top of his head, pointing upward towards the ceiling. He stood there, frozen in place, staring at her, a cigarette still dangling out of the corner of his mouth even while a thin forked tongue quickly darted in and out.

"*What the fuck?!*" Cassondra shrieked, scrambling back so frantically that she almost tripped over a piece of furniture.

"No, it's still me!" Albertson said, reaching out and taking a half-step forward, then returning his attention to his watch. "Hold on! Shit, shit, shit…"

"Who are you?!" Cassondra screamed. "*What* are you? What have you done with Secretary Albertson?!"

"I *am* Secretary Albertson," he shouted back with an almost pleading tone in his voice. "I always have been! I mean, I didn't *replace* him or anything, I—God dammit…" Albertson pulled a screwdriver out of his coat pocket and pried the face off his watch, then started poking at the inner machinery. Finally, Albertson's human appearance flickered back into view, blotting out his monstrous true form, and he snapped the face of his watch back closed and slipped the screwdriver back into his pocket. "*There* we go," he gasped, relieved. The cigarette in his mouth had just about reached the butt, so he pulled it out of his mouth, and flicked it away so that it bounced off the side Donaldson's limp, puffed-up cheek and onto the floor. Then he stomped it out into the carpet, and pulled another one out of his coat. "Okay," he muttered as he slid it into his mouth, lit the tip, and glanced back up at Cassondra. "Where were we?"

"WHAT THE ACTUAL FUCK IS GOING ON?!"

"Right, right, right," Albertson said. He glanced back down at the President's body, then back up at her. "God, this is, like, the worst possible time to do this. Shit, okay, extremely short version: there is no 'real' Jeff Albertson. He didn't exist until I created this identity as a disguise. I haven't hurt anyone, and I have no intention of hurting anyone." He had a nervous, guilty expression, and looked like he *should* be sweating, but he wasn't. With what she knew about him now, Cassondra wasn't sure if he even *could* sweat. "I *promise* to you I am not dangerous, but you're currently the only person on this planet who knows what I really am, and I really, really, *really* need you to keep it under wraps, especially *now*, or else things are going to get so, so, so much worse than they already are, and—"

"All right, what's going on?" Luna Donaldson said, throwing the Oval Office doors open and striding into the room. Her husband, Jacob Kirkman, scurried in after her, making sure that the doors closed behind them. "You said my father was—*shit*." Her eyes had just settled on the body, and so had her husband's. As soon as Jacob Kirkman saw the President lying dead in front of him, his eyes bugged out of his head, then he abruptly fell to his knees and started hysterically sobbing.

"Jesus," Albertson said. "I didn't know Frank and Jacob were so close."

"Oh, they weren't," Luna said. "Jacob just knows that now that my father can't protect him anymore, he's probably going to be indicted." Luna took a couple tentative steps over to the body and nudged it lightly with her foot, her face betraying nothing more than an expression of calm, passive disgust. "So, the stupid motherfucker finally wanked himself to death, huh?"

"It would appear that way, yes," Albertson said.

Cassondra made a small, involuntary whine at the back of her throat.

"How can you all just stand over his *fresh corpse* and talk about him like that?!" she gasped.

"He was my father, dear," Luna said. "He actually *did* fuck my mother." She abruptly turned towards Albertson and pointed back at Cassondra with her thumb. "Who the hell is she?"

"New White House intern," Albertson said, his mannerisms suddenly cool and businesslike. "Having a hell of a first day."

"Lovely. Can she keep a secret?"

"I don't know," Albertson said, staring pointedly at Cassondra with wide, desperate eyes and gritted teeth. "*Can you?*"

Cassondra stared back at him for several long seconds, then started nodding quickly.

"Good," Luna said. "Maybe we won't have to kill her, then. Disposing of one body is difficult enough, it gets exponentially harder with each new one you add."

"Nah, she's a good kid," Albertson said, giving her one last lingering glance just to make sure. "Wouldn't be surprised if all the shit she's seen today has kind of broken her brain, though. So, you know, if she says anything *really* crazy, like she's been having *hallucinations* or seeing *UFO's* or something, that's probably why."

"Jeffery?"

"Yes, Luna?"

"Why are we still talking about the servant girl instead of figuring out what we're going to do about my father?" She snapped her fingers. "Jacob, open up the secret tunnel heading towards Muntz's room."

Jacob Kirkman nodded silently, then scurried over to the wall and pulled down on one of the lighting fixtures like a lever. There was a mechanical whir-click sound in the walls, like ancient clockwork, and a trap door suddenly opened up in the floor on the other side of the room.

"Right," Luna said. "I'll let the two of you boys carry him down. Unless the *intern* is stronger than she looks?" She said the word "intern" like she could barely pronounce both syllables without throwing up.

"No," Albertson said. "I think she's already come into contact with him a little more than she deserves."

Luna glanced over and gave him a questioning look. His hand mimed a "jacking off" motion in the empty air in front of his crotch. Luna's posture abruptly stiffened, and she looked even closer to throwing up than she had a second ago.

"*Eewww*," she said, quickly shaking her head. "*After* he was dead? That's a fate I wouldn't wish on my worst enemy. Here, have some Purell, dear." She slipped a small, clear bottle out of her purse, leaned over, and squirted a blob into Cassondra's hands. It was the same texture as the reason Cassondra needed it in the first place, which didn't make her feel a hell of a lot better. Cassondra gulped as she slowly rubbed her hands together, while on the other side of the room Albertson and Jacob hauled President Donaldson's body up off the floor and Luna watched over them like a stern foreman.

"Um, did you say Muntz's room?" Cassondra stuttered. "Like, as in Patrick Muntz? The Vice President?"

Luna just barely gave Cassondra the dignity of casting her a condescending glance, then immediately rolled her eyes.

“Is she going to be with us the entire time?” Luna snapped.

“Well,” Albertson said, “unless you think it’s a good idea to release a shell-shocked intern who knows the President is dead out into the wild…”

“All right, fine, you’ve made your point,” Luna grumbled. She glanced back at Cassondra, but her expression still intimated that the mere act of having to do so made her feel physically ill. “Yes, dear,” she said. “We’re talking about Patrick Muntz. *As in the Vice President.*” That last part had been done in a mocking impression of Cassondra’s voice, but Cassondra was too strung-out at this point to notice or care. On the other side of the room, Jacob and Albertson had finally wrestled the President’s body into a position where they could comfortably carry it between them—Albertson still had the chest, letting Jacob carry the legs this time—and were starting down the staircase that lead underground into… *wherever* the trapdoor lead. Still grudgingly paying attention to Cassondra, Luna cocked her head and smiled with faux-sweetness. “Would you like your chance to finally meet *him*, too?”

CHAPTER 3

"So, this should be basic civics knowledge that every fourth grader knows," Luna Donaldson said, "but in this administration, it never hurts to make sure." They were walking down a long, stone staircase that spiraled further and further underground from the trap door in the Oval Office. Jacob and Albertson were in front, carrying the President's body, with Luna behind them and Cassondra pulling up the rear. They had, fortunately, managed to get Donaldson's pants back on properly before moving him, in a vain attempt to keep the mess from getting any worse than it already was. The only light in the passageway was provided by open-air torches hanging from wall sconces placed intermittently along their path; Cassondra thought it made the shadows dance around them in weird and eerie formations. "You know who's supposed to replace the President—my father—if he dies in office, right?"

"Yeah, of course," Cassondra said. Just the act of walking down all these stairs and keeping her body moving was helping her regain her senses a little bit. "The Vice President, Patrick Muntz."

"Exactly," Luna muttered. "And therein lies the problem."

"Problem?" Cassondra said as they reached the bottom of the staircase and emerged out into a large underground stone chamber. In the craggy stone walls that surrounded them were several other passageways that Cassondra assumed led to other locations around Washington, D.C., but those other tunnels weren't what she was paying attention to. Instead, Cassondra's gaze was laser-focused on the large iron cage in the center of the room, like the kind old circuses used to show off captive animals. Inside the cage, a human figure was hanging upside down from the bars that closed in its ceiling, completely naked except for what looked like an uncomfortably small thong. There was nothing else in the cage, no furniture or appliances or anything, except for a small metal bucket in the corner that was swarming with flies, which Cassondra figured must be the captive figure's bathroom. He was already staring at them when they entered the room, and as soon as they met his gaze he twisted in place and lowered himself down to the ground in one graceful, spiderlike motion. He didn't break eye contact once, and he didn't blink. It had taken Cassondra's eyes a minute or so to adjust to the dim light in the chamber, but now that she was able to get a horrifying clear look, there was no doubt in her mind that the twisted figure in the cage was none other than Vice President Patrick Muntz.

As soon as he and Jacob Kirkman propped Donaldson's body in a sitting position up against the wall, Albertson raised a closed fist to his mouth and lightly coughed a couple times, then abruptly doubled over and started hacking out the ugliest smoker's cough Cassondra had ever heard, causing everyone in the chamber to jump.

"Can't fuckin' breathe down here," Albertson wheezed as he shakily pulled a cigarette out of his coat and stuck it between his lips. He lit it and took a long, slow breath in, then sighed with satisfaction. Curiously, no visible smoke came back out of his mouth as he exhaled. "Oh, God," he muttered. "Much better."

Luna rolled her eyes, then drew Cassondra's attention back to the man in the cage.

"What you've seen on TV," Luna said flatly, almost nonchalantly, "is Patrick Muntz after he's been *heavily* sedated, and prepped by a team of psychologists for several hours to appear in public. This is the *real* Patrick Muntz."

"*Heh-heh-heh…*" Muntz chuckled, his voice echoing out of his throat in a low, dry rattle. "Ol' Frankie

Donaldson's little *bitch* Luna, coming to pay me a visit. Luna, Luna… *Luna the Tuna*. Do you smell like *tuna*, little girl?" He reached a single long, talon-like hand out through the bars, and even though Cassondra was already standing well out of his reach, she still instinctively took another step back. "Looks like you've brought me a little *treat… treat… treat…*" Muntz hissed. He stared coldly at Cassondra, his eyes drilling through her soul, and licked his lips. "Better not leave me alone with her," he said, pausing to let out a light, breathy laugh. "Mommy doesn't like me to be left alone *with girls*."

Patrick Muntz suddenly started violently convulsing in place, like he was having a seizure, and then slammed his head into one of the metal bars of the cage as hard as he could. "Oh God!" he screamed, somewhere between agony and ecstasy. "I can hear the voices again, Luna!" He bashed his head into the bar again. "It's… it's Jesus!" *Bash*. "Jesus is telling me to do things—*nasty* things—to the young Black lady!" *Bash*. By now, there was a long, vertical welt running down Patrick Muntz's face, and blood was trickling from a laceration in his forehead. Muntz just stood there, staring at them, trembling, until the blood trickled down to the corner of his mouth. He licked in some of the blood, gave one last orgasmic shudder, then resumed his cold, unblinking gaze to Cassondra. "You wouldn't want me to disobey *Jesus*, now would you, little girlie-girl?" he whispered.

Albertson tentatively reached out for Cassondra's shoulder.

"I, um, I think we've seen *enough*—"

"What's that?" Cassondra said weakly, pointing to Muntz's crotch. Now that her eyes had adjusted even more and she'd (unfortunately) gotten a closer look, it didn't look like he was wearing a thong after all. It looked like some solid, rectangular object was being held in front of his crotch with a leather belt. "What's he wearing?"

"That's, um, that's a Bible," Albertson said sheepishly.

"He's wearing a Bible..." Cassondra muttered slowly, "...as a loincloth."

"Yes. Um. We call it his 'Bible belt.' "

Cassondra just stared at the hunched, crazed animal that was the Vice President for several long moments.

She blinked.

She blinked again.

"We cannot let this man become President," she finally muttered.

"Yeah, no shit," Luna said coldly. "That's why we need to keep my father's death under wraps for as long as possible. If people find out, we're going to have no choice but to honor that line of succession, and put... *that*," she gestured loosely towards Muntz, "in the Oval Office. I've got a plan, though. We just need to keep my father's body hidden down here in the catacombs while Jacob and I start going around and—"

"Wait, wait, wait," Cassondra said quickly. "But we just brought his body right past the Vice President! Now that Muntz has seen the President's body, won't he know it's his turn and demand to be put... in... power...?"

Behind Cassondra, Vice President Muntz had begun dancing dreamily around the inside of his cage and singing *I'm a Little Teapot*. He had taken off his 'Bible Belt,' and was now completely naked. And had an erection.

"I'm a little tea-*pot*, short and stout," his voice echoed out into the chamber, unnaturally high-pitched and shrill. "*This* is my handle," he said, grabbing his penis and starting to vigorously masturbate, "and... this... is... my... *spout*..."

"Somehow, I'm not worried about him running to the press," Luna said dryly. "But it's still only a matter of time before someone notices my father's absence, so time is of the essence." She was already walking towards another one of the many tunnels leading out of the central chamber. "Jacob and I will go meet with the Speaker of the House—Christ, I can't even keep track, who's the Speaker right now?"

"Leo Bronstein," Albertson said.

Luna paused for a moment and visibly shuddered, then instantly brought herself back to the task at hand.

"Yes, right, we'll talk to Bronstein," Luna said, "see if we can get some balls rolling. Albertson, you know where the bunker is, right?"

"Yes, Ma'am."

"Great. You and the girl take my father's body there until further notice. We'll reconvene at—"

"You," Vice President Muntz said, his eyes narrowing as his gaze locked onto Jacob Kirkman. "You brought the *boy*, Luna. The one who follows you around. I *like* the boy." He took a couple shaky steps forward, moving jerkily and unnaturally, like he was on marionette strings, until he finally pressed himself up against the bars of his cage and reached out in Kirkman's direction. "I'm gonna eat yer kidneys, *boy*." He hissed, licking his lips. "Eat 'em with ketchup and barbecue sauce. Jesus *wants* me to eat your kidneys. Soft, tender boy-flesh… kidneys are where the *flavor* is!"

"Oh for fuck's sake, let's just get out of here!" Luna said, grabbing Jacob's hand and pulling him out of the chamber. "We all know what we need to do, now *go!*"

CHAPTER 4

Daphne Gould was out working in the field when she saw the big red pickup truck come rumbling down the dirt road, kicking up a cloud of dust behind it. At first it showed no real reason to concern her; people got lost on these back roads fairly frequently and had to stop and ask for directions, or it could even be someone new coming to join the community. Either way, it wasn't her job to deal with them, and she had to have the entire field seeded before sundown to make sure their crops came in on time.

Then she saw thick, white smoke come pouring out from beneath the truck's hood, and before her brain had even had time to fully form the thought, she had already dropped what she was doing and started running over.

Daphne reached the truck just as it rolled to a stop several yards away from the farmhouse and the driver came stumbling out of the cab, coughing hoarsely and trying to wave the smoke out of his face with a baseball cap.

"Sir?" she said nervously. She didn't know exactly what to say next. *Are you okay?* seemed like a stupid question, and so did *Do you need any help?* She decided to just keep quiet until the man stopped coughing long enough to vocalize whatever he needed himself.

"Water," the man said, his voice still rough and raw. "Bring me as much water as you can carry, *now!*"

Daphne froze in place for a second, then suddenly bolted back towards the farmhouse. Even though the house had plumbing, they still kept several five-gallon jugs of water in the basement for emergencies, the kind that office buildings used in their water coolers. Daphne grabbed one of these, hefted it up onto her shoulder, and hobbled lopsidedly back to the truck as fast as she could with the added weight.

The driver ran over to meet her halfway there, grabbed the water just off of her shoulder, and ran back to his truck with it, having already somehow managed to get the truck's hood open while she was in the cellar, even as the white smoke continued to billow out. He ripped the top of the water jug and tipped it over the engine of his car, only releasing a little water at a time to sizzle and pop against the scalding-hot metal. Daphne could hear the harsh *hiss* all the way from where she was standing, and watched as the cloud of smoke and steam ballooned in size before finally dissipating into nothing. By the time she had walked back within earshot, the driver was leaning idly against the side of the truck wiping sweat off his brow as whatever water hadn't immediately evaporated upon contact with the engine slowly trickled its way through the car and pooled around the bottom of the half-depleted jug next to him.

"Radiator," the driver grumbled. His voice was a little deeper now, and nowhere near as wheezy. "Or maybe I blew a hose or something, I don't know." He closed his eyes and put a hand wearily on his temple. "I'll need to wait until it cools down a little more before I can take a look in there. But I was out on the main road when the engine started overheating, 'check engine' light started blinking like crazy, and, well… you saw how much smoke was pouring out of this thing. Figured I was trapped out here in the middle of nowhere until I saw your little house there just *barely* on the horizon—it's a miracle I made it as close to you as I did before she finally gave out on me." His hand thumped appreciably on the side of the truck, then he shook his head with a self-conscious smile and held it out to her. "I'm sorry, I never got the chance to properly thank you for the water, or even introduce myself. Name's Tyler LaFuente."

"Daphne Gould," she said, gingerly taking his hand. "You're welcome. And you're right, this place *is* pretty secluded. What're you doing all the way out here?"

Tyler smiled like he had a dirty little secret.

"Oh, you know… just seeing the country," he said. "But not just the parts that are planted around the big freeways. Those are the parts they *want* you to see. I'm checking out all the places that are a little more out-of-the-way. You know, 'off the grid.' " He gave her a playful wink. "*Hidden*."

"Well, you can't get much further out of the way than here," Daphne muttered. As she talked, she heard the door to the farmhouse open and close behind her. *About damn time someone noticed,* she thought. Tyler seemed relatively harmless, but she still didn't particularly relish the idea of being out here alone with a stranger for an extended period of time.

"Can I help you?" Sal said and he strode up to them, a big, barrel-chested man with a thick moustache that would've looked stupid on anyone other than him. "I heard some of the commotion from inside, is everything all right?"

"His car broke down," Daphne said.

"Truck overheated," Tyler corrected her. "I'm pretty good with engines, should be able to get it up and running again myself once I figure out what the problem is. But that's gonna take at least an hour or two if we're lucky, and I'm kinda stuck her until then."

"Not a problem, stranger," Sal said. "We were just about to sit down for lunch. Would you care to join us?"

Tyler and Daphne both had to go upstairs and wash up before coming down to eat, so they were the last two to make it to the table, and as soon as Tyler sat down, his gaze slowly circling around the table at everyone else in attendance, Daphne could immediately tell what he was thinking. Daphne and Sal were both Caucasian and big-boned; they weren't related but could easily pass as father and daughter or uncle and niece to the untrained eye. Melisa was African-American and still in the early stages of her transition, so she still had what some would consider a relatively 'masculine' appearance despite her long hair and traditionally feminine clothing. Wafiquah was wearing her full burqa—she occasionally relaxed her wardrobe when she was in the house, but having a stranger present made it non-negotiable—and her girlfriend Nasli, who was visiting for the day, had been holding her hand and giving Tyler a death-glare since he'd entered the room. And no one could tell who or what Jacinta was at first glance, but it was clear that they weren't any more "conventional" than anyone else at the table.

Tyler's eyes kept darting from person to person to person as he slowly lowered himself down into the chair, and for a second Daphne thought he was going to let it pass without comment, but then just as he was getting settled in he just barely opened his mouth and mumbled, "You people aren't a family, are you?"

Daphne winced, and she saw Sal and Melisa both react the same way. Nasli started to stand up like she was going to march over and kick Tyler's ass, but Wafiquah kept her in line with a hand squeeze and a sharp glance.

"Er, we are not directly blood-related to one another, no," Sal said, walking back from the oven with a steaming casserole dish full of curried cauliflower in his hands. "But in many ways, we are closer to one another than to the people who are."

"Most of us aren't close with our birth families," Melisa said curtly. "For one reason or another."

"Aw, no," Tyler mumbled, closing his eyes and lowering his head into his hands. "Don't tell me I wandered into a cult!"

Wafiquah suddenly burst out laughing, then immediately put a hand to her mouth and glanced nervously around the room, embarrassed. Nasli was already leaning over the table and piling cauliflower onto her plate.

"Er, *no*," Sal said. "We accept people of all creeds and backgrounds, and openly encourage them to worship as they see fit. I guess the best way to describe what we are would be a *collective* of—"

"A commune," Jacinta said flatly. "But most Americans are afraid of that word, so Sal doesn't like to talk about it without getting his thesaurus out."

Sal hesitated for a second, then nodded graciously.

"...yes," he said. "We are a group of people who have all independently witnessed the many failures of late-stage capitalism and have recognized just how destructive a force it can be on the lives of good, hard-working people, so we have chosen to remove ourselves from it as much as possible. Our aim is to be completely self-sufficient and sustainable out here—we get our power from solar panels on the roof, use collected rainwater as much as we can, grow our own food—that's what Daphne was doing out front when she saw you approaching."

Daphne smiled in spite of herself.

"Yeah," she muttered. "And I'd better double-time it this afternoon if I want to get everything planted before sundown."

"You can do it, Daphne," Sal said. "I believe in you." He returned his attention to Tyler. "I hope you understand, we do not sit in judgment of you—"

"I do," Nasli said, raising her hand without looking up from her plate. Sal just rolled his eyes.

"We understand not everyone is in a position to make the same sacrifices we have—"

"I mean, they might be sooner or later," Jacinta cut in. "After climate change renders every other lifestyle option unsustainable."

Sal sighed.

"Okay, *yes*, that is true," he muttered. "But my point for Mr. LaFuente is, I don't mean for any of this to sound like a 'recruitment' or 'sales pitch.' "

"Yeah," Wafiquah muttered. "The whole concept of a 'sales pitch' kinda goes against the whole 'anti-capitalist' thing."

"What I'm trying to say," Sal continued, "is that I can sense your apprehension, and I assure you it's unfounded." A slight smile. "This isn't some 'horror movie' setup. All we want is to help you fix your car and be on your way."

Tyler sat in place, arms out flat on the table, butt glued to his seat, completely unmoving except for his head as it turned to look at each individual person seated around the table. Then he scrunched his eyes shut and started shaking his head as a high, thin laugh escaped from his throat.

"Oh, this is just *great!*" he said. "So I take it you fellas have got a pretty close eye on the political landscape right now, huh?"

Daphne was pretty sure the word "fellas" misgendered at least half the people sitting at the table, but she elected not to bring it up for the moment.

"That is another facet of our lives here, yes," Sal said. "We attend every single protest we are able to, demanding immigration and civil rights and environmental reform, and we go canvassing in all the neighboring towns before every single election to make sure as many citizens as possible are registered—and willing—to vote. Not to mention that Wafiquah here has just recently passed the Bar Exam, and has been in contact with other lawyers across the country, mounting a series of cases against the Donaldson Administration and its numerous human rights abuses."

"Gonna make the fat-cat motherfuckers *bleed*," Wafiquah muttered through a mouthful of cauliflower.

"We are constantly looking for ways to expand our outreach and improve out political pull," Sal continued. "But as you can see, there aren't *really* that many of us here. While, again, we are by no means recruiting, we are always more than happy to welcome another member to our household-slash-organization, if you were interested in—"

"No, no, it's nothing like that," Tyler said. "It's just, you all seem like a cool-enough bunch of people, you seem really *with it*, you know? So I think you'll all be able to appreciate the *real* reason I'm out here."

Several people at the table exchanged nervous glances with each other.

"Okay?" Sal said skeptically.

"See, what you're doing out here is great," Tyler said. "Or, I mean, what you're *trying* to do, at least. But how effective is it, really? Donaldson doesn't care if a bunch of people with signs don't like him. Hell, he doesn't even care about the courts! He's just gonna barrel on ahead and keep on doing whatever the fuck he wants to do, no matter who tells him no, and he's never gonna face any consequences for it, because rich fucks like him never do. And voting? *Please*. Everyone knows the elections are rigged! He didn't even win the popular vote this time, and there he still is up there in the Oval Office. All the pansy-ass shit you're doing out here—as well-intentioned as it is—it's never going to make any sort of meaningful difference."

Everyone at the table just sat there, staring at him, stunned. Only Nasli appeared to be genuinely paying attention.

"That's why," Tyler continued, "I'm going to do the one thing that actually will make a difference, the one thing that actually *will* end Frank Donaldson's reign of terror and make sure he faces some actual fucking consequences for what he's done to this country and this planet." Tyler stood up from his chair and put his hands on his hips with a satisfied smile. "I got a bunch of guns loaded up into the back of my truck, and I'm driving all the way to

Washington, D.C. along all these hidden little back roads so I can *put a bullet right between Frank Donaldson's beady little eyes*."

"*Woo!*" Nasli said enthusiastically. She lit a cigarette lighter and held it up into the air. "Fuck yeah!"

"N-n-no," Daphne said, slowly pushing herself back from the table. "You can't seriously be talking about *assassinating the President of the United States?*"

"Why not?" Tyler said sharply, his eyes locking onto her. "You know the shit he's done, the shit he still is doing. He's mass-deporting war refugees back to countries where they'll be killed by the constant fighting, he's denying foreign aid money to our allies that need it, he's whipping the little Nazis who support him up into lynch mobs, he's speeding up the destruction of the environment to the point that there isn't going to be a goddamn planet left for the generation after ours, he's *locking up children in cages* down at the border—this man is a literal supervillain. He is evil, he is *literally* destroying the planet we all live on, and for the amount of blood on his hands, he *deserves* to die."

By the time Tyler finished talking, he was panting and sweating where he stood; it was impossible for him to talk about this without getting physically worked up. Everyone else in the room was dead silent. Most of them hadn't even touched the food yet. In the kitchen, a timer on the oven dinged, indicating the next course Sal was cooking was ready. Sal didn't notice.

"No," Daphne stammered. "I'm sorry, but *no*. I don't care how bad you think someone is, how much you think someone quote-unquote '*deserves*' it, you just—you can't legitimately view yourself as having the right to take another human being's life!"

"Aw, c'mon," Tyler groaned. "That son of a bitch only barely counts as human at this point!" He leaned in as close to her as he could with the table between them and stared directly into her eyes. "Look, I hate to bring this up, I really do, but just looking at you, I can tell… you're a transgender woman, aren't you Daphne?"

Everyone in the room stiffened. The atmosphere between them went down a couple of degrees. It was hardly a secret; Daphne was usually pretty cagey about her life pre-transition, but not about the fact that it had happened. And she'd long ago accepted that part of this lifestyle would mean she wouldn't have as much ready access to cosmetics, making it a little harder to 'pass' than she would've liked, but she usually didn't interact with people from outside the farm often enough for it to matter. Her friends around her were alternately staring at Tyler with wide-eyed shock or narrowing their eyes like they were already mentally outlining their very loud, multi-paragraph responses to him.

"Yes," Daphne finally said, coldly. "I transitioned two years ago. I don't see how that's relevant."

"It's *relevant* because that bigot in the Oval Office has been stripping away LGBT rights since day one!" Tyler said. "You of all people should care about what's going on!"

"I *do*," Daphne said sharply. "That's why I'm *here*."

"I'm sorry," Sal cut in before Tyler could continue any further. "But we cannot possibly condone what you are planning, Mr. LaFuente. That's just not how we operate. What you're describing is *barbaric*."

"I dunno," Jacinta said quietly. "I mean, I've certainly heard *worse* ideas…"

" *'Cinta*," Melisa hissed. "*Not helping*."

"Don't worry," Tyler said. "I don't expect you to 'condone' it, at least not publicly. But, on the same note, is there anyone at this table with the inclination—or the ability, for that matter—to actually get in my way or try to stop me?"

Everyone at the table was silent. Tyler bowed slightly.

"That's what I thought," he said. "So your protestations are moot anyway." He smiled at them warmly. "Just as with *your* solution to the crazy, fucked-up world we live in, I know *my* solution isn't for everyone. In fact, that's exactly why I've taken it upon myself. I'm ex-military—U.S. Marine Corps, thank you very much—so I know *how* to pull it off. And I'm not married, I don't have any surviving family, not a lot of friends to speak of, so no one's going to care if I go to prison, or miss me if I get killed doing this. I sacrifice myself willingly, for what I know to be the greater good." He pushed his empty chair back into the table. "And while I am grateful for your hospitality, I'm afraid I don't have much of an appetite right now. Plus, I would of course like to get back on the road as quickly as possible." He turned his back to them and strolled away from them slowly, leisurely, without a care in the world. "So if you'll all kindly excuse me, I think I'm going to head on out and start working on my car."

CHAPTER 5

"The Bunker" that Luna Donaldson had mentioned was exactly what it sounded like: an underground military bunker accessible through the same network of tunnels that apparently connected most of the governmental buildings in Washington, D.C. Getting President Donaldson's body in there had been less trouble than Cassondra had expected—she apparently had more upper-body strength than Jacob Kirkman did, as Albertson kept remarking that she was able to pick up a lot more of the slack than he had been—and they now had the body laid out on a coroner's slab in the bunker's laboratory, still fully clothed, because neither of them wanted to cross that bridge until it was *absolutely* necessary.

After both washing their hands for a *long* time, Cassondra and Albertson were now sitting limply in rolling office chairs on either side of the morgue, just kind of staring in each other's general direction with glazed-over, unfocused eyes. Albertson was, of course, smoking a cigarette.

"So," Cassondra finally muttered, her voice quiet and far-away. "Is now a good time to finally ask?"

Albertson glanced up at her.

"Ask what?" he grumbled.

"Ask *why in the sweet holy mother of fucks* you turned into a blue lizard-dog-person when your watch got damaged?"

"Ah, *fuck*," Albertson groaned, reaching up and rubbing his face with both hands. "Shit. All right. Fine." He lowered his hands away from his face and let out a long sigh. "Okay. How good are you at keeping a secret?"

Cassondra burst out laughing.

"Oh, *you* have no fucking idea," she said.

Albertson cocked his head, puzzled.

"Um," he muttered. "Okay?"

Cassondra shook her head, stifled her last couple chuckles, and cleared her throat.

"Ahem. Yes," she said. "I am very, *very* good at keeping secrets."

Albertson sighed again.

"Okay, fine," he said. He seemed to be marshaling his strength before he said whatever he needed to say. "Now I need you to promise not to freak out, okay? This is going to sound pretty freaky at first, but I promise, it's not as bad as it sounds—"

"You're a space alien sleeper agent sent to infiltrate the government, aren't you?"

"God dammit," Albertson groaned. "You can at least act a *little* more surprised!"

"Jeff," Cassondra said calmly. "With all the freaky, fucked-up shit I've already seen today, you really think *this* is going to be the straw that breaks me?"

"Yeah, yeah, I know," Albertson grumbled. "You've already more than proven yourself. That's how I know I can trust you with this. So, yeah, alien sleeper agent, hole in one. So do you want the whole prepared spiel now or what?"

Cassondra shrugged.

"Don't really have anything better to do right now," she muttered.

Albertson sighed.

"My real name is Theyjey Drizzl," he said. "I'm an advance scout for the Skreeez, an alien race from the planet Katonk that was planning to invade earth. I was sent here to infiltrate the government, mostly doing reconnaissance and sending the information back to the mother ship. 'Jeff Albertson' a completely fabricated persona, with a falsified history running barely-legal businesses that was tailor-made to appeal to President Donaldson. *And it worked.*

Once I got in, I was instructed to slowly work my way up through the government and sabotage it in order to prepare it for the coming invasion." He heisted for a moment. "The thing is, once I got here, it kinda turned out your own government had already sabotaged itself, and I didn't really need to do anything. Then I climbed the government hierarchy *way* faster than I was expecting to, because everyone above me was either fired, got arrested, or just quit in disgust, so, yeah, an alien sleeper agent just kind of… *ended up* as Secretary of State."

"Wait, wait, wait, hold the fuck up," Cassondra said, closing her eyes and waving her hands in front of her face. "Are you saying the earth is about to be *invaded by aliens?!*"

Albertson's gaze shifted nervously to the side.

"Well, about that," he muttered quietly. "I. Um. Like I said, my original job was just to send intel about the planet and the government back to my leaders. And, um… you know what, maybe you should just listen to it."

Without getting up from the rolling office chair, he scooted himself over to her with his feet and held his forearm out in front of him so that his watch was between them. He pressed a button on the side, and the holographic face of another alien appeared floating over the watch face.

"Okay… Advance Invasion Scout Theyjey Drizzl, earth designate 'Jeff Albertson,' this is Captain Krelibon Scooch of the Skreeez Imperial Vessel Ackgatackgatack. We've just received your first intel package on the Planet Earth and the American Government. I'm reviewing the info right now as we speak, and, um… oh, jeez, it looks like you wrote about… oh… oh God… Are they really doing that? *Really?* To their *own people?* Holy shit, what is wrong with these people?! Jesus Fucking Christ on a bike, how could they do that to themselves? Oh Jesus God! Oh fuck! Fuck fuck fuck fuck shit fuck fuck fuck—abort the mission! Abort abort abort! Get us as far away from this fucking mud ball as our thrusters will take us! Jesus fucking Christ, these people are savages! *God*—"

Albertson pressed the button on his watch again, and the hologram disappeared.

"That, um, that goes on for another couple minutes, but I think you get the idea."

"So they abandoned the invasion?" Cassondra said.

"Yep," Albertson said, leaning back in his chair and folding his hands behind his head. "After taking one good, long look at the human race, they unanimously decided that this planet was way more trouble that it was worth and immediately packed up and left." His eyes narrowed. "They left so quickly, in fact, that they kinda *forgot* to take *me* back with them."

"Oh," Cassondra said slowly. "They just *left you here?*"

"*Yep*," Albertson said. "But since part of my mission duties when I was impersonating the Secretary of State were to, you know, actually *perform* the job duties of the Secretary of State, and since Donaldson's cabinet was always kind of a clusterfuck, I was the only one in the government who was actually doing my job. And then I was the only one covering for half a dozen *other* people's jobs, while they spent all day going to the orgy-parties in the capitol building, and… basically I've been running the entire United States government almost single-handedly for, oh…" He closed one eye, concentrating. "…about six months?" He gave her a nervous smile and attempted to chuckle. "A-*heh*."

Cassondra just stared at him for a couple seconds, wide-eyed without blinking, then shifted her gaze down to her feet.

"Jesus," she muttered.

After that, they were both quiet for a long time, both independently contemplating the silence that hung heavily in the air between them.

"Um, Cassondra?" Albertson finally murmured.

"Yeah?"

"Are you okay?"

"No," she said succinctly.

"Oh," Albertson said. "Um. That makes sense, I guess. It's just, like, this is your first day as a White House intern, isn't it?"

"Yeah."

"And, like, just within the first couple hours, you've found a dead body, had a conversation with an actual cannibal, and uncovered a secret alien invasion plot to take over the planet."

"Uh-huh."

Albertson paused for a moment.

"You just seem to be taking it really well, is all," he muttered. "You know, all things considered."

"I'm screaming on the inside," she said quietly.

"Oh," Albertson said. "Yeah. Yeah, I guess that's fair." Another pause. "I, um, I think you might be in shock, actually. Like, medically in shock. We might want to have a doctor check you out at some point."

"You know what I can't stop thinking about?" Cassondra said. She was sitting bolt-upright with her hands clutching her knees, and her eyes were still glazed over, focused on some vague point in the space immediately in front of her. "That message you showed me from your *alien overlords*, were they actually speaking English, or did you run it through some sort of translator?"

"Oh, yeah, we use translators," Albertson said, rubbing his Adam's apple. "Little mechanical implant right here. Our throats aren't even capable of making most of the sounds used in terrestrial languages without them." He tapped the face of his watch. "I took the liberty of running that transmission through the translation software for your benefit."

"Cool, cool, I figured it was something like that," Cassondra said, slowly nodding to herself, still staring intently at nothing in particular. "So why does your alien language from your completely alien culture have a one-to-one translation for the phrase, 'Jesus fucking Christ on a bike?' "

"Oh, yeah," Albertson said flatly. "Jesus has visited and spread the Gospel on every planet with sentient life. Christianity is recognized as the one true religion throughout the entire civilized cosmos. Didn't you know that?"

Cassondra snapped to attention.

"Wait, *what?*"

"Yeah," Albertson muttered. "Specifically, Lutheranism. In fact, the supreme spiritual truth of the universe has been empirically deduced by the greatest theological minds of a thousand different worlds, and the Third Lutheran Church of Duzat County, Indiana is the only religious institution on earth that gets it a hundred percent right."

Cassondra just stared at him for several long seconds, until her eyes finally narrowed.

"You're messing with me," she said.

Albertson smiled.

"Yes I am," he said. "But admit it, I had you going there for a second or two."

Cassondra just stared at him for a second longer, then a smile slowly spread across her face as well and she descended into a bout of uncontrollable giggling.

"You *asshole!*" she sputtered, punching him lightly on the arm. By now he was laughing along, too.

"I'm sorry," he chuckled. "I had to bring you back down to earth somehow." He paused for a moment. "Um. You know. So to speak."

"Yeah, no, I get what you mean," Cassondra said, wiping a tear out of the corner of her eye. "So what *was* your captain guy actually saying when he went on that tirade?"

"Well, we have *really* advanced translation software," Albertson said. "So, like, when we swear or talk about religion or anything like that, it just finds the closest comparable analogue from your culture and swaps that in instead."

"Oh, shit, really?" Cassondra said. "So every time you say 'Jesus,' what are you *really* saying?"

"It… it doesn't matter," Albertson said. "It wouldn't translate."

"Aw, *come on*," Cassondra whined. "What is it?"

Albertson let out a frustrated sigh.

"All right, fine," he grumbled. "Whenever I say 'Jesus,' or whenever you *hear* me saying 'Jesus,' I'm actually invoking the name of Gotagk the Vociferous."

"Gotagk the Vociferous?"

"Yeah," Albertson said sheepishly. "He was the one who introduced grundlefloo to the Skreeez people on the third night of the Dorpus-moon—look, it's a local thing, it doesn't translate, okay?"

"Uh… sure," Cassondra muttered. She paused for a moment. "What about 'fuck?' "

"Oh, yeah, that one's different too," Albertson said. "It is *so* weird that you people use your own reproductive process as a swear word, you know that? Like, the biggest insult you can throw at something is to compare it to a process that's both pleasurable *and* necessary for the continuation of the species?"

"Okay, fine," Cassondra said. "What's your version, then?"

"Our nearest equivalent is the word for when someone takes a shit in their own mouth."

Cassondra just stared at him for a couple seconds in total silence.

"See!" Albertson said. "That makes much more sense as an insult!"

"Why does your language have a specialized word for that though? Like, how often was that relevant to daily life?" She paused. "You know what, I don't want to know."

With some effort, and despite every sore molecule of her body screaming at her to reconsider, Cassondra managed to slowly push herself up from her chair and started pacing stiffly around the room to stretch her legs.

"Mother of God," she muttered. "I had no idea things were going to get this crazy when I took this job."

"Yeah, I know what you mean," Albertson grumbled.

"No," Cassondra snapped, startling Albertson with her sudden anger. "You have *no* idea what I mean!" Her eyes widened as she realized what she was saying. "Sorry. I'm sorry," she said quickly, lowering herself back down into her chair. "I don't… I just…" She paused, simultaneously on the verge of laughing and crying. "It's been a *really* stressful day for me, okay?"

"Oh, *absolutely*," Albertson said. Just as he was saying this, the last of his cigarette finally burned itself down to the butt, which he spit out and tossed aside before immediately pulling another one out of his jacket.

"Oh, for God's sake," Cassondra said. "Do you *have* to do that all the time?"

Albertson glanced up at her, the unlit cigarette hanging limply from his mouth, lighter held at the ready.

"Do what?" he said.

"The smoking!" Cassondra snapped. "God, it just figures, doesn't it? Aliens visit earth and the first thing we do is get them addicted to nicotine."

"Oh!" Albertson said. He lit the cigarette and then hastily stuffed the lighter back into his coat. "No, you don't understand, I *need* these."

Cassondra rolled her eyes and crossed her arms in front of her chest.

"Dude, people have been quitting smoking for *decades*," she muttered. "It's really not impossible. I mean, you've already got that awful smoker's cough."

"*No*," Albertson said evenly, staring at her intently. "My home planet's atmosphere is loaded with chemicals that aren't as plentiful here on earth: carbon monoxide, ammonia, methane, *et cetera*. I *literally* need to be constantly smoking in order to breathe properly. That God-awful cough is what happens when I *haven't* had a cigarette in too long."

Cassondra threw her hands up.

"You're fucking kidding me!" she said.

"Afraid not," Albertson muttered.

"You can't just use a mask or breathing apparatus or something?"

"Well, when I'm sleeping, yeah," Albertson said. He patted his face. "It's a little hard to hide under the hologram, though." He smiled meekly. "Sorry I have to make everyone else put up with it. If it helps, because of my biology, I don't exhale as much secondhand smoke as a conventional smoker."

"You know what?" Cassondra said, getting up from her chair. "That's fine. *Fine!* I don't care anymore! I don't care!" She marched across the room and stood against the wall with her back to him and her arms folded in front of her chest, then called back over her shoulder. "*I don't care!*"

Albertson had to stifle a chuckle. He shook his head and sighed, then returned his attention to the President's body on the slab in front of him.

"So, what do you think we should do about Donaldson?" he muttered.

"I dunno," Cassondra grumbled. "Leave him here? Let him rot?"

"Jesus," Albertson said. "I thought you liked President Donaldson."

"Liked him?!" Cassondra gasped, whipping around. "He was a racist, misogynistic piece of crap who was running this country into the ground! Why the fuck would I *like* him?!"

"I don't know," Albertson stammered. "I mean, none of the stuff you just said about him is *wrong*, but if you hated him so much, why did you apply to work for him?"

Cassondra closed her eyes and let out a long sigh.

"That's a really long story," she said. "Maybe I'll tell you at some point, since you're helping me so much, but in the meantime…that hologram thingy of yours. Can you change its appearance? I saw it flicker through a couple different disguises when it got damaged earlier."

"Yeah," Albertson said, looking down at his watch. "It has a couple different settings. Why?"

"Can you hologram-disguise yourself to look like President Donaldson and do public appearances in his place until we've gotten all of…" She gestured at Donaldson's body. "…*this* sorted out?"

Albertson was still looking at his watch. His eyes went wide.

"Oh," he said. "*Oh!* God, what is wrong with me? I genuinely didn't think of that."

"Yeah, I'm a genius," Cassondra grumbled. "So, you think you can do it?"

"Yeah, I think so," Albertson said, standing over the President's body. He held out his watch and pressed another button, and a laser beam flashed down and began running back and forth over Donaldson's face, scanning it. "This might take a little time, though."

"That's fine," Cassondra muttered, slumping back down into her chair. "That's the whole reason we're down here, remember? So no one can interrupt us."

And just before Albertson could agree, the door swung open and the First Lady suddenly barged into the room.

CHAPTER 6

"What the hell is *he* doing here?" Irene Donaldson demanded, her eyes bugging out as she stared at her husband's body on the slab.

"*I can explain!*" Cassondra and Albertson blurted out in almost perfect unison, Cassondra jumping to her feet and Albertson throwing his hand behind his back to hide the alien-technology "watch."

"This… this…" the First Lady stammered, "this is supposed to be the only place I can get *away* from him!"

Albertson and Cassondra shared a glance, only for a moment, then their gaze returned to her.

"What?"

Irene started pacing back and forth in front of them.

"All day, every day, since I married that asshole and came to this country, I've had to put up with him, grabbing me, ordering me around, threatening to *deport* me, and that was before he even entered politics! I didn't ask for this! All I wanted was some rich American sugar daddy whose wealth I could inherit after he died! I didn't sign up to be the *First fucking Lady!*"

Albertson and Cassondra shared another glance.

"Um…"

"I am *so* sick of this man's bullshit!" Irene continued, pointing accusingly at her husband. "I started avoiding him, just wandering the halls, doing anything I could to keep busy. Then I started *hiding*, and that's when I found the catacombs, and started bringing lemon cakes from the kitchen down for Muntzie."

"Wait," Albertson said, "you've been doing *what?*"

"And then, when I found this bunker," Irene went on, "I thought I'd finally found a safe space where I could just come down here and chill for a while every time I needed a break! But *no*, now I barge in one day to find that my asshole husband has invaded *this* too, just like he's taken over every other aspect of my life, all so he can, what, *take a nap?*"

"Uh… *yeah*," Cassondra said, running over to the slab. "That's it! Your husband is just down here taking a nap!" She leaned down and lightly slapped Frank Donaldson's cheek a couple times. "Mr. President," she said, just loudly enough. "Your wife is here, sir! It's time to wake up!" She worked her hands under Donaldson's shoulders and started to pull him up. "Here, Mr. President, let me give you a hand! I know how bad your back is."

Albertson shot her a silent *What the hell are you doing?* look. Now that she knew his secret, it really was astounding how much nuance his hologram and translation software were capable of in terms of gesture and facial expression. She just shot him a weak, nervous, smile back, and pushed Frank Donaldson the rest of the way into a sitting position.

"I know it's hard to open your eyes so soon after taking your eye drops, sir," Cassondra said loudly. "But your wife, the lovely First Lady, is standing right in front of you—"

"*Save it*," Irene snapped. "I've had enough of letting other people talk for me. I'm ready to speak for my damn self." She shifted slightly so that her feet were an exact shoulder's-breadth apart, faced her husband head-on, and cleared her throat. "Frank," she said sternly, "I want a divorce."

Albertson and Cassondra both just stared at her, wide eyed, their mouths hanging open slightly. Albertson subtly nudged Donaldson's body, making it look like he was shifting his weight in his seat.

"No, don't say anything, you bastard," Irene snapped. "You dragged me into this political mess without ever once asking if I was okay with it, you fuck other women *all the damn time*, and then you bring home whatever venereal diseases they've got and give them to *me* half the time! Oh, but all of that pales in comparison to what you did to our son, Frank." She leaned in close, her index finger centimeters from Donaldson's face, and hissed out so quietly it was barely audible, "I will *never* forgive you for what you did to our son."

Irene stood back up and took a half-step back, her eyes locked on him and dripping with hate.

"So I'm leaving you, Frank," she said. "I don't care what you say or what you do or how you try to get back at me, I don't care if you *do* fucking deport me, I don't. Whatever happens to me from this point on is *nothing* compared to the hell that you've already put me through." She leaned in close again, even closer than before, and grabbed her husband by the lapels of his coat. "What do you have to say to *that*, huh big man?"

The sudden jostling made Donaldson's mouth fall open and his tongue flop out, hanging limply to the side. A second later, because of the expanding gasses in his decomposing stomach, he let out a low belch that echoed and reverberated through the small room and lasted for several agonizingly long seconds.

Tears welled up in Irene Donaldson's eyes. She let go of her husband's jacket with one hand but held on with the other, drew back her fist, and decked him so hard that he went flying off the slab, smashed his head against the corner of a nearby counter, and landed on the floor in a tangled heap of limbs.

"*You son of a bitch!*" she shrieked. He'd landed in such a way that his open legs were facing her, and she dove her foot into his crotch as hard as she could, again and again, screaming, "I hate you! I hate you! *I hate you I hate you I hate you* I hate you I hate you..." Irene fell to her knees and covered her eyes, tears streaming down her face as she filled the room with wet, ugly, gasping sobs. Then she abruptly got back to her feet, spit on her husband's crumpled form, and managed to choke out, "*I hope you burn in Hell, Frank!*" before she ran out of the room, the soft *clack-clack-clack* of her fashionable shoes against the cavern's stone floor disappearing into the distance.

CHAPTER 7

Albertson and Cassondra waited for the room to once again grow completely silent. Then, once the last vague echo of Irene Donaldson's footsteps had finally dissipated into nothing, they still couldn't think of anything better to do than just sit in the silence for a little while longer.

"Well," Cassondra finally muttered, her eyes locked on the door that the First Lady had just run out through. "*That* happened."

"*Jesus,*" Albertson whined, lowering his head into his hands. "What the fuck is wrong with *everybody? People?* What the fuck is wrong with *people?*"

"I didn't even know Donaldson *had* a son," Cassondra muttered.

"Neither did I," Albertson said, suddenly looking up, his expression distressed. "And I have much better resources than you. Like, government ones *and* alien ones. Whatever the hell he did to that kid, it must've been covered up by a pro."

"Heh. Tell me about it," Cassondra grumbled. "So, keeping the body here might not be as good a hiding place as we thought."

"Yeah, no kidding," Albertson said. "I don't really know where would be better, though."

"Oh, come on," Cassondra said, "you *can't* be telling me that there aren't any good places to hide a body is *Washington fucking D.C.!*"

"Well it's not just *hiding* him, it's *transporting* him there too," Albertson said. "And so far, we've been having pretty bad luck with people interrupting us at the worst possible time—"

The phone rang.

They both paused and stared at it. It wasn't either of their cells. There was an old-fashioned, beige landline telephone installed into the wall of the bunker that neither of them had noticed before. There was a little red light installed into the receiver that flashed every time it rang.

It rang again.

Cassondra and Albertson exchanged a glance, then Albertson reached forward, took the receiver off the hook, and pressed a button to turn the speaker on.

"Hello?" he said.

"Uh, hi," a voice on the other end said. Cassondra couldn't quite tell if it was a man's or a woman's. "Is this the White House?"

Another exchanged glance.

"Yeah," Albertson said. "After a fashion. May I ask who this is?"

"Oh, no, no, no, I want to keep this anonymous," the voice said. "Like, I'm calling from a random payphone and everything—took me three tries to find one that still worked—anyway, I wanted to call in an anonymous tip that someone I know is planning an assassination attempt on the President of the United States."

A long pause hung in the air.

"Really?" Albertson finally said.

"Yeah!" the voice replied. "There was this scary-looking drifter who came through my town, his name is Tyler LaFuente, and he'd stockpiled all these weapons and ammo, and he said he was driving to the capitol in this big red pickup truck of his so he could assassinate President Donaldson. He didn't say this in so many words, but I bet he's planning to do it during that big rally the President has planned tomorrow—"

"Ah, God, the rally!" Albertson hissed to himself. "I forgot about the rally!"

"What?" the voice on the phone said.

"Oh," Albertson muttered. "Nothing, sorry. Go on?"

"Oh, okay," the voice continued. "So this LaFuente guy, he was ranting about all this political stuff, and I think he was crazy!"

"Well, thank you for telling us… *citizen*." Albertson said awkwardly, with a hurried tone of voice. "I'll be sure to pass it along to the proper channels. You are a true American hero." He glanced over at Cassondra. She was giving him a look of pure bewilderment. He returned his attention to the phone and gulped. "May I ask how you got this number—" There was a loud click as the person on the other end hung up, and then all they heard was a dial tone until Albertson places the receiver back on the hook.

"Well, that doesn't complicate things at all," Cassondra said dryly. "Do you think it was legit?"

"I don't know!" Albertson said. "Somehow they got the phone number for the emergency line in a secret underground bunker that they shouldn't even know exists, so God only knows what they do and don't know. I just… I don't… *gah!*" He fell back into his chair, hunched over, and put his face in his hands. "I'm starting to crack up a little, Cass," he stammered, his voice shaking. "Things just keep *happening*, and I'm the only one trying to do anything about any of it, and I have to keep so many balls in the air at once, and if I let *any* of them fall a whole lot of people die, and, and…" He suddenly looked up, his eyes wide and sunken. "Donaldson had a speech planned at the Capitol tomorrow. One of those big, stupid rallies he does to rile up his supporters. I forgot all about it, because usually I don't have to pay attention to stupid shit like that, but how is he going to give it *now?!* God, what if I have to use my hologram to impersonate President Donaldson and give the speech in his pace, and then that lunatic coming after him shoots *me* in his place! Then I'll be dead, and they'll do an autopsy on me and find out I'm an alien, and then they'll think Donaldson was an alien this entire time, and then they'll think all the awful things he did during his presidency were really an alien plot to destroy the world, and they'll declare war on Katonk and my entire home planet will be destroyed because I couldn't do anything right—"

Cassondra slapped him.

He stopped talking.

He blinked a couple times.

"Listen," she said. "This has been a really, really long *motherfucker* of a day for everyone involved. Both of us are at our breaking points. If we don't take a second to just chill the fuck out and collect our wits, we're going to explode."

"But," Albertson sputtered, "but Donaldson…"

"Isn't going anywhere," Cassondra said. "And right now, there's some weird fluid leaking out of his mouth that I *really* don't want to touch. His creepazoid of a daughter and her little imp of a husband are off doing whatever political machinations they have planned, I don't really care what. As near as I can tell, the world isn't go end if we take a thirty-minute break." She reached down into her bra and pulled out a little baggie full of something green and fluffy. "So," she said, "I've got some weed. Wanna go find someplace quiet and get high?"

CHAPTER 8

Cassondra licked the edge of the Zig-Zag paper, then finished rolling the joint and handed it to Albertson.

"Here," she said. "You sure you're gonna be able to breathe okay with this instead of a regular cigarette?"

"Yeah, it's enough of the same chemicals, I should be fine," Albertson said. "I'm kind of surprised you're so adept at rolling these, though, though, with how much of a shit-fit you threw about *me* smoking."

"Hey, this is *marijuana*," she said matter-of-factly. "You smoke *tobacco*. Tobacco is *disgusting*."

Albertson just shrugged and slid the joint between his lips.

"Whatever," he muttered as he lit the other end with his ever-present lighter, then he took a deep breath. He held it like that for a second, then blinked a couple times and coughed, but no visible smoke came out of his mouth. "Oh, God," he said, taking the cigarette out of his mouth and glancing down at it. "That's the *good* shit."

"Yeah, I got some connections," Cassondra said. "Now gimme." Albertson handed her the joint and she took a long puff herself. Then, as she handed it back to him, she said, "Wait, I'm not gonna get any alien cooties from this, am I?"

"Nah, nothing you're susceptible to," he muttered. He took another puff. "Our biology is so different it would be like a human getting infected with bark beetles." A third puff. Cassondra chuckled. He glanced over at her. "What?"

"The way you're suckling on that thing after I slobbered all over it. So much for you being a 'germophobe.' "

Albertson chuckled back.

"Yeah," he said. "Plus the fact that I've been *carrying a dead body around* for the last couple hours." Puff. "In case you haven't already guessed, that excuse was bullshit. I really don't like shaking hands because then people will feel that my skin texture is all scaly and doesn't feel like a normal human's. The hologram can only do so much." Another puff.

Cassondra's eyes narrowed.

"Okay, seriously, stop hogging it," she said, reaching over. Albertson leaned back to keep just out of her reach.

"I literally need this to breathe," he said flatly. "If I don't hog this joint, I will die."

Cassondra leaned back and folded her arms over her chest.

"Fine," she grumbled.

A gentle breeze picked up. They were outside, sitting on the roof of the White House, overlooking the National Mall. It was unusually empty for this time of day; no tourists, no school groups, no government officials rushing to or from work. Just a couple homeless people rifling through garbage cans and wide stretches of Washington, D.C.'s open landscape.

Albertson finally handed the joint back to Cassondra and she took another puff, then idly stared at him for a couple long seconds.

"Take off the hologram," she said.

"What?"

"Take off your hologram," she repeated. "Or, like, turn it off, or power it down, or whatever the right word is. Let yourself 'go natural' for a second."

"Are you insane?" Albertson said. "If anyone sees an alien chilling out on the roof of the White House—"

"No one will see," Cassondra said, gesturing out towards the empty National Mall. "Or anyone who will is just a crazy hobo no one will believe anyway. Come on, it must drive you nuts, hiding yourself like that all the time."

"Well, yeah, kinda," Albertson admitted. "But, I mean, I've never even let it down outside before."

"Really?" Cassondra said. "Oh, well now you *have* to do it."

"God, I don't know," Albertson said, then let out a small cough. "Hey, give me the joint again."

"Only if you lower your hologram."

"Cass, I could *literally die*."

"Okay, okay, here," Cassondra said, handing the cigarette back. "But you should still lower your hologram."

Albertson took a long pull from the joint, then sighed as he exhaled. His breath was still clear; his lungs must have just been absorbing all the chemicals in the smoke.

"All right, fine," he said. He pressed the hidden button on his watch and his human visage flickered away, once again revealing the alien one underneath.

"Yayyy!" Cassondra said, holding up both her arms. "Doesn't that feel better?"

"I'm sorry, do you have any idea how holograms work?" Albertson said. "I don't 'feel' anything different. It's not a physical costume. It's all just about bending light."

"Yeah," Cassondra said. "But that isn't what I meant. Do you feel better *in your soul?*" She placed her palm flat on Albertson's chest. He glanced down at it, then back up at her.

"God, you are so stoned right now," he chuckled.

"Some might say I'm *not stoned enough!*" she said. "Gimme!" She leaned over and grabbed helplessly in the joint's general direction while Albertson held it out of her reach.

"Hold on, I need one more drag," he said. He held it to his lips and sucked in as much smoke as he could, then handed it back to her. "Okay, I should be good for another minute or two."

"Glad to hear it," Cassondra said, taking the cigarette back from him. She took a puff almost as long as his, then the two of them went silent as they sat next to each other, there on the White House roof, staring off contemplatively across the Washington, D.C. skyline as the sun sank slowly towards the horizon.

"God, the sunsets are gorgeous up here," Albertson said. "I mean, all the sunsets on your planet are beautiful. The atmosphere back home is so smoky and cloudy, I'd never seen anything like them until I came here. But here, specifically—in this specific city, on this specific roof—they beat everywhere else in the universe."

"You come up here a lot?" Cassondra said.

"Yeah," Albertson muttered. "Not as much as I used to, though. Sometimes, when Donaldson would threaten another world leader, or say something stupid in front of the press, and everyone was running around in 'damage control' mode, this was the only place you could go to get a couple minutes of peace and quiet. Even out in the Rose Garden, I had to fight off reporters or panicked aides sometimes, but no one ever thought to look for me up here."

"Yeah, sunsets are nice," Cassondra said quietly. For a while, all she did was watch as the enormous, red-orange sun slowly crept down towards the horizon. Then she turned back to him. "Jeff?"

"Yeah?"

"Why do you do it?"

"Do what?"

"Your job," Cassondra said. "You have one of the most miserable jobs on earth, cleaning up the messes of a crazy person on a national—if not *worldwide*—scale, the stakes are enormous even when there's *not* an emergency like the one today, I can see the stress is eating you alive...

why didn't you quit this 'undercover' job the second your alien bosses left and move to the Bahamas or something?" Almost as an afterthought, she added, "there are lots of pretty sunsets there, too."

Albertson let out a long, careful sigh. His sighs had been sounding progressively more exhausted as the day had gone on, and Cassondra hardly had to question why.

"For a while, while I was trying to 'blend in,' I was practically the only person in the government who was actually doing my job. Hell, I still am a lot of the time. Almost everyone else is just funneling money into their own personal interests, or just doing shit that doesn't actually help anyone except themselves."

"Yeah, you mentioned that," Cassondra said. "That you're basically keeping the entire government running singlehandedly."

"Right," Albertson said. "Which means if *I* disappear, you people are *fucked*."

Cassondra arched an eyebrow.

"Really?" she said. "You're doing that much?"

"Well," Albertson muttered, "as Secretary of State I can pretty much guarantee that I've prevented *at least* two wars that Donaldson almost started, with another three or four in the 'maybe' pile. And since I learned how to forge Donaldson's signature, and started signing laws and executive orders in his stead,"… he started counting things out on his fingers as he talked… "I've kept the government from shutting down three times, I've kept welfare and social security running, I've tightened a lot of environmental regulations—can't invade the planet if you idiots don't leave us anything worth invading right?" He chuckled, then sighed. "It all sounds like mountains of paperwork and boring legal stuff—*and it is*, believe me—but I've been doing a lot of good in my position, Cass, and helping a lot of your people." He started fidgeting uncomfortably in place. "I guess I just don't think walking away from it would be responsible."

"But why do you care?" Cassondra stammered. "They're not *your* people! In fact, you explicitly came here *as their enemy!* Why would you go to so much trouble, driving yourself to distraction for their benefit?"

Albertson smiled wistfully to himself and shrugged.

"I didn't join the Skreeez military to be some big, strong invading 'Hero of the Empire,' " he said. "I mostly did it because my hometown sucked, and I needed any way out I could find. Truth be told, I spent most of my military career as a desk jockey. I'm pretty sure I only even got this assignment because one of my superiors really didn't like me. She used to tell me all the time that I 'wasn't a model soldier,' " His expression suddenly darkened. "And she was right. I'm *not* a model soldier. I don't *like* seeing people suffer. And I've been seeing *way* too much of it since I arrived on this planet."

A silence hung in the air between them. Albertson quietly puffed away on the joint, watching the sunset, until Cassondra's arm reached over, asking for another puff herself.

"You seem awfully interested in this topic," he said, handing the joint over to her. "Are you dealing with some stuff I should know about?"

Cassondra let out a long, haggard sigh, then took as deep a pull as she could manage and held it in for as long as possible before coughing the smoke back up.

"Okay," she said. "You have been really, really open with me about aspects of yourself that are *probably* classified, right?"

Albertson shrugged amiably.

"That's one word for it, yes."

"Okay," Cassondra said. "So, if I tell *you* deep dark secrets about *myself*, you can keep those classified as well?"

"Of course," Albertson said. "Aside from, you know, *not wanting people to suffer and die*, I care way less about human affairs and politics than you'd think."

"Oh, this isn't just *politics*," Cassondra muttered. "You aren't the only one here who isn't what they seem, space boy."

Albertson arched an eyebrow as she handed the joint back to him.

"Oh?"

"Yeah," she said. She took in a deep breath of fresh air and then let it out slowly. "Okay. I'm not just doing this White House internship for shits and giggles. I have a very explicit reason for being here. I..." she hesitated for a moment. "I'm actually a spy for the Chinese government."

Albertson just stared at her for several long seconds, blinking.

"China," he finally said.

"Yes."

A pause.

"You're not Chinese," he said.

"I know."

"You're Black."

"Yes, I am already aware of that, thank you," Cassondra said. "What do you call a spy who you would never, ever suspect to be a spy?"

"A pretty damn good spy," Albertson muttered, lying back onto the roof with his hands folded behind his head, the joint sticking straight up out of his mouth. "Okay," he said. "I'm intrigued. *Details*."

Cassondra sighed.

My actual birth name *really is* Cassondra Warren. I'm a natural-born U.S. citizen. I was born in Detroit. My biological mom gave me up for adoption almost immediately after I was born, and I was adopted by a Chinese couple who had just moved to the States. Turns out they were spies who had been sent over for the explicit purpose of adopting a natural-born U.S. baby and raising them to be a spy to infiltrate the government on China's behalf."

"Jesus," Albertson said, sitting back up. "Are there more kids like you running around? Should I be worried?"

"Yeah, they're out there, but I don't have a list of names or anything," Cassondra said. "They did their best to keep us in the dark about each other so that we couldn't rat each other out if we got caught. Last I'd heard, though, I was the most successful one, in that I actually got a position *in* the White House. I think we've got one guy interning for the Missouri State Legislature, another guy just never got good enough grades to get into any government programs, one girl totally burned out and became a performance artist—anyway, my assignment wasn't all that different from yours: collect data, send reports back to the motherland, climb the ladder and let the natural process of promotion net me higher and higher positions until I had an actual position of power and could start enacting changes on China's behalf some ten or fifteen years down the line." She glared at him. "But then I walk into to work on the first day of my 'mission' and the President is fucking dead, so as near as I can tell my mission is either obsolete or I've already done such a good job that there's no need for me to continue any further."

"So you came into this job kind of already accustomed to weird shit," Albertson said, knowingly waging his finger in her direction. "*That's* why all the craziness today hasn't reduced you to a whimpering puddle of jelly."

"Well I sure as shit wasn't expecting *this!*" Cassondra said, a little louder than she intended, gesturing wildly at her surroundings. "Just like you, I'm a *reconnaissance* spy. I wasn't trained to *kill* people, or to haul fucking *corpses* around secret underground tunnels! So yeah, even *with* my training, today has been a bit much for me." She folded her arms for a second, then immediately unfolded them and reached out. "Give me the joint again."

"All yours," Albertson said, handing it over. "So, all this talk about questioning whether you should have empathy for people who aren't 'your people…?' "

Cassondra took a long pull from the joint and then sighed out a small could of smoke.

"My parents didn't raise me in a vacuum," she said. "They knew I'd never be able to convincingly pass as an American if I wasn't still exposed to American culture. So they let me have friends, they even had me going to public school for a while—they were surprisingly not strict for Chinese-foreign-spy-parents—but the entire time, they never let me forget that these people I was hanging out with and interacting with were the enemy, and that the country I was living in was evil, and that it was my *destiny* to bring *ruin and destruction* down upon—they could get a little over-dramatic sometimes."

"Eh. I've heard worse," Albertson muttered, holding out his hand.

"But I still grew up with these people," Cassondra continued, handing the joint back to him. "They shared their lives with me. They were my *friends*." Her eyes were getting watery, and she started to sniffle. "One of my friends had a single mom, who still managed to feed and clothe five kids despite having *nothing*. Another friend watched her brother die in a hospital because her family couldn't afford the medical bills." Her eyes narrowed and her fists clenched. "*Another* friend watched her brother die in the street, because the cops shot him for having the same skin color as me." She turned back to Albertson. "My parents were definitely right about some things: this is a twisted, fucked-up country that doesn't do jack-shit for its own citizens. It is a corrupt nation built on slavery and oppression, and it *does* deserve to be torn down, brick by brick." She swallowed hard. "I don't give a *fuck* about America," she said, "but I would like life to be a little better for the people living in it."

Albertson raised his hands and gave her a light applause.

"Bravo," he said. "Encore! Encore!"

"Oh, shut up," she grumbled.

"I'm sorry," he said. "So does this mean your abandoning *your* mission, too? Does the fact that you're even telling me about your mission in the first place mean you've already abandoned it?"

"I don't know," Cassondra groaned. "I've spent my whole life getting groomed for this shit against my will, and now, because my parents forced me into it, within the last twelve hours I've been ejaculated on, threatened multiple times, watched the President fucking *die*, forced to move a dead body, probably committed any number of federal crimes, and now I'm on the roof of the White House getting stoned with a fucking space alien." She got to her feet, walked to the edge of the roof, extended her middle fingers, and proudly flipped off the sunset-hued D.C. skyline with both hands. "I GIVE ZERO FUCKS RIGHT NOW!" she screamed at the top of her lungs. "YOU HEAR ME? I GIVE ZERO FUCKS!"

Way down on the ground below them, one of the homeless people wandering around the National Mall pumped his fist and shouted back, "Right on, sister!" Cassondra collapsed onto her back, onto the roof, panting hard and laughing deliriously. She didn't see him stand up, but she felt the shadow as Albertson loomed overhead, looking down at her.

"Well," he said, monkeying with his wristwatch until his human disguise flickered back into view, "we know for a fact things aren't going to get better for people if that Muntz lunatic actually ends up in the Oval Office. And, honestly, I have no idea how we're going to stop him from ascending. I just know that we *do* have to, and that even compared to what we've already been through today, whatever we have to do next is going to be a clusterfuck the likes of which the world has never seen." He held out a hand to her. "So. A foreign spy and a *literal* alien invader: the only two people left who can save America?"

"Let's fuckin' do it!" Cassondra said, and she grabbed Albertson's hand so he could pull her to her feet.

CHAPTER 9

Luna Donaldson strode authoritatively through the halls of the Capitol, with Jacob Kirkman trailing behind her. He was trying to keep up, but was hugging himself and trembling so hard that it was causing him to lag behind her. Luna finally rolled her eyes and stopped walking for a second, waiting "patiently" for her husband to close the gap between them, her face in her hands.

"Christ," she muttered under her breath, quietly enough that she couldn't hear. "If I had to marry into old money, I should've just picked one of Donald Trump's brats.

When Jacob finally did catch up to her, she abruptly whipped around and slapped him so hard that he almost lost his balance.

"You weasely little *shit*," she snapped while he clutched his jaw and stared up at her, dumbfounded. "You think I'm not scared too? I've had my hand in just as many cookie jars as you have. Without my father's position guaranteeing us protection, the ethics committees are going to start investigating *both* of us, and they're not going to like what they find in *my* background any more than *yours*."

She closed her eyes and started shaking her head, slowly, then let out a dry, ironic chuckle in spite of herself.

"You're freaking out because you think *you're* not going to do well in prison," she said, "and you're right, you *aren't*. But I promise you, women's prison doesn't look too fondly on pampered little rich girls like me, either."

Jacob started to nod, but Luna took a large step forward, stamping on the ground in front of him so hard that he scrambled a couple quick steps back.

"But do you see me acting like a little *bitch?*" Luna said. "Do you see me whining and whimpering and cowering now that I'm working without a net for the first time in my miserable little life? *No!*" She grabbed Jacob's collar and pulled him in so close that droplets of spittle landed on his glasses as she hissed out her words through gritted teeth. "You see me rolling with the punches! You see me taking advantage of a bad situation!" She pushed him away from her without letting go of his collar, then immediately yanked him back, jolting him in place. "You see me getting off my spoiled little rich-girl ass and *doing* something about it!"

With the hand she'd been using to hold onto him, she shoved him away from her, letting go of him this time, causing him to stumble haphazardly backwards, crash against the opposite wall spine-first, and collapse to the floor in a heap.

"I will take care of this," she said, looming over him. "I know what I'm doing. As long as you do what I say, neither of us have anything to worry about." She slid a thin butterfly knife out of her coat pocket, casually flicked it open, and whispered, "But if you *fuck* this up for me..." She was on the ground lightning-fast, on top of him, pressing the impossibly sharp blade of the knife up against his neck. "If you don't grow some fucking *balls* and learn how to play international politics without wetting yourself like the whimpering little man-baby that you are..." She pressed the tip of the knife into his skin just hard enough to draw a single drop of blood. "I. Will. Fucking. *End*. You," she whispered, her voice almost seductive. "And then I will tell Air Force One that I need to leave the country immediately for 'security reasons,' and I will be sipping cocktails on the beach in Aruba while some gorgeous pool boy fucks my brains out before they've even discovered your body." She jerked the knife away from his throat just as suddenly as she'd thrust in there in the first place, daintily wiping the drop of blood off the tip before folding it back up. "*Or* my father's."

She got back to her feet and stood over him, glaring down at the whimpering mess at her feet while she casually slid the butterfly knife back into her pocket.

"So," she said, "are you ready to help me, Jacob?" She reached down, grabbed his hand, and yanked him to his feet. "Will you be able to actually take command of a situation for once, and act with the goddamn confidence and motivation that people expect from their leaders?" She leaned in and wrapped her arms around him, rocking him slowly back and forth, almost like they were dancing to music only they could hear. "Cause I'll tell you a little secret, Jakey," she whispered into his ear, her voice suddenly deep and sultry. "I don't *want* to go to Aruba. That's really just my last resort. I want to say here, and stay in power, and stay with you, and keep raking in more and more money until the two of us own the world." Jacob smiled and leaned in, letting his cheek press warmly against hers. Then he felt the blade of the knife press up against his side, and a cold sweat started to form along his brow. He hadn't even seen her take it out again. "But if that turns out not to be possible," Luna hissed. "I will be *more* than happy to settle for what's behind Door Number Two."

"Ms. Donaldson?" a voice said from down the hall. "Luna, is that you?"

Flick. The knife was closed again, and back in her pocket.

"Oh, thank God!" Speaker of the House Leo Bronstein said, his heavy dress shoes clacking loudly against the floor as he hobbled towards them. Bronstein had always walked with a pronounced limp, but refused to use a cane; Luna vaguely remembered hearing something about an old war injury. She didn't remember many the details, and she didn't particularly care. "I've been looking all over for you!"

Luna disengaged from her husband.

"Leo!" she said brightly. "So you got my message?"

"Of course I did!" Bronstein said. "Your father is really, finally ready to negotiate government subsidies for the soybean farms that are being negatively impacted by his trade war?"

"Er, yeah," Luna said. "He can't wait to talk about that. He's just been chomping at the bit, in fact!"

"That's incredible!" Bronstein said, reaching up to straighten his glasses, his mouth wide with shock. "He's always been so stubborn about it before! What the hell happened to change his mind?"

Luna forced her smile to look demure and humble. She felt like she was going to throw up.

"Well, I sat down and had a little talk with him," she said. "He always listens to me, you know—we have this special daddy-daughter bond—and I guess I was just finally able to bring him around."

"You are an *angel!*" Bronstein said, wrapping his arms around her and pulling her in for a bear-hug. "You've just guaranteed my reelection! What can I ever do to repay you?"

Luna winced as Bronstein's cold, wrinkly hands brushed against the back of her neck.

"Please don't touch me," Luna said.

"Ah, come on!" Bronstein said, patting her amiably on the back. "We go so far back, since before your father even got into politics." Bronstein pulled back slightly, but still kept his hands on her shoulders and held her across from him at arm's length, his eyes gazing into hers through his big, thick coke-bottle glasses. "You remember those visits from your 'Uncle Leo' back when you were a little girl, don't you? You sure weren't squeamish about hugging and kissing *then*, now were you?"

"Uh… yeah… I guess not… ha-ha," Luna muttered, still subtly trying to pull herself out of his grasp.

"So, don't just stand there," Bronstein said, still not letting go. "Talk to me. This plan your father suggested, how exactly does it work?"

"The plan?" Luna said nervously. She hadn't expected the bastard to actually want details. "Well, um, it's a hell of a plan, I can tell you that much." She daintily reached up and pulled one of Bronstein's hands off of her shoulder, but he clamped it back on a moment later. Ever so subtly, she could feel her entire body starting to tremble. She was struggling to keep her mind from spiraling into a full flashback. "Really good for the *farmers*."

"Yeah, but give me details," Bronstein said. He was getting closer to her again, inch by inch. She could smell his breath. "What exactly does he have in mind?"

Luna's heart hammered in her chest. She was right on the verge of losing her shit… and then she suddenly wasn't. An eerie, numbing calm suddenly washed over her, just like it had all those times when she was younger. Luna sighed.

"I don't know," she said flatly, reaching up and brushing both of Bronstein's hands off of her shoulders, one after the other. "Why don't you go ask him yourself?"

Luna suddenly jolted herself forward, and Bronstein let out a choked, startled gasp as the blade of her knife slid cleanly into the flesh of his stomach.

CHAPTER 10

"Shit, it doesn't look like the hologram's going to work," Albertson said, tinkering with his watch while he and Cassondra walked back through the underground catacombs. "When you smashed it earlier, you took out the scanner. I can't scan in Donaldson's face to make a disguise that looks like him."

"Really?" Cassondra said skeptically. "And you're *not* just saying that because you don't want to put yourself at risk for an assassination attempt?"

"No, it really is the watch," Albertson said. "But even if it weren't, not wanting to get shot would still be a perfectly valid reason to back out of that plan."

"Uh-huh," Cassondra muttered.

"Look!" Albertson said. "I'll show you." He fiddled with the watch, and his face abruptly flickered into Frank Donaldson's, but it was distorted almost beyond recognition. His nose was so big it took up half of his face, like he was staring directly into a fisheye lens, and his eyes were on the sides on his head like a bird's or a fish's."

"*Argh!*" Cassondra shouted, jumping back.

"See," Albertson said, his face flickering back to his usual disguise. "I'm afraid I'm stuck looking like this for the time being."

"Hrmph," Cassondra grumbled, "I'd make a nasty joke about your appearance, but I know your appearance is fake and you're intentionally *trying* to look like a dumpy old guy anyway, so it wouldn't really mean anything."

"Well, it's the thought that counts," Albertson grumbled. "And besides—oh, shit!"

"What?" Cassondra said.

"Look ahead," Albertson muttered. "The door to the bunker is hanging open!"

"*Shit!*" Cassondra yelled, bolting down the twisting stone corridor ahead of him. "Why is the secret underground bunker so hard to lock people out of?"

"Donaldson insisted on changing all the security codes to 1-2-3-4," Albertson wheezed, running after her. He never would've admitted this to Cassondra, but it wasn't just the disguise; he'd let himself get pretty out of shape by his own species' standards too. "He said it was easier to remember!"

"That fucking moron!" Cassondra said, screeching to a stop in front of the bunker door. "If he wasn't already dead, I'd—*eewww…*"

"What?" Albertson said, slowing down as he caught up to her, out for breath. "God, I need a cigarette—*Oh, Jesus!*"

The pig, Squeally Dan, had waddled his way into the bunker and was chewing on the left leg of Frank Donaldson's corpse. He'd already eaten the entire left foot, having somehow pulled it out of its shoe with his snout.

"Aw, Danny, *no*," Albertson cooed as he slipped in and pulled the pig away from his meal. "You don't want to eat that, buddy. It's not good for you."

"How did the pig get in here?!" Cassondra screamed. "Did he just randomly paw at the keypad and *just happen* to hit the right combination?! Were the fucking *President's* security codes so simple that fucking *pig* could figure them out?! I don't—How do you even—*Aaarrrggghhh!!!*"

Albertson was cradling Squeally Dan in his arms. He and the pig both glanced up at Cassondra's outburst.

"I thought the whole point of the weed was that it would calm you down," Albertson said.

"You hogged most of it, you pig," she grumbled, crossing her arms. "No offence to Squeally Dan."

"None taken," Albertson said. "He is but a peaceful traveler through life, who has learned how to turn the other cheek."

Cassondra was slowly shaking her head.

"You need help, dude," she muttered.

"All my coworkers are assholes, and everyone I knew before then is eleven billion light years away," he snapped. "If the pig wants to be friends, *I will be friends with the pig*." He walked towards the door, still cradling Squeally Dan like a baby. "Now in case you haven't been able to tell, Dan is hungry, because with all the craziness today I haven't had time to feed him, and if I don't feed the pig, nobody feeds the pig—"

"No," Cassondra said, "I think Squeally Dan is probably pretty full now, because he just ate *a human goddamn being's entire goddamn foot*."

Albertson sighed.

"I guess we do have more pressing matters right now, don't we?" he grumbled, then he lowered the pig back down onto the ground and gave it a little swat on the butt. "You run along, buddy," he said. "I'll catch up with you later and give you a little treat, okay?"

Squeally Dan snorted in the agreement, and then trotted away. Albertson stepped back into the bunker and closed the door behind him. Cassondra was on the floor, scrunched up into something resembling fetal position, her hands mechanically running themselves through her artificially-straightened hair.

"I'm surrounded by crazy people," she whispered under her breath.

"Hey, I'm an alien," Albertson said, strutting past her. "What's everyone else's excuse?" He knelt down over Donaldson's crumpled body, wrapped his arms around the corpse's torso, and tried to haul it back up onto the slab. "Hey, um, a little help here?" he grunted. "This guy's kind of heavy."

"Do I have to touch his leg-stump?" Cassondra moaned, glancing up.

"If you can figure out a way to get him up here *without* touching it, be my guest."

Somehow, with a lot of pushing and pulling, they did finally manage to get Donaldson's body back up onto the slab, and as soon as the heavy lifting was done, they both slumped back down into their rolling office chairs from before.

"So," Cassondra grumbled. "If you can't impersonate him at the rally tomorrow, what do we do now?"

"Shit, I don't know," Albertson said. "Can we just cancel the rally?"

"Jeff," Cassondra said, "you know Donaldson was a media whore. The man never met a camera he didn't like. You can't go two days without seeing his face on the news." She hesitated. "Well... *couldn't*, at least. If he suddenly disappears, people are going to notice, and start asking questions." She paused for a moment, thinking. "I dunno," she finally muttered, "do you think we could just tell everyone he's sick?"

"Oh, God," Albertson grumbled. "That would be worth than saying nothing. Donaldson's surrounded himself with nothing but sycophants and yes-men. They'd be trampling over each other to be the first person to wish him '*Get well soon*,' or to be the person who brought him the biggest bouquet so they could earn his favor. We'd be fighting off a damned parade."

"Oh, God," Cassondra said. "Well, okay, but what if we just, like, left him lying in bed, let everyone come in to pay their respects, and then kicked them out because he was 'contagious' or 'needed to rest' or something? That way at least he makes his appearance but doesn't have to, you know, *move*." She gulped. "Plus, we are going to have to publicly admit that he's dead *eventually*, and if it was already common knowledge that he was sick, that might soften the blow a little bit."

"Hmm..." Albertson said, scratching his chin. "You really think that would work? You really think people wouldn't notice that he's dead?"

Cassondra shrugged.

"His own wife didn't," she said. "You'd think if anyone would be able to tell, it would be her." The corner of her mouth turned upwards into the hint of a dark, self-conscious smirk. "I mean, this is Frank Donaldson we're talking about. He already looked kind of like a bloated corpse, even when he was alive."

Albertson sighed.

"You're not wrong," he muttered. "We would have to do some preparation, though. Embalm the body, see what we can do to preserve it. You know. Cover up the smell."

"Oh, God," Cassondra groaned, leaning over. "I was okay until you said that." She put a hand over her mouth. "Finally broke the seal. I think I'm gonna hurl."

"Oh, you don't have to help with any of that stuff," Albertson said, standing back up. "Most of the equipment I'd need is already in this bunker, plus some alien tech I've got stashed around. I should be able to take care of that on my own." He held up one of Donaldson's arms, then let it drop limply back onto the slab. "We also might want to remove some of his organs. That'll at least slow down decomposition." He glanced back at Cassondra. "Plus, if we hollow him out, he'll be a little easier to carry around."

Cassondra only barely made it to the wastebasket in time before blowing her groceries.

"Well excuse me for being practical!" Albertson said while Cassondra evacuated her lunch. His gaze returned to the body lying in front of him. "Transporting him is going to be a problem too," he said, stroking his chin. "We can't just keep hauling his limp body around like a sack of potatoes. One glimpse of that, and people are going to know exactly what's going on."

Cassondra spat into the trash can a couple times, then wiped off her mouth and glared up at Albertson.

"Well," she grumbled, "what alternative have we got?"

Albertson continued staring down at the body for another couple seconds of silent contemplation.

"How old are you?" he finally muttered.

"What?" Cassondra said, narrowing her eyes. "Twenty. Why?"

"Oh, I made a point of studying a lot of earth culture before coming here," Albertson said, "but I've found that sometimes young people aren't as up-to-date as I am." He glanced over at her again. "Tell me, have you heard of this movie from the eighties called *Weekend at Bernie's*?"

CHAPTER 11

President Frank Donaldson "walked" down the halls of the White House with Secretary of State Jeff Albertson and White House Intern Cassondra Warren on either side of him. He had his arms draped over both their shoulders, as if they were old buddies. (Or, alternatively, as if he were blackout drunk and needed them for balance. Either cover story worked, and Cassondra didn't really care which conclusion bystanders jumped to.) His right leg was affixed to Cassondra's left with rubber bands that couldn't be seen unless someone looked really closely, and his empty left shoe was attached to Albertson's right with double-edged tape, so that when they walked, it looked like he was walking along with them. (Neither of them had wanted the side with the chewed-off leg stump, but Albertson eventually had to relent that it would be easier to stick Donaldson's empty shoe onto his own loafer rather than to Cassondra's high-heel.)

They hadn't run into anyone else, so far. The catacombs below D.C. had, obviously, been empty, and once they'd finished rigging up Donaldson's body and maneuvered him back topside, it was already well past midnight, so there was hardly anyone left doing business in the White House.

"Hey," Cassondra grumbled, lurching forward with her side of Donaldson's body, pivoting around Albertson's stationary foot. "We've pretty much had *cart blanche* with this guy since he died."

"Yeah, I know," Albertson said, taking a step of his own now. "Thank God."

"Well, yeah, I mean obviously, it's a good thing," Cassondra muttered. "But where the hell is the Secret Service?"

"Oh, the Secret Service has been running on a skeleton crew for month. They barely exist at all anymore."

"What?" Cassondra said. "*Why?*"

"Same reason it's so hard for us to get interns," Albertson grunted. "Can you think of anyone who would actually be willing to *give their life* for this asshole?"

"So what?" Cassondra stammered. "They all just *quit*, and no one else applied to take their place?"

Albertson shrugged, causing Donaldson's left arm to slump unevenly.

"Pretty much," he said, then his head immediately perked up at attention. "Oh, shit, someone's coming."

Albertson and Cassondra both stood up as straight as they could with the added weight on their shoulders and forced themselves to smile. Somewhere in the back of her mind, Cassondra realized that Albertson was technically always 'faking' his expressions and could just tell his hologram to show a perfectly convincing smile, while she had to actively concentrate on controlling her body language and expression. Her life suddenly felt *that* much more unfair.

Cassondra tried to focus her attention on the person approaching them, a young, impeccably-groomed white guy carrying a stack of papers. She didn't immediately recognize him.

"Low-level White House aide," Albertson whispered to her under his breath. "No one important."

"Oh! Good evening, Mr. President!" the aide said cheerfully as soon as he was in earshot. "You're looking wonderful today! Did you get a new haircut?"

Cassondra rolled her shoulders a little, causing Donaldson's right arm to flip up for a second in a motion that could've easily been interpreted as a wave, a mock-salute, or those douchebaggy finger-gun things. As soon as he saw the President's gesture of casual acknowledgement, the aide hugged his papers a little closer to his chest, let out a restrained little gasp, and started to blush. He picked up his pace as he walked past the three of them, and as he walked away down the other side of the hallway, Cassondra thought she could hear the man whisper, "*He noticed me,*" under his breath and giggle euphorically to himself.

"Well, um," Cassondra muttered. She shot Albertson a nervous smile. "At least it worked?"

"Yeah, but that wasn't exactly the most discriminating test subject," Albertson grumbled. "I'd like to see if he can pass a couple more people's scrutiny before we consider ourselves in the clear—"

"Mr. President!" another voice called from down the hall. They both turned towards the source of the sound, then shuffled around each other so that Donaldson turned towards it too. The President's head lawyer, Neil Downe, the one who appeared on the TV news shows every other day to defend Donaldson's latest act of insanity, came striding around the corner, his tie hanging loosely around his neck and his shirt visibly stained with sweat. "What are you doing up so late? It's after midnight! You should be in bed watching TV!"

"W-w-well," Cassondra stammered, "he got a call, that, um, he was urgently needed down here… because…"

"He hired another Russian call girl," Albertson said evenly, without breaking eye contact with Downe, "but she got lost on the way in, so we're out looking for her."

"Oh!" Neil said. "Nice! Just like the good ol' days, eh, Frankie? God, and you've still… you know, you've still *got it*, even at your age?" He held up his forearm and clenched his fist; at first Cassondra didn't know what he was doing, but then she remembered seeing some idiot frat boy at her college use that gesture as shorthand for getting an erection. "*You know…?*"

Albertson and Cassondra both subtly dipped forward to make Donaldson's head bounce back and forth on his neck, so that it looked like he was nodding.

"Aw, good for you, buddy!" Neil said, reaching forward and giving Donaldson a friendly clap on the shoulder. "You go get her, you stallion you! I'll keep an eye out, see if I can spot her for you." His eyes darted to one side, then the other, and he subtly licked his lips before returning his gaze to Donaldson. "So, uh, what's this one look like? Blonde, right, like the last couple?" He cupped his hands under his own chest. He was starting to sweat. "Big, uh… you know, *big*… what're we talkin', C's, D's? *Double*-D's?"

"That's classified information," Cassondra blurted out quickly. "What we want to know is, what are *you* doing here at the White House so late?"

Downe just stared at her.

"Um, sorry," Albertson said. "She's new." He turned to her, craning his neck to look at her past Donaldson's limp head. "Mr. Downe sleeps in the Oval Office at night, ever since his wife kicked him out of the house. One of the couches folds out into a futon."

"Oh," Cassondra said. "Well. Um. It's been a pleasure talking to you, Mr. Downe, but, um… the President needs to… you know…"

"Yes!" Neil said. "Of course!" he scurried past them, on towards the Oval Office. "Best of luck, sir! I'm sure you'll find her soon! And I'm sure she isn't planting bugs like the last one we lost!"

"*Hush!*" Albertson stage-whispered down the hallway to him. "You know the President doesn't like it when you bring that up!"

Neil Downe opened his mouth like he was about to say something else, then just nodded his head in assent, turned around, and scurried back around the next corner.

Cassondra let out a sudden gasp and took a couple slow, careful breaths, like she'd been holding her breath for the last several minutes.

"Holy God," she breathed. "That was his lawyer!"

"Yeah," Albertson said. "I know."

"But, I mean, he and Donaldson have known each other for *years!* How were we able to fool *him?!*"

"Because, for obvious reasons, Donaldson can't talk right now," Albertson said, "and we can only make him do a few vague, confusing gestures. The best we can do is make him look and act like an aloof, temperamental, uncommunicative jerk." He offered a thin, wistful smile. "So yeah, don't be surprised if it takes people a while to notice the difference."

Cassondra thought on this for a moment.

"*Riiiiiiiiight,*" she finally said, stroking her chin with her free hand. "Jesus Christ. Is this actually going to work?"

"Well, it sure as hell isn't going to last forever," Albertson said. "Despite my best efforts in the lab, we've only got another couple days at most before he's so decomposed that even the most devoted kiss-ass won't be able to ignore it anymore. And even now, the fewer people who see him the better. We should avoid news cameras like the plague."

"But at least for the next couple days…?" Cassondra said, allowing the briefest hint of hope to creep into her voice.

Albertson closed his eyes, lowered his head, and sighed.

"Yes," he said. "At least for the next couple days, we should have this—"

Albertson's phone rang.

"Ah, fuck," he grumbled, fishing around in the breast pocket of his coat until he finally fished it out and glanced at the screen. "It's Luna." He tapped the "answer call" icon, and then turned on the speaker. "Talk to us," he said.

There was a pause.

" '*Us?*' " Luna's voice said on the other side of the line. "Oh, God, don't tell me that servant girl is still with you."

"I didn't really know what else to do with her," Albertson said. "Besides, she's as much a part of this now as we are." He smiled bemusedly to himself, then shot Cassondra a knowing glance. "She can have her moments when she's useful."

Cassondra rolled her eyes.

Luna's annoyed sigh came out of the phone as a garbled rush of static.

"Albertson, can you *please* stop sleeping with that poor little intern long enough to focus on *our problem?*"

Albertson and Cassondra both did a double-take.

"What the fuck did you just say—"

"Albertson, I need you to come meet me in front of the Capitol," she said. "*Now.*"

"Uh," Albertson stammered, staring back and forth between the phone in his hand and Donaldson's slumping head next to him. "It would be a little easier if you could come meet us here back in the White House. Or, like, *a lot* easier."

"Albertson, stop being a pussy and get your ass over here!" Luna snapped. "Bring the fucking girl if you have to! I don't care! If you're afraid of exposure, you can get here using the tunnels."

"No," Albertson grumbled. "Oval Office is off-limits. Neil Downe has already come in for the night."

"*Fuck,*" Luna barked, but it didn't seem to be directed at anyone in particular. "All right. We can work around this. I still need you to come to the Capitol, though. Be here in half an hour." She paused for a moment. "That isn't a *request.*"

"Luna, I really can't—"

The phone went dark. Luna had hung up. Albertson sighed and slipped the phone back into his pocket, then gave Cassondra a clearly-forced, nervous smile. That almost caught her off-guard; could he really *not* use his hologram to fake emotions? Was his translation software really so sensitive it picked up all the nuances of a *forced* smile?

"So," he said, trying and failing to sound jovial and nonchalant. "How do you feel about going on a late-night stroll?"

<u>CHAPTER 12</u>

It was a cool, crisp Washington, D.C. night, with the wind just barely rustling the leaves of the surrounding trees and a distant, high-pitched hum ringing ever-presently from the unseen multitudes of crickets and tree frogs who only deigned to make the presence known well after nightfall.

By the time Albertson and Cassondra finally managed to hobble up the Capitol steps with Donaldson's body in tow, Luna and Jacob were already up there waiting for them. Luna had her arms folded in front of her chest, and was tapping her foot impatiently.

"I told you to be here thirty minutes after I called," she hissed. "It's been almost an *hour*. What have you—"

Her eyes went wide and her face went ghost-white as soon as she caught a glimpse of her father. Or, at least, what was left of her father. Jacob Kirkman abruptly doubled over and threw up on the Capitol steps.

"Uh, *hi*," Albertson said sheepishly. "Sorry we're late. But we may have come up with a solution for—"

"*A solution?!*" Luna screamed. "How is this a…?" Her head was shaking so hard she couldn't finish the sentence. She raised a hand to her forehead, unable to take her eyes off of Donaldson's body. "How did you even think to do this?" She started glancing back and forth between Albertson and Cassondra, her gaze still occasionally stopping on the body between them. "You are two sick fucking people, you know that?"

"Hey, don't look at me!" Cassondra snapped. "This whole thing was *his* idea!"

"Hey, it fooled his lawyer," Albertson said. "And one of the aides. And—oh, yeah—*his wife*."

Luna's entire posture stiffened, and her face scrunched up with a cross between fear and disgust. Cassondra privately decided that it was the exact same physical reaction she would've expected if a metal bar had been rammed up Luna's ass. She let her brain linger on that thought for just a couple seconds.

"My mother," she drawled out slowly, as if the words were physically making her sick, "has *seen him?*"

"Yeah," Albertson said.

Luna's arms flailed in Donaldson's general direction.

"*Like this?!*"

"Yeah," Albertson said again. "She legitimately couldn't tell the difference."

Luna was shaking her head, staring off at nothing in particular. She slowly lowered herself down and took a seat on one of the top steps. Cassondra glanced over towards Jacob, just to keep track of him, and found that he'd fainted, and was now lying face-down in his own puke. She briefly considered rolling him over so he didn't suffocate. Maybe if he didn't get up in another couple minutes she'd nudge him with her foot.

"I know they haven't been sleeping in the same bed for years," Luna said. "But this is…" She scrunched her eyes shut, shook her head a little more vigorously, then stood back up. "You know what, I'm just not going to think about that right now."

"Yeah," Cassondra muttered weakly. "That's basically how the rest of us are staying sane."

"Okay," Luna said, clapping her hands as she walked back towards the Capitol building. "I was going to ask you for help with cleaning something up in here, but it looks like you two clearly have your hands full, so I guess Jacob and I can take care of it on our own." She stopped and glanced around. "Wait, where is Jacob?"

"Over here," Cassondra said. She'd kept one eye on him the entire time; he still hadn't gotten up. The bubbles in the puddle of vomit had stopped too. That probably wasn't a good sign. "Here," she said, "let me see if I can nudge him awake." She still had one leg attached to Donaldson's, but she tried to reach out with the other one, basically doing the splits in place. He was lying further away from her than she'd originally thought.

"Cass?" Albertson said. "Cass, what are you doing?"

"Just… trying… to wake him… up…"

"Well you need to tell me these things!" Albertson said, pivoting Donaldson's body around towards her. "We need to work in tandem in order to keep this going. Donaldson's already balanced pretty precariously as it is."

Cassondra's ankle was bent at a pretty weird position, but she felt the tension slowly releasing as Albertson shifted Donaldson's weight. She was about to take another step towards Jacob when she suddenly heard a familiar low, quiet grunting echo out from inside the Capitol Building.

Everyone's heads snapped to attention as Squeally Dan happily trotted out onto the steps and stared at them all quizzically. Luna immediately rolled her eyes.

"Oh, God," she groaned. "What the hell is that *thing* doing here?"

Albertson furrowed his brow, visibly annoyed with Luna's aloofness.

"He shows up in weird places," Albertson said. "I think there are entrances to the catacombs only he knows about. Like, little pig-sized cracks in the bedrock, or maybe he even burrowed down himself. I've actually been trying to figure out for a while now how he—"

"I really, really don't care," Luna grumbled. "Make him go away, please."

Albertson sighed, then clapped his hands a couple times.

"Go on, Danny! Scat! I can't play with you right now!"

Squeally Dan immediately perked up and started trotting towards Albertson. Albertson unconsciously took a step back, increasing the strain on Cassondra's ankle.

"No, don't come *towards* me! I don't have any treats right now! Come back later, Danny! Daddy's busy!"

Halfway to his rendezvous with Albertson, Squeally Dan abruptly stopped, pivoted in place, and instead ran up to Jacob Kirkman, who was still lying face down in the puddle of vomit. Or, more specifically, Squeally Dan ran up to the puddle of vomit itself, and started sniffing at it greedily.

"*Oh, God, Danny, don't do that!*" Albertson choked. "That's just sick!"

Jacob Kirkman suddenly let out a loud groan, shifting slightly in place. He turned his head to the side and started coughing and spitting, then opened his eyes to see Squeally Dan's expectant face hovering inches from his own.

"*Waugh!*" he shouted, pushing himself up and scrambling away from the confused pig. But he wasn't looking where he was going, and before Cassondra could move, he crashed into her leg with his full weight.

Cassondra let out a startled yelp as she crashed heavily to the ground. The weight of Donaldson's body landed on top of her, but only for a moment, as the commotion had made Albertson lose his balance too and he was stumbling away from her in the opposite direction. *Towards* the stairs. Cassondra tried to scramble back to her feet, but it was too late; the rubber bands holding her and Donaldson's legs together stretched to their breaking point and snapped one by one, as the stump of Donaldson's other leg slipped out of the empty shoe that was taped to Albertson's.

"Oh *nooo*," Cassondra stammered as she stumbled forward, her hands fumbling for anything they could grasp onto in order to keep President Donaldson from plunging down the Capitol steps. Her fingers found Donaldson's cartoonishly long necktie and wrapped around it, hoping a good solid yank would be enough to pull him back from the brink. The line of silk went taught for just a fraction of a fraction of a second and the President's body hung in suspended motion over the top step… and then with a loud, wet, sickening *pop* the necktie went slack again, and they all watched with muted horror as Donaldson's disembodied head bounced down the Capitol steps, followed moments later by the rest of his body.

"*Shit!*" Albertson shouted, scrambling back to his feet as quickly as he could and running down the stairs after them. "Shit shit shit shit shit shit shit shit—"

Jacob Kirkman was also suddenly overcome with the compulsion to intervene—perhaps to secure the President's head while Albertson took care of the rest of the body—and started down the steps as well, but as neither of them was really paying attention to the other one, he and Albertson collided with each other halfway down the staircase and proceeded to tumble the rest of the way down ass-over-teakettle, finally landing in a heap on top of Frank Donaldson's now-decapitated body.

Then Squeally Dan scampered down after both of them.

Luna and Cassondra both facepalmed in almost perfect unison.

"I don't know what you're indignant about," Luna said as she and Cassondra both walked—*slowly, carefully*—down the Capitol steps. "It's your fault any of that happened in the first place."

"I'm sorry!" Cassondra stammered. "I just reached out and blindly grabbed for something, I didn't know that was going to happen! I didn't know what I was doing!"

"Yes," Luna said coldly. "That much is obvious. You wouldn't have even had to grab for him at all if you hadn't been standing there doing calisthenics in place while trying to hold onto my father's body."

Cassondra scowled.

"Well pardon me all to hell," Cassondra said. "I'm sorry I tried to stop your husband from drowning in his own puke."

"You'd better be," Luna grumbled as they reached the bottom of the stairs, where Albertson, Jacob, and Donaldson looked like nothing but a tangled pile of limbs in the darkness. Luna just kicked Jacob in the ribs, causing him to gasp out a muted squeak, and he crawled weakly off the top of the pile, leaving only Albertson and Donaldson. Cassondra breathed a silent sigh of relief that Albertson's hologram-watch had held up during all the commotion. He also still, somehow, had a lit cigarette in his mouth.

"All right, Jeffery," Luna said, making no attempt whatsoever to hide the palpable disgust in her voice. "Are you planning to get up any time soon?"

"No, no," Albertson muttered back, his voice weak and wheezy. "I was actually thinking I could just lie here until I die, if that's quite all right."

"You realize you're still lying on a human corpse, right?"

"Oh, God, *eww!*" Albertson gasped, scrambling off of Donaldson's body. Luna reached over to help pull him back to his feet, which he shied away from, which only made her non-verbally insist even more. Cassondra rolled her eyes and knelt down to help pick Donaldson's body back up, and then she froze.

"Jeff?" she said, unable to keep her voice from quavering. "Luna? Where's his head?"

"What?" they both said in unison, their attention snapping back to Donaldson's body.

"It landed right next to me," Albertson said, looking around frantically. "It should be right—*Danny!*"

Cassondra heard that familiar quiet snorting, and followed Albertson's gaze until she saw Squeally Dan sitting quietly off to the side, happily clutching President Donaldson's head in his mouth.

Albertson gulped and lightly clapped a couple times, trying to keep his voice low and soothing even though it was trembling so badly he could barely get the words out.

"C-c-come here, Danny," he cooed. "Bring that over here, yeah? I've got an even better treat for you if you just bring us back that head—"

"*If you don't drop that fucking head right fucking now,*" Luna screamed, lunging at Squeally Dan, "*I will fry you into bacon myself!*"

Squeally Dan immediately leapt to his feet and bolted away, before Luna could even get close. She was left huddled down on the ground on all fours, panting desperately to catch her breath, while the pig disappeared into the nearby bushes and took the President's head with him.

CHAPTER 13

Cassondra was sitting at the bottom of the Capitol steps with Luna Donaldson while Albertson and Jacob both searched through the bushes for Squeally Dan and/or the President's disembodied head. Luna had gotten eerily quiet ever since the decapitation had happened, and she and Cassondra were both trying really hard not to look at the raw neck stump on the President's body just barely within their field of vision.

"Ah, there we go," Albertson said. Luna and Cassondra both immediately turned to look in his direction, but the expression on his face already told them his news wasn't as good as they'd hoped. As soon as he noticed they were watching, he pulled up a section of the bushes to reveal a deep underground burrow just big enough for Squeally Dan to squeeze into. "I told you he had his own ways of getting underground," Albertson said. "Little bugger's probably in the catacombs by now."

"Okay," Cassondra called back over her shoulder. "So, what, should we go down and start looking for him now?"

"Cass, do you have any idea how big and sprawling that tunnel system is?" Albertson said, walking out of the bushes. "With only four of us looking, and Danny clearly having ways in and out we don't know about, it could be days before we find him. And even if one of us does find him, he's already shown that he can outrun us if he wants."

"Oh, Christ!" Luna gasped. It was the first thing she'd said since Squeally Dan had disappeared. "We're never going to find it!" Her words were coming out as more of a high-pitched whine now and she had her hands on the side of her head as she slowly rocked back and forth in place. Cassondra almost did a double take, startled. She had never seen *Luna* having a breakdown before; she hadn't even thought the woman was capable of it. Even though there was absolutely no love lost between her and Luna, seeing the woman like this just didn't feel right. Cassondra narrowed her eyes and tried to look away. "We've lost my father's *head,*" Luna continued, "and now there's going to be no hiding it, everyone's going to *know* he's dead, and Jacob and I are going to be investigated, and then we're going to go to prison, and that fucking monster Patrick Muntz is going to end up in charge of the country, and—"

"Luna!" Cassondra snapped. "We don't have time for this shit! You need to get it together, *now!*"

"Aw, come on, Cass," Albertson said, shuffling over and sitting down next to her. "We've both had to talk *you* down from nervous breakdowns today. Don't begrudge the rest of us a moment or two to freak out."

Luna sniffed loudly once, then twice, then rubbed her nose on her sleeve.

"I think there's only one collective nervous breakdown," she said, her voice still a little shaky, "and we've just been passing it back and forth to each other all night." She took a long, slow breath, then finally stood back up. "Okay," she said, still sounding a little unsure. "Okay."

"You good now?" Albertson said, looking up at her as he remained seated for a little longer.

"Oh, God, no," Luna said. "Tonight has added *years* to the amount of therapy I already need because of my father." She took in a deep breath and let it out slowly. "But I think I can continue to function for another couple hours, yes."

"Glad to hear it," Albertson said, pushing himself back up to his feet. "So, *do* you think we should keep looking for the President's head? If we get a larger search party together, we might be able to do a more effective sweep of the catacombs."

"No, no, the fewer people know about any of this, the better." She shot him a nasty side-eye. "If that *animal* of yours really did take it underground, at least we don't have to worry about anyone else finding it."

"Unless Squeally Dan gets bored down there and decides to bring it back up here," Albertson said.

"True," Luna muttered, "but with the amount of wear-and-tear he's putting it through, it'll probably be rotted beyond recognition by then. Anyone who finds it will just think it's a random disembodied head."

Cassondra gulped, and then calmly raised her hand.

"What?" Luna said sharply.

"I'm sorry for being short with you a moment ago," Cassondra said. "I was okay until you said the word 'rotted.' But I think I would like my turn to use 'the nervous breakdown' now."

"No," Luna snapped, "you can still be useful to us. The four of us are still the only ones who know what's really going on with my father, so we need all hands on deck until this is finished."

"Finished?" Albertson said. "What does 'finished' mean, exactly? What's the endgame of all of this? Because right now, it looks like all we can possibly do is keep killing time until someone inevitably realizes Donaldson is dead and Muntz takes over."

"*No!*" Luna barked. "That is *not* going to happen."

"Really?" Albertson said. "Because that's the only way I can see this ending. Unless, of course, you have some other secret machinations brewing that you haven't told us about, *hmmm?*"

Luna stood in place, bristling, her mind cycling through a dozen different ways to go on the defensive, then relented at the last moment and just narrowed her eyes.

"*Of course* I have machinations I haven't told you about, you *lout*," she said, her tone of voice icy but measured. "What kind of fool do you take me for?"

"What the fuck?" Cassondra said indignantly. "A second ago you were lying on the ground in a blubbering mess, now you're suddenly back in supervillain mode treating us all like your henchmen again? What the hell is wrong with you?"

Albertson was shaking his head.

"Just let it go, Cass," he grumbled.

"No!" Cassondra said, taking a defiant step towards Luna. "We've seen the mask slip, Luna. We know you don't *have* to act like Bitch Queen of the Amazons when it doesn't suit you, so why do you keep putting it on? We're on the same side here!"

Luna's eyes just narrowed.

"Just because we all happened to stumble into the same awful situation doesn't mean I should *trust you*," she said, her eyes flicking back and forth between the two of them like a snake. "And before you ever address me like that again, I would advise *both* of you to *remember your place*."

Cassondra was about to respond, but Albertson discreetly put a hand on her shoulder and theatrically rolled his eyes for Luna to see.

"You know what, *fine*," he said. "I'm not even going to press. You can *keep* your cutesy little '*secrets*,' I've got more important shit to worry about. We *both* do." He took his hand off Cassondra's shoulder and straightened his tie, then turned his back to Luna, taking a few steps towards what was left of President Donaldson's body. "At least tell me you got some sort of arrangement worked out with Bronstein."

Luna's entire body suddenly stiffened.

"Yes," she said slowly. "The Speaker. He and I have reached, um… an *arrangement*." She paused for a moment. "A *secret* arrangement. That I can't tell you about."

"Whatever," Albertson said, kneeling down over Donaldson and grabbing the man's legs. Cassondra quickly followed suit, hurrying over and grabbing Donaldson's arms, so that they two of them were able to hoist him up off the ground again. Albertson glanced up at Luna just for a moment, and pointed at his own face. "See this?" he said. "This is me not caring. Go have your fun playing baby's first espionage."

Luna just scowled at him. Jacob Kirkman, having finally picked himself up, staggered over until he was standing next to her. As soon as she saw him, Cassondra had to stifle a pitying laugh. It looked like a strong breeze could've blown the man over.

"You may laugh now, Albertson," Luna Donaldson said as she put an arm around her husband's shoulders. "But if you don't start playing your cards right and showing some respect awful damn fast, you're going to see what happens to those who cross Jacob and I, and I promise you, our retribution will be swift and—"

Jacob took one look at the President's raw, bleeding neck stump and immediately fainted again, his head bouncing off of one of the stone steps of the Capitol with a hollow *thunk*.

"*Oh God damn it!*" Luna Donaldson shrieked. "Just *go*," she said, covering her face with one hand and using the other to shoo them away. "You two take care of my father's current *situation*. Jacob and I have more work to do here." And as she and Albertson carried Frank Donaldson's body away, Cassondra could just barely make out his daughter muttering, "…as soon as the little pussy wakes up…"

Albertson and Cassondra were both silent for a while as they made their way back to the White House, for lack of anywhere better to go, but as soon as she was convinced they were safely out of earshot, Cassondra quietly muttered, "I don't think we can trust her."

"Oh, really?!" Albertson said. "What was your first clue? Was it when she looked us dead in the eye and *told* us to our faces that we couldn't trust her, then spent the next five minutes doing her best Lady Macbeth impression?"

"Well, actually, it was a little before that," Cassondra muttered. "But your sarcasm is duly noted and I will shut up now."

"No, I'm sorry, it's fine," Albertson grumbled, his face scrunching up in such a way that suggested he would be facepalming if his hands were free. "It's just been a really, really stressful day—obviously—and I think tempers are flaring all around."

"Yeah," Cassondra said quietly. "Sorry if I snapped at you earlier, or if I snap at you again later. It's just, you know, what you said. Stress."

"I figured," Albertson said. "Don't worry, I'm not holding it against you."

"Thanks," she murmured. Then, after another lengthy pause, "Um, so, side note: this guy's neck stump is dripping blood on me, and I'm *kind of* about to start freaking out again."

"It's not blood," Albertson said. "I took care of that, remember? It's just embalming fluid."

"Oh, well pardon me all to hell," Cassondra said. "The strange fluid that's leaking out of the *dead body's fucking neck stump* is dripping on me, and I would like it to stop before I lose what precious little composure I have left and start running around in circles and screaming again. Is that *specific* enough for you?"

"Oh for God's sake—look, my arms are getting tired too, let's just set him down for a sec, okay?"

They both abruptly dropped Donaldson's body at the same time. He landed on the soft, dewy, early-morning grass with a resounding *thud.*

"So, obviously, we need to patch him up," Albertson said, "before we do anything else with him. Like, public appearances, obviously, but even basic transport is going to get more and more difficult if he keeps falling apart on us." He gestured towards her with a quick little gentlemanly flourish of his hand. "As you just stated so eloquently."

Cassondra smiled, curtseyed, and then flipped him off, still smiling.

"Which *means*," Albertson continued, "we need to start looking into, um—How do I put this delicately?—*replacement parts*."

"What are you saying?" Cassondra said, shuffling up next to Albertson and staring down with him at Frank Donaldson's body.

"I'm *saying*," Albertson muttered, "that we need to find the President a new head."

CHAPTER 14

They'd been driving for hours.

Albertson was behind the wheel of the beat-up old Civic he'd bought shortly after coming to earth, with Cassondra slumped over in the passenger seat next to him, snoring loudly. Albertson, fortunately, only needed to sleep every three days or so because of his alien biology, so he was able to get them all the way from D.C. to the woodsy part of upstate New York in just under four hours, while Cassondra grabbed the last four hours of sleep she was probably going to get for a while. One of the advantages of driving in the middle of the night was that there had been no traffic, so they were getting close to their destination just as the thin light of dawn began to peek through the trees lining either side of the road.

In fact, Albertson had just been pondering what great time they were making when the engine of his car started sputtering, and thick, black smoke started pouring out of the engine.

"Oh, no," he said out loud, leaning forward to place his hand on the dash. "C'mon, Bessie," he whispered. "You can do it, girl. Come on…" There was a loud *bang* from the engine that visibly loosened the car's hood, and he could feel the car already starting to slow down. "Ah, *shit*," Albertson groaned. "Come on! Oh, no no no no no!"

"Whazzat…?" Cassondra muttered groggily, without opening her eyes. "We almost there or what—"

The entire car lurched violently, instantly jolting Cassondra awake.

"What the fuck?" she sputtered, sitting bolt-upright and bracing her hands against the seat. "What's going on?"

"The fucking car," Albertson hissed, repeatedly stomping on the accelerator to no visible effect. They were still slowing down. He finally managed to pull to the side of the road just as they slid to a full and complete stop. Without saying another word, they both got out, shuffled around to the front of the car, and pulled the hood open. More smoke billowed out to greet them, but the output seemed to be slowing down now that the engine had turned off. Cassondra coughed as the remaining cloud dissipated, but Albertson just pulled the cigarette out of his mouth for a second and took a deep breath. After another moment of silence, he breathed out slowly through his nose, then replaced the cigarette. "Well," he finally muttered. "This isn't good."

"Yeah, no shit!" Cassondra said. "Do we have any idea how close the nearest gas station is?"

"We passed one about five miles back," Albertson muttered, still gazing down at the smoldering engine. Cassondra slumped forward, closed her eyes, and sighed.

"I mean, a five mile walk is *doable*," she grumbled. "But what does that do to our timetable?"

"Destroys it, basically," Albertson said. "Obviously, we needed to get up here and then back down to D.C. as quickly as possible. Which is why I was pushing ninety most of the way here." He took a step back. "Which was apparently pushing it too much for this piece of *crap—*" Albertson kicked the fender of the car as hard as he could, then immediately fell to the ground and clutched at his foot. "*Arrggghhh!* What do they make these bumpers out of?!"

Cassondra just rolled her eyes.

"Why do you drive a piece of crap car like this, anyway?" she said. "I mean, you've got a pretty high-paying job."

"I wasn't expecting to be on this planet for very long," Albertson grunted as he got back to his feet. "I didn't think I'd need anything that would last more than a couple months. And then buying a new one just felt…" He sighed. "I dunno. *Wasteful.*"

"*Wasteful?*" Cassondra said. "What do you even spend your money on?"

Albertson shrugged.

"I don't really need anything other than the essentials," he said. "So what I don't spend on food, rent, and cigarettes, I donate to charity." He smiled weakly. "Animal shelters and Greenpeace, usually. All anonymous, of course."

"So you're telling me that you're functionally broke right now?"

"Oh, no, I don't give *everything* away," Albertson said. "I've still got a good, oh, two hundred dollars saved up. Maybe two hundred fifty, since I haven't been eating out much lately."

Cassondra facepalmed.

"Perfect," she grumbled. "Well, we're out in the middle of nowhere, and the only people who know we're here are Luna and Jared, who I don't really think we can call for help."

"Yeah, no," Albertson said. "Showing weakness in front of them is a bad idea."

"So I guess I'll start hiking to the gas station," Cassondra continued, stepping out onto the road, "and pray that the entire country doesn't collapse in the extra day or two it's going to take us to get this sorted—"

"Wait! Cassondra!" Albertson said, desperately gesturing towards something further down the road. "I see headlights!"

Cassondra turned around. Sure enough, there were two bright orbs off in the distance hurtling towards them, coming down the road in the opposite direction they'd been going. Cassondra immediately broke into a dead run towards the oncoming car, waving her arms wildly and screaming at the top of her lungs.

"*Hey! Stop! We need help! Heeeyyy!*"

The approaching vehicle—which they could now see was a bright red pickup truck—blared it's horn a couple times, then swerved to the side of the road with an ear-splitting tire screech, coming to a stop just a couple feet away from Albertson's car.

"Jesus Christ, girl!" the driver shouted, throwing the driver's-side door open and climbing out. "The hell is wrong with you? You trying to get run over?!"

"I'm sorry! I'm sorry!" she said, jogging back over to him. "It's just, our car broke down, and we're kinda stranded out here, and we don't know where the next rest stop is, and you're the first person to drive by, and we really just need help, or a ride, or *something*." She realized her nose was running, and wiped it off on her sleeve. Neither of them had particularly liked the idea of pulling a four-hour car trip in their business clothes, so Cassondra had changed into a college hoodie and sweatpants before their departure, while Albertson was wearing a yellow plaid button-up shirt, jeans, and a baseball cap tucked low over his eyes. He'd actually, physically *changed* into them, too; his clothes weren't part of the hologram.

The stranger glanced over at their car and clicked his tongue, then strode over, pulled the hood open, and leaned down over the engine.

"Oh, yeah, this is easy," he said. "I can fix this in a couple minutes, right here."

"Wait," Cassondra said, "really?!"

"Yeah," he muttered, turning around and walking back to his truck. "Just let me get my tools." He reached into the bed of his truck—which was covered by a cammo-patterned tarp—and pulled out an old red toolbox that had definitely seen better days, and loped back over to them. "What did you say your name was again?"

"Uh," Cassondra stammered. "*Monique*." She held out her hand.

"Tyler," he said, taking her hand and shaking it. Then he let go of her, and held his hand out towards Albertson, who had been hanging to the back for fear of being recognized, since he still looked like the Secretary of State. "What about you?"

Albertson hesitated for a moment before he realized Tyler was wearing work gloves, and wouldn't be able to directly feel his skin.

"Oh, uh, I'm John," he said, leaning forward and shaking Tyler's hand.

Tyler arched an eyebrow. "I'm sure you are," he muttered as he let go of Albertson's hand. Cassondra didn't know what he meant at first, then realized that most people would assume there were only so many reasons for a girl her age to be out in the middle of nowhere with a significantly older man she clearly wasn't related to, and most of them weren't particularly savory. On one hand she felt the need to defensively correct him, but at the same time realized that letting people jump to their own conclusions about her and Albertson probably helped their cover.

"Nice to meet you both," Tyler said, turning back towards their car. "What're you folks doing out here this time of morning?"

Cassondra had trouble deciphering his tone; outwardly he was being friendly, but there was still something vaguely accusatory in the way he talked to them. Maybe it was just the assumptions about them she'd already deciphered, or maybe he could tell they were still up to something else shady. Or maybe he was just still a little upset about being stopped. She needed to tell him *something*, though, and if he was already getting suspicious of them, it was probably best not to layer any more lies on top of it unless absolutely necessary.

"Well, um… okay," she said. "You know the comedian Kate Phoenix?"

"Phoenix?" he said, pulling a tool she didn't recognize out of the toolbox and leaning over the engine again. "Isn't she the one who got in trouble for, like, making that fake disembodied head of President Donaldson?"

"Yeah!" Cassondra said, suddenly brightening up. "I'm actually surprised you remember! That bit was a while ago."

Tyler smiled broadly, and a hearty chuckle echoed out from beneath the truck's hood. "That was fuckin' brilliant, though!" he said. "Anything that takes that asshole down a peg or two is golden in my book."

Cassondra forced herself to laugh.

"Yeah, well, don't tell anybody, but she actually lives in a secluded little house up around these parts."

"No shit?" Tyler said, setting one of his tools down and reaching for another one out of the box. "Well, I can't blame her. This part of the country is just gorgeous."

"Yeah," Cassondra muttered. "And, um…" Okay, *now* it was time to start making shit up. "We're from Hollywood," she said. "And we have a role we'd like to discuss with her in an upcoming movie. But she's super busy, you know, being an entertainer and all. So first thing in the morning was the only time in her schedule when we could set up a meeting." She gulped. "Which is why, you know, it's *really* important that we get there in a timely manner without any delays."

"Ah, I gotcha," Tyler said. "I'm kind of on the time clock myself. I'm trying to be in Washington, D.C. by this afternoon."

"Oh, really?" Albertson said. "Well, you're on the right track. Just got a couple hours ahead of you."

"Yeah, I know," Tyler grunted, as he strained to twist something on the car's engine back in place. "Which is why having to stop for you folks so suddenly threw me for a little bit of a loop. But, that shouldn't be a problem anymore, because I believe I'm just about..." He stood back up, leaned back for a second to admire his work, then slammed the hood of the car back down. "Done!" He turned back towards them, hands on his hips, beaming with pride. "All right, folks, you should be good to go."

"Oh my God," Cassondra gasped, shuffling up to the car in a state of awed deference. "It's really fixed?"

"Well, the vehicle's on her last legs, so you're gonna have to replace her pretty soon anyway," he said, "but she should at least go for a while longer without breaking down on you."

"Oh my God, thank you so much!" Cassondra shouted, throwing her arms around Tyler. He laughed and patted her on the back, then disengaged from the hug.

"No problem, folks!" he said. "When y'all get to Ms. Phoenix, tell her you met her number one fan!"

"Will do," Albertson said, walking over to shake Tyler's (still gloved) hand. "And, again, *thank you.*"

While they were shaking, Tyler stared at him, his eyes slowly narrowing.

"Hey, fella," Tyler said. "Anyone ever tell you that you look like—whatshisname—Jeff Albertson? The Secretary of State or something?"

Albertson froze for a second mid-handshake, just staring back blankly at Tyler, then theatrically rolled his eyes.

"All the damn time!" he said. "I am so sick of hearing it! I don't even see the resemblance, but everyone else is always going on about it!"

Tyler let go of Albertson's hand and laughed as her turned back towards his truck.

"Yeah, I get that," he said. "People are always comparing me to that actor guy, Woody Harrleson, but I don't see it neither." He shrugged. "Ah, well. You know how people are."

"Yeah," Albertson said, waving to Tyler as he climbed back into the cab of his truck. "I mean, I think I might be related to Albertson. We're fourth cousins or something. But *his* side of the family stayed on the east coast while mine moved out to Los Angeles, and, I mean, big Catholic families, you know how hard it can be to keep track of everyone sometimes."

Tyler gave them one last wave through the windshield of his truck, then pulled back onto the road and sped away, leaving Cassondra and Albertson to watch as the dust cloud disappeared into the distance.

"Layin' it on a little thick there, Jeff," Cassondra finally muttered.

"Yeah, what can I say," Albertson grumbled. "I'm not good at ad-libbing. All the 'Jeff Albertson' stuff, my whole fake identity was made up by someone else in the Skreeez military and just kinda handed to me."

Cassondra let out a long sigh.

"You're a sleeper agent," she said, "who's not good at acting or ad-libbing?"

"…yeah…"

A pause.

"Are you sure, that your planet didn't just send you here to get rid of you?"

He waited a good couple second before answering.

"No," he finally said. "No, I am not sure of that."

Cassondra just stood in place, nodding to herself, then turned to get back in the car.

"Yours was brilliant, though!" Albertson said as he pulled open the driver's-side door to join her. "All that Hollywood stuff, you came up with that on the spot? That was great!"

"Mm-hmm," Cassondra muttered, nodding. "And as far as I'm concerned, it's our official cover story."

"You really think she'll fall for it?" Albertson said as he turned the key in the ignition and the engine once again purred to life. It was the most beautiful sound either of them ever heard.

"Christ, I hope so," Cassondra groaned, leaning back in her seat and scrunching her eyes shut. "It's literally the only plan we've got right now."

"It's still a pretty shitty one, though," Albertson admitted.

"Yeah, well, the shitty plan is the one you use when you haven't got any other options," Cassondra muttered. "How much longer till we get to her house?"

"GPS says another twenty minutes or so," Albertson said, straightening his phone in the little stand that was suction-cupped to the dashboard. "Why?"

"Want to see if I can squeeze in another catnap before we get there," Cassondra yawned, twisting in her seat to try and make herself comfortable, but the uneasiness was visible on her face. "Don't know if I'll be able to, though."

"Something bothering you?" Albertson said as he pulled back onto the road. "I mean, aside from all the obvious stuff."

"Eh," Cassondra grumbled. "That guy who helped us. Tyler or Tyson or whatever his name was. Did he seem, like, familiar to you at all?"

Albertson shrugged.

"Not really. Why?"

"I don't know, there's just this weird feeling tickling the back of my brain, like I should be remembering something, but I'm not." She yawned again, and snuggled down into the seat as much as she could. "Oh, well," she muttered. "It's not a priority right now. If it's important, it'll come back to me later."

CHAPTER 15

Cassondra and Albertson were both sitting on Kate Phoenix's couch, wearing enormous, shit-eating grins. They'd changed back into their work clothes before knocking on her door, so they both looked like professionals. Kate Phoenix was sitting across from them in her bath robe, staring at them bleary-eyed through the steam rising up from her coffee.

"I am so sorry," she grumbled as she lifted the mug to her lips so she could take a sip. "I totally forgot about this meeting. My personal assistant must've forgotten to tell me about it, or I would've set an alarm to wake up."

Actually, Albertson had used alien technology to remotely hack her phone and add it to her calendar, so that it looked like the meeting had been scheduled weeks ago. Still, it had taken a little bit of convincing when they'd first showed up at her door to stop her from calling the police.

"So," Kate said, "what's this movie about, anyway?"

"Well," Albertson said, "uh…"

"It's a science fiction movie," Cassondra cut in. "About an alien invasion."

Kate rolled her eyes.

"Oh, yeah," she said. "There've only been a million of those."

Cassondra felt herself getting flustered for a second, but managed to force it back down.

"Well, um, see," Cassondra continued, "all the other alien invasion movies, they're about planet vs. planet, right? I mean, like, the *entire* alien planet vs. *all* of earth. And, like, in *Independence Day*, it's a whole big thing where all the countries have to come together to fight off the aliens together."

Kate's eyes narrowed.

"Yeah?"

"Well, *we* think that's totally unrealistic," Cassondra said, proudly pointing at herself with her thumb. "All those different countries uniting under one cause? *Never gonna happen.* On our planet *or* theirs. So in *our* movie, it's just *one single country* on the alien planet that's invading, while the rest of the alien planet doesn't really care—and they're *only* invading the United States. Europe, Asia, and the Middle East never get touched by the aliens. Some of them even offer alliances with the alien country. Our alien invasion isn't '*us vs. them*,' it's one tiny little fraction of us vs. one tiny little fraction of them. And while we're asking the rest of the world to stand with us and fight off the invaders, the rest of the world couldn't care less because it's not happening in their back yard, you know? And it may even be advantages for some of them to let the U.S. get blown up by aliens."

Kate Phoenix leaned back in her chair, stroking her chin.

"Okay," she said. "You've got my attention. What have I got to do with it, though?"

"Well, um," Cassondra stammered, "well, we were thinking of this scene, just a quick little thing at the beginning, like a 'cold opening' before the credits, where the first flying saucer comes down in Washington, D.C., and President Donaldson shuffles out to get the paper, and this alien runs up and zaps him with a death ray, and his head comes flying off, and then you're standing there, and you catch the head, and you pose in the same way you did in that photo where you were holding the fake Donaldson head, and, and everyone will think it's funny because they remember the picture, and then you scream and the credits roll, and, um, um…" Cassondra gulped. She was sweating profusely. "I guess it's really more of a 'cameo' than anything else, but, um…"

Kate was shaking her head slowly.

"I don't know," she said. "Are people really going to get it? The whole fracas about that severed head thing was years ago. Does anyone even still remember it?"

"YES!" Albertson said, suddenly sitting bolt upright. "We were just talking to someone on the way here, a totally random guy we ran into when we had to stop, and when we mentioned your name the President's severed head was the first thing he brought up!"

"Oh," Kate said, her expression brightening a little. "I had no idea I'd left such and impact." Her eyes narrowed again. "Wait, you didn't tell him I live up here, do you?"

"What?" Albertson said, his eyes darting back and forth. "No! Of course not! Ha-ha, why would we ever—"

"*Look*," Cassondra cut in quickly. "If you're having trouble visualizing it, we could do a little reenactment of the scene right here, right now, to show you how it'd play out." She raised a hand to her mouth and hoarsely cleared her throat. "Do you. Um. Do you happen to still have the severed head prop lying around?"

"Oh, I must," Kate said, pushing herself up from her chair. "Let me go check in the garage, give me a second."

"Great!" Cassondra said. "And while you're there, my friend John is going to put on the alien costume."

"Wait," Albertson said, "I'm going to *what?*"

"We've got some great special effects people working on this movie," Cassondra called after Kate as the woman walked into the other room. "I swear, you'll love it!"

"Cass, are you *insane?!*" Albertson hissed, trying to keep his volume down just in case Kate was still within earshot. "I can't let any more people know what I really look like! I'm still not a hundred percent comfortable with having *you* know!" He gestured around at their surroundings. "Especially if you're gonna pull bullshit like this!"

"Look," Cassondra said evenly. "We can't do half-measures with this. We *need* that head. It looks *super* convincing, and neither of us is going to be able to mock up something that looks that good in the time we have left. We need to do whatever we can to convince her to hand it over, and we need to do it as quickly as possible, so we might as well come out swinging."

Albertson just stared at her for a moment, then finally lowered his head and sighed.

"God dammit," he muttered, and he reached down to flick a switch on his watch. A moment later, his human visage flickered away and he was sitting there in all his blue, scaly glory. "If I end up on a dissection table in Area 51 because of this, I'm blaming you."

"Of course," Cassondra said. Then, after a pause, "Wait, you have high-level government clearance. Are there actually aliens at Area 51?"

"Oh, absolutely," Albertson said. "None of my people, though. Most of them were Malathoosians. Totally different planet." He leaned back in his seat, folded his arms, and pouted a little bit. "Those guys were assholes, too. I went down to ask if they could give me a ride home once, and they just started pointing and laughing at me."

Cassondra had to stifle a chuckle.

"What, are your two races warring or something?" she said.

Albertson shrugged.

"I don't know if 'warring' is he right word," he grumbled. "I guess we kinda act like two rival frat houses. One time they released a virus on Katonk that gave everyone on the planet this really itchy rash on their butt that spelled out 'Malathoos Rules' in discolored scales—"

"Okay, I found it!" Kate said, striding back into the room, holding the papier-mâché head. "Now what did you want—holy shit, that *is* good alien makeup!"

"See!" Cassondra said, beaming. "What did I tell you?"

Kate set the head down on her coffee table, then walked up and leaned in close to Albertson's face.

"This looks *so real!*" she said. "How did you get it on so quickly?"

"Most of it's a latex mask," Cassondra said, "then we touch up with some quick makeup and a couple glued-on prosthetics. Looks even better on camera!"

"I'll bet!" Kate said as she stood back up. "Okay, so what did you want to do with the head, now?"

"So here's how the scene's going to work," Cassondra said, jumping up from the couch and grabbing the fake head. "I'm President Donaldson, see?" She held the fake head in front of her own and started waddling forward. "And I'm walking out of the White House, early in the morning, to get the paper—"

"Um, I don't think the President has to get his own paper," Kate said. "I don't think President Donaldson even reads the paper. Hell, I don't think President Donaldson can *read*."

"Suspension of disbelief," Cassondra said. "Now, just as he's reaching down to get the paper, and alien jumps out of the bushes! With a ray gun!"

Albertson glanced around the room. There was a bowl of fruit on the coffee table. He pulled out a banana and pointed it at Cassondra.

"Um," he muttered. "*Zap!*" He shook the banana.

"Oh no!" Cassondra shouted, falling to the floor as she tossed the head over to Kate. "President Donaldson is dead!"

Kate Phoenix snatched the severed head out of midair, held it out at arm's length, and let out a blood curdling scream, then collapsed back into her chair, laughing so hard she could barely breathe.

"Yeah, okay," she finally wheezed. "This sounds fun. I'm in."

"Great!" Cassondra beamed. "Thank you so much, Ms. Phoenix! We'll have our people send the contract to your people! This movie is gonna be epic!" She paused for a moment, and cleared her throat. "Now, um, I realize this may be kind of an odd request, but would it be all right if we took the head back to the studio with us?"

Kate glanced down at the papier-mâché head in her hands, then back up at them, skeptically.

"Why?" she said. "Can't you just make your own? I mean, your guys did such a good job with that alien makeup, mocking up your own fake head should be a no-brainer."

"Well, um, yes, of course!" Cassondra stammered. "But you see, um…"

"Our makeup and prop guys are in the hospital," Albertson said. "They were just in a car accident. Both of them. At once. They were in the same car. They carpool to work. They're gay lovers, actually, but the prop guy is asking us to keep it under wraps because he's not totally out of the closet to his family—"

"We'd like to let the *new* prop guy examine your version of the head," Cassondra cut in. "For reference." She walked up to Kate and leaned down so that her face was inches from the head, admiring it. "Because, I mean, you did *such* a good job with this thing!"

Kate blushed.

"Well, acting is my profession," she said, "but I've always had a soft spot for arts and crafts, you know? I've always felt that it's important for *artistic* people like us to have a secondary creative outlet that they do just for fun, and aren't trying to sell or profit off of." She gave them both a dreamy expression. "Do either of you have creative hobbies that you do to unwind outside of the studio?"

"Oh… oh, yeah," Cassondra said. "I, um, I paint butterflies."

"I write pornographic *Harry Potter* fan-fiction," Albertson said flatly.

"Nice," Kate said. "Hermione-on-Draco?"

"Hermione-on-Harry-*and*-Draco. *At the same time.*"

"*Niiice!*" Kate said. "So you *do* understand!"

"Uh-huh," Albertson said. "And sometimes, like, they even forget Hermione is there and just start going at it with each other—"

Cassondra discretely reached over and smacked Albertson lightly on the forearm to shut him up. Kate Phoenix was staring down pensively at the papier-mâché head in her hands. After what felt like an eternal moment of contemplation, she finally sighed and handed it over to Cassondra. "Okay," she said. "I know my baby will be in good hands with you. Just make sure you bring it back in one piece, okay?"

"Of course!" Cassondra said, plucking it greedily out of Kate's grip. "We should have it back to you in," she glanced at Albertson, "what, a month, two months at the most?"

"Yeah, sure," Albertson said. Under his breath, Cassondra heard him mutter, "we'll have either solved this mess or we'll be in prison by then, so yeah."

"Great!" Kate Phoenix said. "And I'll tell my agent to keep an eye out for your contract! What did you say the title of this movie was?"

Albertson and Cassondra exchanged a glance.

"It, uh, doesn't have a title yet," Cassondra said. "It's too early in the production."

"Yeah," Albertson said. "Right now, the studio is just calling it, 'Untitled Jim Carrey Project.' "

"Oh!" Kate said, brightening up even more. "Jim Carrey is in it?"

"No, actually," Albertson said. "I can see why you'd think that, but they're just calling it that that to throw people off."

"Anyway, we need to get going!" Cassondra said, reaching out and vigorously shaking Kate's hand while she still kept the fake head tucked under her other arm. "We need to get back to L.A. ASAP so we can start hammering out the details of this deal." She and Albertson were already inching their way back towards the door. "You understand, of course."

"Yeah," Albertson said, "and I need to get home and feed my pig." His eyes went wide as he paused for a moment, then put a hand on his forehead and gazed off for a second. "Oh my God, it's been a full day since I gave him a proper meal! No wonder he keeps stealing things, the poor little guy is starving! I mean, I guess he has had a *little* bit to eat since then, but I don't know if any of that stuff was good for him. And he can probably forage if he has to, but then there's no telling what he'll come across and try to eat! One time he got into one of the interns' pot brownies, and I don't know what made him sick, the chocolate or the pot, but I had to rush him to the vet, and it's a lot harder than you'd think to find a vet who'll treat potbellied pigs, and—Oh, God, this is the longest I've ever left him alone, I hope he's doing okay without Daddy to take care of him."

"*Please* stop referring to yourself as 'Daddy,' " Cassondra groaned. Her hand was on his shoulder, trying to discreetly pull him out the front door. "Now come *o-on*," she said in a sing-songy voice that only barely betrayed the true level of strain she was under. "We need to get going!"

"Wait," Kate Phoenix said, thoughtfully scratching her chin. "You're getting back on the plane? Right now? How are you expecting to get a severed head through airport security—?"

Cassondra slammed the front door shut, then finally allowed herself a brief moment to exhale before she and Albertson ran back to the car.

CHAPTER 16

"Christ," Cassondra breathed, almost reverently, once they'd gotten back on the road. She was driving this time, shaking her head slightly as her hands gently turned the wheel to match the curve of the road. "What was that shit about the pig back in Kate Phoenix's place? You're just as bad at telling the truth as you are at lying!"

"I'm worried, okay!" Albertson said defensively from the back seat of the car. He was lying down across the back with a moistened paper towel pressed against his forehead, claiming he had a stress headache. "Nobody else takes care of Squeally Dan! I have no idea how he's going to fare when I'm not around."

"I'm worried too," Cassondra said. "Only *I'm* worried about the fate of the country and/or the *world* if we screw this up."

Albertson scoffed.

"Oh, well, *yeah*," he said, sitting up as much as the cramped space in the car would allow. "I am too. I just thought that was obvious enough that I didn't need to keep saying it."

"No, actually," Cassondra said. "I think I kind of *would* like periodic reminders that the *literal alien invader* is actually on my side, thank you!"

"Okay, fine!" Albertson snapped back. "Earth Earth Earth! I love Earth! Definitely in my top ten favorite planets, maybe even top five! I like Earth Day, earthworms, and Earth-toned color palates!" He lay back down and closed his eyes. "There. Happy now?"

"Yes," Cassondra said flatly. "And speaking of alien shit, your hologram's still down."

"What?" Albertson said, then he glanced down at his blue, scaly hands. "Oh, shit, right." He tinkered with his watch until "Jeff Albertson" came back into view. "You don't suppose she recognized me in there, do you? When I was still in my human form?"

"If she did, she didn't say anything," Cassondra muttered. "Good news is, unless you're Hillary Clinton or someone who was already well-known, not a lot of people know or care who the Secretary of State is at any given moment. Add that to how Donaldson's cabinet gets shuffled around more often than a deck of cards…"

"Yeah, I'll take it," Albertson said, gently repositioning the paper towel on his head. "It's pretty much the only stroke of good luck we've gotten lately."

Cassondra snorted.

"Yeah, no kidding," she muttered. "But seriously dude, you are *so* piss-poor at lying! How have you not blown your cover before now?"

Albertson actually laughed at this.

"You have no idea how often I ask myself that same damn question," he said. "Christ, even *I* think I'm kind of an idiot sometimes."

"Exactly!" Cassondra said. "Like, no offense, but how is someone who screws up as often as *you* the most competent person in the Donaldson Administration?" She paused for a moment. "Actually, no, never mind. That part still make sense."

Albertson's eyes narrowed.

"Um, wait, which part am I not supposed to be taking offense at, again?"

"Whichever part makes you happy, dude," Cassondra chuckled. "Though I guess if you talk the exact same way when you lie as you do when you're telling the truth and just stressed out—like you were when you brought up the pig—that would actually make you a *great* liar. Because giving people too many false positives is still a good way of obscuring what you are and aren't making up out of the blue."

"Um, thank you? I think?" Albertson said, arching an eyebrow. "Is there a point to this?"

"Yes," Cassondra said firmly. "The very important point I'm trying to make is that I *genuinely* couldn't tell if the 'Harry Potter fan-fiction' thing was a lie or not, and the answer to that question is going to have a dramatic impact on how I interact with you in the future."

"*What?*" Albertson sputtered. "Yes, of course it was a lie!"

"So *that's* the first place your mind went when you were told to make up a creative hobby?" Cassondra said. "God, that's almost *weirder*, somehow!"

"Oh, come on!" Albertson said. "What was it you told her? You 'paint butterflies?' What a cliché answer! *Anyone* could paint butterflies! It's so generic! If you really want to be convincing, you need to make up something that sounds stupid and embarrassing, because that'll sound more authentic, because who would *make up* a stupid and embarrassing hobby that they don't actually do?"

"Well, you would, apparently!"

"Exactly!" Albertson snapped, then paused for a second, thinking. "Wait, what—"

Before Albertson could continue his thought, the car hit a monster pothole that almost sent him tumbling out of the backseat. Cassondra reflexively threw her arm protectively in front of the papier-mâché Donaldson head, which was seat-belted into the passenger seat next to her.

"Jesus," Albertson grumbled as he swung his legs around so that he was actually sitting in the seat properly. "Be careful, would you? This thing's already a hunk of junk. We don't want it to fall apart on us before we make it back to D.C."

"Yeah," Cassondra muttered. "I don't think we can rely on a friendly, well-meaning stranger to save our asses a second time around." She cleared her throat. "Believe me, I'm not *trying* to drive like an idiot." She patted the papier-mâché head next to her. "I mean, we can't risk anything happening to this thing, after all, now can we?"

Albertson glanced around the back of the seat and stared at the head.

"God, that thing's creepy," he said.

"More realistic than I was expecting, too," Cassondra grumbled as she side-eyed the head. "Let's hope we don't get pulled over on the way back. I have no idea how we'd explain this."

Albertson stared at her quizzically.

"Why would we get pulled over?" he said. "You're a good driver. You haven't broken any laws."

"Yeah," Cassondra said. "But I'm Black."

Albertson cocked his head slightly, confused.

"Why would that make you more likely to be pulled over?"

Cassondra just stared back at him through the rearview mirror.

"Jesus Christ," she breathed. "You really are from another planet."

"Yes!" Albertson said. "Yes, I am! So cut me some slack if I'm still not *totally* a hundred percent fluent in earth culture, all right?"

"Okay, but, like, you were working in the government!" Cassondra said. "How could you *work in the government* and still not at least pick some of this shit up?"

Albertson just shrugged.

"I don't know, I never heard it brought up," he said. "How often do your *human* lawmakers openly talk about this stuff?"

Cassondra just stared out blankly at the road for a couple seconds, then lowered her head and sighed.

"God dammit," she muttered. "Fuck this country so hard."

"Look, if all this is because you're worried about the head getting us in trouble, we can just move it into the trunk—"

"I do not take my eyes of the papier-mâché head," Cassondra growled. "I don't care if I have to strap it to myself like a baby in a papoose. Today has already been enough of an exercise in Murphy's law, I'm not even giving the *chance* for anything else to go wrong." Cassondra shook her head. "But, I'm sorry, I kinda got lost on a tangent. There's a lot more wrong with this country than we can fix with just a papier-mâché head."

"Well, yeah, obviously," Albertson said. "But, I mean, Donaldson's already dead, so as long as we can keep Muntz from taking his place—"

"No," Cassondra said. "It is so much deeper than just 'bad man in power doing bad things.' Muntz and Donaldson aren't the cause of this country's problems, they're the symptoms of it. How do you think those two assholes got elected in the first place?"

"They cheated their way in, didn't they?" Albertson said. "They gamed the electoral college so they could win the election without needing to win the popular vote."

"Exactly," Cassondra said. "Which means there was already a system in place long before they showed up that enabled them to win even though the majority of people didn't want them to. And that all the people who were in power before them looked at this system for centuries, knowing full well that it could be used to rob people of their democratic autonomy, and decided that they didn't really have a problem with it." Cassondra took in a deep breath and let it out slowly. "Which isn't to say that there weren't still plenty of people who *did* vote for him," she grumbled.

"Right," Albertson said. "I've been trying to make sense of that ever since I got here. I mean, from the moment he started his campaign, it was so obvious that

Donaldson wasn't fit to be President. You could see it from space!" He paused for several seconds, then flashed a wan smile. "Get it? Because, I'm, *like*, literally from space, so I can personally vouch that—"

"Yes, I got it, thank you," Cassondra grumbled. "Donaldson caught on because he gave everybody in the country permission to give into their worst impulses. He made racism and misogyny 'okay' again for all of his supporters, and he gave his opponents an enemy they could freely, unambiguously *hate* with that same level of vitriol without needing to feel an ounce of guilt: *himself*."

"Jeez," Albertson muttered. "That's kind of a really cynical way of looking at the world, isn't it?"

Cassondra just glared at him through the rearview mirror.

"Donaldson *won*, didn't he?"

Albertson stared at her, blinked a couple times, then just lowered his head and sighed.

"God dammit," he said. He seemed to be having trouble finding the right words, then finally sputtered out, "*How?* Do you people actually *enjoy* being miserable?"

Cassondra almost laughed at this, but it was a rueful, melancholy laugh.

"Believe me," she said, "I've listened to a lot of people go on a lot of rants about Donaldson. I've seen some really close friends and people I care about losing sleep over it and driving themselves to distraction. And, I mean, most of them are completely, one hundred percent *justified* in being angry and scared. This guy has done some horrible, heinous shit, literal crimes against humanity. I just…" she hesitated. "I wish there was something in their lives that they *enjoyed* with as much fervor and passion as they *hated* Frank Donaldson."

"Shit," Albertson muttered. "I'm sorry."

Cassondra just sighed.

"Isn't your fault," she grumbled, so quiet he could just barely hear her. "When you asked if we 'enjoy being miserable,' you aren't totally wrong. Losing your shit and getting worked up about something… I don't wanna say it feels *good*, but it can certainly be *cathartic.* All the stress and anxiety that builds up because of the exploitive capitalist hellscape we live in, mostly caused by things we have little to no control over, it makes sense that you'd want to find a target to vent some of that pent-up rage at." Her eyes narrowed. "Especially one who makes himself up as a walking, talking symbol of everything in society you dislike in the first place."

"Oh," Albertson said. "But what about his supporters, then?"

"Oh, they're just fuckin' stupid," Cassondra said. "They know that the world sucks too, because they have fucking eyes, but they don't want to take a close enough look at *why* it's fucked up. Because then, they might have to acknowledge that some of the aspects of society they *like* and that they always thought were okay are actually perpetuating the parts that are oppressing them, and that would require them to—horror of horrors—*change their minds*. So when some idiot comes along and tells them that it's actually a whole lot simpler than that, that it's actually *women* and *people of color* making their lives harder, they lap it up like dogs eating their own puke." Her hands were starting to tremble on the steering wheel as she gripped it tighter and tighter, and she was starting to raise her voice. "And then they spend their whole lives fighting *against* progressive policies that would actually *help* their sorry asses if they would just *listen* for *ten goddamn seconds*—"

"Whoa, there," Albertson said, reaching forward and putting a hand lightly on her shoulder. "Do we need to make a stop? Your driving's starting to get a little erratic there."

"I," Cassondra stammered, tightening her grip on the steering wheel, "I'm fine, thank you. Whew. Maybe we should stop talking about this for a little bit."

"Yeah, maybe," Albertson said. "Breathe, girl. Put some music on or something." The trees around them had been thinning for a while now, and Cassondra could see they were coming up on their entrance back onto the main highway. "We've still got a long drive ahead of us."

CHAPTER 17

It was a little after 1:00 PM when Albertson and Cassondra finally arrived back in Washington, D.C. They didn't stop to talk to anyone or change back into their professional clothes, they just made a bee-line straight for the nearest building that housed an entrance to the underground catacombs and made their way back to the bunker where they were storing Donaldson's body. Since the moment they'd left the car, Cassondra had been keeping the papier-mâché head clutched protectively close to her chest for fear of losing it.

"The bunker's probably our best bet, for the time being," Albertson said. "I called Luna a couple hours ago and she said she'd keep us updated, but I haven't heard anything from her since then. Which either means something happened to her, or she's trying to keep us in the dark intentionally."

Cassondra rolled her eyes.

"Right," she groaned. "Because we're only dealing with a governmental crisis that threatens the continued stability of the country itself. Why would she stop playing stupid power games with *her own allies* over a little old thing like that?"

Albertson snapped to attention and held up a single index finger, asking for her silence.

"Do you hear that?" he said.

"Hear what?"

Cassondra closer her eyes and concentrated. There was a low flickering sound created by the flaming torches that illuminated the passageway. Albertson's and her own breathing. And something a little further in the distance, so faint she could only barely differentiate it from the background noise. It sounded like something rough scrabbling against the stone floor. And then something high-pitched and nasal, like… *oinking?*

"Squeally Dan?" Albertson said, immediately brightening up. "You still down here, buddy?!"

Sure enough, the little pot-bellied pig rounded a bend in the tunnel a couple yards ahead of them, saw Albertson, and immediately came barreling towards them, squealing with joy.

"*Danny!*" Albertson shouted, getting down on his knees and spreading his arms so the little pig could jump up into his lap. Cassondra just stood over them, glaring down at them disapprovingly, her arms crossed in front of her chest.

"I can't help but notice he doesn't have the head anymore," she said coldly.

"Oh, I'm sure it's around here somewhere," Albertson said. "Besides, we've already got a replacement, don't we? And by now, after all the trauma and decomposition and pig bites, our fake head probably looks more like Donaldson did when he was alive than his actual head does anyway."

"Fine," Cassondra sighed, but Albertson's attention had already returned fully to the pig cradled in his arms.

"How you doin' buddy?" Albertson cooed. Squeally Dan stretched and preened as Albertson scratched him behind the ear and under the chin. "Have you been stuck down here the whole time? Aw, man, we need to get you back up into the sunshine, little dude!"

Cassondra rolled her eyes.

"Jeff," she said, as calmly as she could manage, "I appreciate that you have something in your life that makes you happy, but we really, really, *really* need to get moving."

"Yeah, yeah, I know, I know," Albertson said, keeping his arms wrapped around Squeally Dan as he stood up. "I'm just going to keep an eye on him until we get topside. He shouldn't slow us down any."

Cassondra sighed again.

"Fine," she grumbled. "Just *come on.*"

She started marching towards the bunker again—she'd been down here enough times to more or less memorize the layout for herself—and gestured for Albertson to follow her, which he did. After just another couple minutes, Cassondra's phone started ringing, and she pulled it out so fast she almost tore the pocket out of her coat.

"It's the Wonder Twins," she said, glancing at the screen.

"Um, I mean, I get the joke," Albertson said, "but they're *married*, so calling them 'twins' brings up some *really* weird mental imagery."

"Hello?" Cassondra said, holding the phone up to her ear.

"Where are you?" Luna Donaldson's voice barked. "Have you gone into the bunker yet?"

"What?" Cassondra said. "No, we're on our way, but we're still in the tunnels—"

"Oh thank God," Luna said. "The bunker has been compromised. Whatever you do, DO NOT go in there."

"Oh, shit," Cassondra said, feeling her heart rate slowly starting to climb. "Did someone discover Donaldson's body?"

"No, Jacob and I have my father's body," Luna said. "We got it out of there just in time. But there are people watching the room now, we can't go back." Luna stopped for a couple seconds, breathing heavily. Wherever she was and whatever she was doing, it sounded like she was exerting herself. "Where are you?" she finally said. "Like, where exactly in the tunnel system?"

"Crap, I don't know," Cassondra said. "We came in through the entrance under the…" She glanced back at Albertson. "National Portrait Gallery?"

"National Portrait Gallery, yeah."

"National Portrait Gallery," she said into the phone, "and we've been heading back towards the central chamber, where Vice President Muntz is caged up, but we aren't quite there yet."

"Okay, I know where you are," Luna said. "Somewhere in the Northeast Passage. Just stay where you are. Jacob and I will be there shortly and we'll (**huff**) have the body with us." Oh, Cassondra realized, *that's* why Luna sounded out of breath: she was trying to carry a dead body. "I heard you talking to someone else a second ago," Luna continued. "Is Albertson there with you?"

"Yeah, of course he is," Cassondra said. "Why?"

"Because I tried calling him three times before I called you," she hissed. "His phone isn't turned on." And with that Luna ended the call.

Cassondra slowly turned to glare at Albertson as she slid the phone back into her coat pocket.

"What?" he said.

"Check your phone," she grumbled.

He pulled it out and glanced at it, then pressed the button a couple times, then glanced at it again, puzzled.

"Oh," he said. "I guess the battery died."

"*Yeah, I guess*," Cassondra muttered, sitting down on the stone floor and backing up against one of the stone walls of the tunnel. "Everything's okay," she said, closing her eyes. "Or at least as close to 'okay' as we're going to get. She and worm-boy are coming to us. We can just hang out here and chill for a little bit."

"Oh thank God," Albertson said, walking over and sitting down next to her. "My back is killing me. How the hell is driving for ten hours so exhausting? All you're doing is sitting on your ass!" As soon as they were next to each other, Squeally Dan tried to stretch out of Albertson's arms and take a bite out of the papier-mâché head in Cassondra's; she pulled it out of the way just in time, then glared at the pig.

"If you fuck this up again," she growled, without breaking eye contact with the animal, "I'm gonna have bacon for breakfast tomorrow."

"I, um, I think I'm just gonna scoot a little bit to the side, here," Albertson said, hastily shuffling himself a couple feet away from her without properly standing up.

"Good idea," Cassondra grumbled.

They weren't waiting for very long at all before they heard footsteps echoing down the tunnel, coming from the same direction they expected Luna and Jacob.

"Think that's them?" Albertson muttered. Cassondra was leaning back against the wall with her eyes closed, trying to squeeze in one moment of last power-nap before everything got crazy again.

"If it's not," she said, without opening her eyes, "I'm just gonna sit here and let them shoot us, so this whole mess can finally be over with." Now she dared to open her eyes, just in time to see Luna Donaldson come storming around the bend with Jacob Kirkman limping after her as quickly as he could, trying to carry the body all on his own. Luna looked pissed-off, but that wasn't necessarily a clue to her emotional state so much as a perennial description of her face's natural appearance.

"*You idiots!*" she shouted at them.

"That is us, yes," Albertson mumbled, staring up at the curved ceiling above his head without making any attempt to stand up. Squeally Dan was asleep in his arms. "What did we do this time?"

"I just got a call from the Press Secretary," Luna hissed, her voice suddenly transitioning from a scream to a whisper, "asking when my father is going to be ready for the big rally he had scheduled for this afternoon?"

Albertson closed his eyes and thumped his head back against the wall.

"Ah, shit…"

"You forgot to cancel the speech?!" Luna screamed.

"We were busy!" Albertson screamed back. Squeally Dan started wriggling around in his arms, startled by the noise, but Albertson stroked him along the back and cooed under his breath until the pig calmed down.

Jacob Kirkman's wobbling knees finally gave out and he had to let go of the President's body, dropping it like a limp sack of potatoes on the floor of the tunnel and then collapsing against the opposite wall, wheezing and gasping for air. Luna just put her face in her hands and let out a long, slow breath.

"Well, it's too late to cancel it now," she said. "The crowds and the press have already gathered. They're expecting him there in less than an hour. If he cancels something this last-minute, they're going to immediately know something is up."

"Well, I mean," Cassondra sputtered, "can't we just say it was an urgent matter of state? An emergency meeting with a foreign leader or something?"

Luna arched an eyebrow.

"Would my father ever realistically cancel a chance to publicly aggrandize himself for the sake of *doing his job?*"

Cassondra let out a loud groan.

"God dammit," she muttered under her breath. "What is this speech even about?"

Luna rolled her eyes.

"What are *any* of my father's speeches about?" she said. "He's the greatest person on earth, anyone who doesn't support him is stupid and wrong, the media is out to get him, any politicians who don't openly support him deserve to be lynched for treason…" She sighed and rotated her hand in a loose circular motion. "*Et cetera, et cetera*. Only less coherent than that, somehow."

"Well," Albertson said slowly, "we've got the head." Cassondra nodded and helpfully held the fake head out for Luna to see. "So it'll at least be a *little* easier to fake his appearances now."

Luna leaned down and took the head from Cassondra's hands and held it out at arm's length as she examined it.

"Jesus Christ," she whispered. "This really *is* a good likeness of my father. The craftsmanship is amazing. Even the hair looks real. Or, I mean, as real as my father's actual 'hair' ever looked, anyway." She glanced back down at them. "Where the hell did you get this?"

"Trade secret," Cassondra said, before Albertson could answer. "But I'm glad you approve." She swallowed. "Next problem: that is an inert chunk of papier-mâché. In order for it to be a convincing face—especially Frank Donaldson's face—we're going to need the lips to move."

"I think I can help with that," Albertson said, raising his hand as high as he could without upsetting the pig. "You carry a knife, right Luna?"

Her eyes narrowed.

"Yes, I do," she said. "And don't you ever forget it."

"Duly noted," Albertson muttered. "I'm going to need to borrow it for a sec. Also any makeup compacts that either of you are carrying, and we don't happen to have any rubber bands, do we?"

"Uh, yeah," Cassondra said. "I carry some for my hair."

"Great," Albertson said, standing up. "Let's trade off. I take the head, you take the pig."

"Uh, sure?" Cassondra stood up as well and scooped Squeally Dan out of Albertson's arms, then Luna handed him the head.

"The knife, too, if you don't mind," Albertson said, holding out his free hand.

Luna just glared at him for a second, then grudgingly reached into her pocket and pulled out the butterfly knife.

"If you leave so much as a smudge on the blade," she said as she passed it over to him, "you are going to become a lot better acquainted with this weapon than you would like to be."

"Once again: duly noted," Albertson said, and then he stabbed the knife into the back of the fake Donaldson head, eliciting a simultaneous flinch from both Luna and Cassondra.

"What the hell are you doing?" Cassondra hissed. "We only have one of those! If we fuck it up—"

"I won't," Albertson said, focusing on his work as he continued to work the blade further and further into the papier-mâché. "I know exactly what I'm doing. But that's why I need the makeup, to cover up the hole in the 'flesh' after I'm done."

"Okay," Cassondra said slowly. "But then what do you need the rubber bands for?"

"Oh, simple," Albertson muttered, pausing his action with the knife for a second to glance up at them. "That's how I'm going to rig his lips to move."

CHAPTER 18

"Look," Albertson said, flipping the head over as soon as he was done, "I was able to rig it so that the mouth moves when you press this little lever on the back of his head, like a ventriloquist's dummy."

"The lever" had been made out of an old golf pencil Jacob had in his pocket, and sure enough, when Albertson flicked it up and down with his thumb, the Donaldson-head's mouth opened and closed just as he'd described.

Luna and Jacob had "gone up for air" several minutes ago, which at least in Jacob's case wasn't a lie—he had looked pretty green in the gills—so now it was just Albertson and Cassondra down in the catacombs. And the President's body. And Squeally Dan.

"I can set my hologram so that it doesn't show my own lips moving," Albertson continued. "That way, I just give the speech for him, and make it look like it's coming out of his mouth." He smirked. "I mean, that's basically what I've been doing in the government for the last several months anyway, only now I'm doing it in person instead of just through paperwork."

Cassondra drew in a sharp, worried breath through her teeth.

"I don't know," she murmured. "Are you sure you can do a convincing-enough impression of him?"

Albertson rolled his eyes.

"Cass, *everyone* can do Frank Donaldson. Every actor, every comedian, most average schmucks on the street. He's like Schwarzenegger or Christopher Walken, he has one of the easiest-to-imitate speaking patterns on the face of the earth."

"Okay," Cassondra muttered, but she still couldn't hide the note of skepticism in her voice. "Just try not to make him sound *too* coherent, you know? This is still Frank Donaldson. If he suddenly starts making sense, people are going to know something's up."

"Of course," Albertson said. "What do you think I am, some kind of amateur?"

"Well, gee, I don't know," Cassondra said. "Is this the first time you've impersonated a world leader on live TV by converting their actual, physical corpse into a literal ventriloquist's dummy?"

There was long pause.

"…yes…" Albertson said sheepishly.

"Then I guess you *are* an amateur at this," Cassondra said. She leaned back against the wall again and sighed. "You know," she muttered wistfully, "you keep talking about how you've been secretly running everything in Washington behind the scenes for the last couple months, because everyone else up there is out to lunch. Which, I mean, I don't doubt." She glanced up at him. "But if you actually had as much power as you say you did, why is everything in this country still so fucked up?"

"Well," Albertson said, "*because everyone else was out to lunch*. There's a difference between 'running things' and 'keeping things running.' You can't expect me to singlehandedly handle a workload that was originally meant to be spread between a dozen people and do it *well*." Finally satisfied with his work, he knelt down and plopped the papier-mâché head onto the President's neck-stump and started re-tying his neck tie in order to securely fasten it on. "Plus, I wasn't autonomous," he muttered as he worked. "I was the only person there who was actually doing his job, but there were still dozens of other people who weren't doing their jobs, *per se*, but still had plenty of power to do whatever the hell else they wanted. First and foremost: the President himself. I tried to do as much good as I could, but there were so many destructive forces in the administration fighting against me, most of the time that just meant cleaning up other people's messes and putting out fires before they had a chance to impact normal people's lives." Albertson gulped. "Did you know that Donaldson attempted to declare martial law on three separate occasions while he was in office?"

"Oh, Christ," Cassondra groaned. "No I didn't, but it doesn't surprise me."

"Yeah," Albertson muttered. "I was able to stop those in time, but just barely. Believe me, I *tried* to shut down the camps at the border, and strengthen gun control, and slip some environmental bills through, but checks and balances are a double-edged sword. They were able to check me just as much as I was able to check them." He wiped off his brow. "Even with the added 'power' of not having that many people paying attention to me or really caring what I did, there was only so much I could get done."

Cassondra smirked.

"Wait," she said, "so you're saying there actually *was* a 'Deep State' conspiracy working against the President?"

"Well, I mean," Albertson muttered, "I'm trying to stop him from actively destroying everything. Does that count as 'going against his agenda?' "

"Yes, I think it does, actually," she said. "As near as I can tell, fucking up everything around him was the closest thing to an 'agenda' that man ever had. I wouldn't be surprised if he added 'fuck everything up' onto the end of his shopping list every week."

"You're not wrong," Albertson said as he put the finishing touches on Donaldson's neck, covering up the seam with makeup and making sure it looked *just* right. "At least, not in spirit. And that's just what you were able to glean from the news, as an outsider. Imagine what I saw dealing with the son of a bitch on a daily basis." He paused for a moment, leaning back to admire his work. "And besides, Cass, you know damn well he didn't do his own shopping. Even if he didn't have servants and staff to do that shit for him, he only barely ever ate home-cooked meals."

"Yeah, yeah, we all know he was a slob," Cassondra grumbled.

"Is there a problem?"

"I don't know, you know how I feel about hating someone too much, even someone as bad as Donaldson. And the way everyone keeps talking about him, insulting him, cussing him out, taking the piss out of him while *his fucking body* is right here in the room with us, it feels—I don't know what the right word is—self-indulgent? Sacrilegious?" She gulped. "That kind of shivery feeling you get when you step on someone's grave? Like no matter who it is or what they did, you're doing something fundamentally *wrong?*"

"No, I get what you're saying," Albertson said. "Even when the anger is wholly justified, you have to be careful not to let yourself get consumed by it. I totally understand that. But, again, you never had to deal with the man in person. This isn't just some far-off mental abstract for us. A lot of us built up *a lot* of frustration from our interactions with this man. And not just 'daily annoyance' frustration, either. We're talking 'I watched this man *gleefully* make decisions that cost people their lives and I was powerless to stop him' frustration. So you'll have to excuse us for wanting to blow off a little steam."

"Oh," Cassondra said quietly. "Yeah, I guess I can understand that, at least in theory—"

Without warning, Albertson drove his fist into Donaldson's stomach as hard as he could, causing the entire body to spasm wildly for a moment.

"*That was for the camps at the border, you weasel-fucking bastard,*" he hissed between clenched teeth.

Cassondra's face was in her hands.

"Just tell me when you're done turning him into a puppet," she said weakly.

"Actually..." Albertson muttered. He stood up with his hand firmly grasping President Donaldson's back, and it looked like Donaldson was standing up with him. The two of them together looked like a perennial photo op, two fake-smiling politicians, one with a friendly hand on the other's back in the kind of stoic half-hug that characterized political allies desperately trying to pretend they liked each other. "What do you think?"

"That's terrifying," Cassondra said flatly.

"Really?" Albertson said in Donaldson's voice, moving the puppet-head's mouth as he talked. "I think it's pretty convincing."

"Yeah," Cassondra muttered, turning away from him. "That's *why* it's terrifying."

"Aw, come on, Cassondra," he continued, still in Donaldson's voice. "Don't be scared!"

Donaldson's arm reached out and his hand flopped limply onto her shoulder.

"*Jesus fuck!*" Cassondra screamed, scrambling backwards away from the hand. "How... how did...?"

Albertson was laughing so hard, he almost lost his grip on Donaldson's body.

"I'm sorry, I'm sorry," he said. "I should've warned you first, but... I'm sorry, I just couldn't resist." He cleared his throat. "I was able to jury-rig a couple pulleys out of Jacob Kirkman's old fidget spinner, and ran a string down Donaldson's arm, so I can make him gesture while he's talking, too." Donaldson raised his hand and waved at her. Again, in the Donaldson voice: "I think it's pretty convincing, don't you?"

Cassondra leaned forward, bracing her hands on her knees.

"Oh God," she said. "I think I'm gonna throw up again."

"Well, if you do," Albertson muttered, "Squeally Dan's probably just going to trot over and lick it up—"

"*Hooaarrrkkk!!!*"

"Oh, Jeez, um… sorry," Albertson said sheepishly. "I, um, probably shouldn't have said that, huh?"

"Fuck… you…" Cassondra grumbled, wiping off her mouth while Squeally Dan dutifully scurried over to the new puddle on the floor. "For the love of God, can we please just get this nightmare over with?"

Almost on cue, her cell phone rang. It was Luna again.

"Hello?" Cassondra gasped, fighting back the urge to hurl again as she brought the phone up to her ear.

"Are you two almost done?" Luna's voice echoed out of the phone. "The crowd is starting to get testy."

"Yeah," Cassondra said. "Perfect timing, actually. Where should we meet you?"

"Come up through the catacombs entrance under the Capitol building," Luna said. "Jacob will meet you there and escort you to the stage where '*my father*' will deliver the speech." She hesitated for a moment. "Do you really trust in Albertson's ventriloquism skills enough to pull this off? Do you really think this is going to work?"

"Do we have an alternative if it doesn't?"

There were a couple moments of silence, followed by a prolonged sigh.

"Just tell Albertson not to say anything important," Luna grumbled. "This isn't a policy speech. Hell, my father doesn't even give policy speeches. This is just another one of his damnable rallies to the loyal sheep who voted for him. All you need to do is spit out a bunch of meaningless platitudes and do a bunch of lame macho posturing to whip the crowd up into a frenzy."

“Heh,” Albertson muttered without looking over, “isn’t that just what every politician does?”

“I heard that,” Luna said through Cassondra’s phone. “For once, I’m not just busting your balls here. I am genuinely concerned that you won’t be able to pull this off.”

There was the faintest glimmer of something resembling actual vulnerability in Luna’s voice, but it was only there for a moment.

“Hey,” Cassondra said, trying to keep her voice as smooth and level as possible. “We got this.”

“I would feel a lot more confident if you could say that without your voice cracking.”

“Fuck,” Cassondra whispered under her breath, then back into the phone: “Hey, sorry, no more time to talk, see you up there in a few!” Cassondra abruptly hung up the call before Luna could finish the first word of her exasperated reply. She turned her phone onto “Do not disturb” mode before slipping it back into her pocket.

“That’s a really irresponsible thing to do right now,” Albertson said as he shuffled over, lugging Donaldson’s body with him.

“So is literally everything else we’re doing right now,” Cassondra said. “Speaking of responsibility, what are you going to do with the pig, now?”

They both glanced over at Squeally Dan, who was sniffing idly at a mushroom growing out of the cavern floor.

“Probably best to just leave him down here for the time being,” Albertson said. “He’ll just get in the way if we bring him with us, try to eat Donaldson’s foot again or something. He’ll find his way back out eventually through one of his secret hidey-holes, or I can come back down and get him once all the shouting upstairs is done with.”

“Fair enough,” Cassondra said. “Now it sounds like they’re almost ready for you up on that stage. It’s time for you to get out there and *try not to fuck this up!*" She tried to make herself sound enthusiastic, but the smile she gave him was still weak and unsure. "The fate of the planet might *actually* depend on this! So, you know… *no pressure*."

CHAPTER 19

The crowd roared as President Frank Donaldson walked out onto the stage, smiling and waving at them all, escorted by his close friend and trusted ally Secretary of State Jeff Albertson. Anyone could see that the bond they shared was almost brotherly; even as the President took his place behind the podium, the Secretary seemed reluctant to leave his side.

"My fellow Americans!" President Donaldson called out to the crowd, eliciting a renewed wave of raucous cheering. There couldn't have been more than a thousand people out there, but a series of large mirrors has been discreetly set up around the speaking area to make the crowd look significantly larger. "I have been talking all morning with my good friend here Secretary Albertson," the President continued. Albertson rolled his shoulder to make it look like Donaldson's limp arm was patting him on the back. "He really is a smart man! One of the smartest men in Washington!" Behind the stage, where the crowd couldn't see them, Luna and Cassondra rolled their eyes in perfect unison. "I don't know," Donaldson continued, "many are saying Secretary Albertson is almost as smart as me!"

Several people in the crowd laughed good-naturedly, which quickly rose into another rolling cheer. Albertson smiled and laughed and "humbly" motioned for them to settle down. Cassondra felt the nausea starting to build again.

"What do you say?" President Donaldson said. "Should we let him stay on stage?" A smattering of cheers and applause responded. "Well, okay," Donaldson said with a cautious, admonishing tone of voice, "but you better be on your best behavior, Mr. Secretary!" Albertson gave a comical, exaggerated shrug. The crowd laughed and cheered.

"Oh my God," Luna groaned from backstage. "He really does do a good impression of my father."

"Yeah, I know," Cassondra grumbled. "Doesn't it just turn your stomach?"

Luna snorted out a stifled laugh.

"You think *you're* sick of hearing Frank Donaldson talk?" she muttered. "You've only had to deal with him for the last year or two, since he became a part of the news cycle. I've had to listen to that voice every day of my life for the last thirty years."

"I'm so sorry," Cassondra said. "Do you need a hug?"

"Don't get cheeky with me, girl."

"I'm not," Cassondra said. "That was a sincere offer. I figure you've never gotten one before, you might like to know what it's like."

Luna just glared at her for a moment, grumbling something under her breath that Cassondra couldn't quite hear, then returned her attention to the speech.

"Well folks, it's mission accomplished!" President Donaldson continued from the stage. "The lying news media has been trying to take me down for ages, but I'm still up here winning! You see folks, there are the things they know, the things they think they know, and then the things they don't know, and the things they don't know that they don't know! I am one of those things! They think they have all these 'facts' and 'evidence' against me, but even if they do, I know in my heart that I've done nothing wrong! And see, folks, that's what they'll never understand!"

"Yes," Luna said.

"What?" Cassondra hadn't really been paying attention; she was too focused on the speech.

"The hug," Luna said. "I changed my mind. I think I do want it after all."

Cassondra didn't really know how to react.

"Oh," she said. "Really?"

"Yes," Luna said quietly, without taking her eyes off the stage. "My father is dead, and I don't even know if that makes me sad or not. But right now, I am staring at his corpse, watching a man I don't even like drag it around and put words in his mouth, and…" She paused for a long moment, just watching the stage. "And he's presenting Frank Donaldson as more of a real, likeable human being than even my father himself could manage half of the time. Right now, I am imagining Christmas morning with my father, only instead of my real father it's Secretary Albertson using my father as a puppet, and…" She took in a deep breath and let it out slowly. "And to be brutally honest with you, and with myself, I am genuinely not sure whether that perverted mockery on stage wouldn't actually be an *improvement* on some of the real Christmases I had with my family. So yes. I would like that hug."

"Oh," Cassondra said. "Um. Okay." She took her eyes off Albertson/Donaldson's speech for a second, leaned over, and wrapped her arms around Luna's torso. Luna subtly flinched for just a moment, but otherwise didn't fight it. After a moment, she slowly raised her arm and awkwardly, mechanically patted the back of Cassondra's head. The entire time, Luna kept her eyes locked on what was happening on the stage, without even blinking.

"Um, I don't mean to pry," Cassondra said as she started to pull away, "But doesn't your husband… I mean, doesn't Jacob ever—"

"We sleep in different beds," Luna said coldly, abruptly pulling herself the rest of the way out of the embrace and folding her arms in front of her chest.

"Hey, that's not *exactly* what I was asking," Cassondra said, raising her hands and taking a step back. "I just mean, does he ever, like, touch you? Like, in a good way? Just, you know casually?" Luna shot her a glare.

"Hey, I don't mean it as a sex thing!" Cassondra said quickly. "Just, like, holding your hand, or patting you on the shoulder when you're sad, or… *anything?*"

"We're not close," Luna grumbled, turning her back to Cassondra.

"…you're married…"

On the stage, the speech was reaching a crescendo.

"You're all my people!" President Donaldson said, waving at the crowd in a sweeping gesture with his free arm that wasn't still draped over Albertson's shoulders. They all cheered. "That's why we all get along so well! You're all here for me, and you know that I'm here for you!" Donaldson paused for a second, as if in hesitation. "But maybe it's time to be a little nicer to the other people, don't you think?"

Almost immediately, the cheering died down. People in the crowd started staring at each other, confused. Luna immediately whipped around and glared up at the stage.

"What the fuck is that idiot doing?!" she hissed. "He's going off script!"

"Hold on," Cassondra said, putting a hand on Luna's shoulder. "I want to see where Albertson's going with this."

Luna smacked Cassondra's hand away.

"He's pushing his luck," she said. "His sheep are never going to buy it. We can't afford to rock the boat right now!"

"We know the people who don't believe in me are losers, and they're wrong," President Donaldson said. The people in the crowd started smiling again, and a couple laughs echoed forth from the mass of people. "But that's no reason to be mean to them all the time. The anger and the name-calling and the violence—*especially* the violence—has gone too far! We have fun at these rallies—I mean, that's why we're all here, right? To have fun? We're not actually getting anything *done* by being here, I'm not discussing policy or saying anything you all haven't already heard me say a thousand times before. We're just shouting our opinions at people we know already agree with us, because it's..." Albertson glanced off-stage to Cassondra for just a moment. "...*cathartic*. But we can't forget that the rest of the world is still out there! The *real* world!"

Low, suspicious grumbles started emanating from the crowd.

"See, he's losing them," Luna said. "He's already used at least half a dozen words that my real father didn't even know how to spell."

"*Hey!*" President Donaldson called, cutting off the nascent protest. "Are you saying I'm not entertaining?" He put a hand on his chest. "Am I not a *fun guy* to be around?"

A smattering of laughter. Smiles again. On the stage, President Donaldson seemed to be getting emboldened, and his loyal ally Secretary Albertson was getting worked up along with him, the two of them beginning to slowly rock back and forth in place, arms still over each other's shoulders.

"Come on!" Donaldson shouted. "How about it, people? Do you like me?"

The crowd roared back in approval.

"Do you *love* me?"

The roaring got louder.

"Do you trust me?"

"*YEAH!!!*" They all shouted back in unison.

"Do you *believe* in me?"

"*WE BELIEVE IN YOU!!!*"

President Donaldson swept his arm against the podium in front of him, knocking it on its side and sending it rolling lopsidedly off the edge of the stage with a hollow crash. The cheers were deafening, just one constant note of adulation held aloft in the air by a thousand different voices.

"Are you ready to do whatever I say?" Albertson's impression was starting to slip and sound like his normal voice, but no one in the crowd seemed to notice. "Cause if you love me and you trust me and you believe in me, then you'd better be ready to obey me too! And I say, it's time to stop being so mean to people! Stop insulting the people who disagree with us! Stop trying to solve our problems with violence!"

"He's trying to speak their language," Cassondra said, her gaze fixed on the stage in fascination. "He's trying to turn their own fucked-up cult logic back around on them."

"It won't work," Luna said, re-crossing her arms and staring coldly at the stage. "Just watch. I know my father's followers."

"*You!*" President Donaldson said, picking a man out of the front row of the crowd and pointing to him dramatically. "Are you with me?!"

"I sure am, Mr. President!" the man shouted back, on the verge of tears. He was standing close enough to the stage that his replies could be heard clearly through the shotgun mic pointed at the crowd.

"When you leave this rally today, when you go back into the real world, are you going to do your part to take some violence and hate out of the world?"

"*Damn straight, Mr. President!*" the man screamed. The dam had burst, and he was openly weeping with joy.

"That's my man!" Donaldson said, victoriously pumping his fist. "And how are you going to do that?"

"I'm gonna go out and kill some niggers!" the man hollered back through an enormous, gap-toothed grin. "Cause they're the most violent people I know!"

Even with the hologram camouflaging his mouth, Albertson's expression visibly changed. His jaw sank, his entire posture shuddered, and the cigarette actually fell from his mouth. Next to him, Donaldson's head lolled limply to the side as Albertson's hand lost its grip and drooped down behind his torso.

This only barely registered to Cassondra though. She felt light-headed. Her entire body was trembling. Out in the crowd, people were laughing and emphatically high-fiving the guy in the front. All the noise suddenly sounded like it was far away and underwater. Cassondra didn't remember falling, but suddenly she was on the ground behind the stage, on her hands and knees, the world spinning around her as Luna tried to help her back to her feet.

"*Abort! Abort!*" Luna screamed, to whom Cassondra didn't know. "Cut the mics! Kick out the reporters! Get him off the stage! Disperse the crowd! Just *end this speech now!*"

Everything was shaking. Cassondra could barely swallow. On the other side of the stage, a sizeable portion of the crowd was chanting "*Kill them all! Kill them all! Kill them all!*" and pumping their fists into the air. Albertson was trying to back away as quickly as he could, but he was still carrying the dead weight of Donaldson's body and didn't dare let the charade fall with this many people watching. Cassondra tried to raise her head and stare out at the sea of faces who didn't even know she was there. That's when she saw it.

Behind the crowd. Like, *far* behind them. The Washington Monument, with the afternoon sun hovering blindingly behind its tip. There was something on top of the monument, a silhouette, a *human* figure. Luna was saying something to her, her tone of voice attempting to be reassuring but clearly teetering on the verge of a breakdown of her own. Cassondra didn't hear the words. She was too busy watching as the human figure leapt off the top of the Washington Monument and… *flew?*

No, not quite. He was *gliding*. He was wearing one of those base-jumping suits with the carbon mesh webbing under the arms that let people ride the air like a flying squirrel. The crowd gathered for the speech barely noticed as his shadow sailed over their heads, too busy chanting "*KILL! KILL! KILL! KILL!*" with their attention focused on President Donaldson and on each other, until the mysterious glider finally landed perfectly on the edge of the stage, used the momentum to carry him forward into a summersault, and sprang back to his feet in front of the President, gun already drawn and pointed directly between Frank Donaldson's eyes.

"*Sic semper tyrannis*," Tyler LaFuente hissed between gritted teeth, and he pulled the trigger, obliterating President Donaldson's papier-mâché head.

For a full three-count, the crowd was completely silent, just staring at the stage in muted, wide-eyed, slack-jawed horror.

Then the chaos started.

Albertson's hand had slumped just low enough to avoid getting blasted apart along with Donaldson's head, but the gunfire had gotten close enough to singe the sleeve of his jacket. The crowd started screaming incoherently; what had moments ago been one unified voice dissolved back into hundreds as Donaldson's headless body slumped out of Albertson's arms and onto the floor. Albertson took several slow steps back, as if in a daze, his hands trembling, then doubled over and started coughing and hacking, fishing around desperately in his coat for another cigarette. Tyler LaFuente dropped his gun to the ground and fell to his knees, hands held in flat up in the air as the sparse security rushed onto the stage, tackling and cuffing him. Luna was on her hands and knees as well behind the stage, crying, screaming helplessly into the ground. Spectators were pushing their way out of the crowd and running off in all directions, blindly, aimlessly, ready to run everywhere as long as it took them away from here.

Cassondra was calm.

All the running and screaming and crying felt far away, somehow. The Secret Service had already wrestled Tyler LaFuente off the stage, and Albertson was off huddled on the corner, puffing on his new cigarette as if his life depended on it. Which, she supposed, it did. Luna Donaldson was literally in fetal position, her face buried in her arms, whimpering the phrase, "We're all fucked," over and over again. Cassondra walked up the stairs leading to the stage and stared out at the ocean of faces that had just moments before been calling for her death, and now only barely noticed her presence. Then she looked down idly at the once again headless body of President Frank Donaldson.

"Well," Cassondra mumbled under her breath to no one in particular, "I guess Ms. Phoenix isn't getting her prop back."

CHAPTER 20

"Okay," Luna said, her voice deceptively calm. "So let me see if I've got this straight." She was sitting behind the President's desk in the Oval Office, with Jacob anxiously pacing back and forth behind her. Albertson was sitting at rigid attention on one of the couches in front of her, his face still wearing the exact same expression as it had been the moment President Donaldson was shot. Cassondra was sprawled out on her back on the other couch, staring listlessly at the ceiling. Next to her on the couch was a box of pre-sharpened pencils, and every couple seconds she would pull one out of the box and throw it at the ceiling point-first. She had already gotten five to stick up there. "You two received a credible warning about an assassination attempt on the President's life at least a day in advance?"

"Yep," Cassondra said. Another pencil lodged itself in the ceiling with a hollow *thunk*.

"Uh-huh," Albertson muttered weakly.

"Not only did you not take this threat seriously, you neglected to even mention it to me, or Jacob, or literally anyone else affiliated with the White House or the United States government.

"Yep," Cassondra said. Another pencil. *Thunk.*

"Uh-huh," Albertson muttered. "But in our defense, he was already dead—"

"*Ahem,*" Luna said sharply. "I am asking simple 'yes' or 'no' questions, Mr. Albertson. The commentary is not necessary." She cleared her throat. "Now, just to make sure we are all on the same page: The two of you both elected, in fact, to *completely ignore* the credible warning about an assassination attempt on the President's life?"

"Yep."

"Uh-huh."

Thunk.

"Then, not long after you received this credible warning about an assassination attempt on the President's life, the winds of fate just randomly happened to bring you into personal contact with the assassin about whom you had been warned during your little jaunt up to New York."

"Yep."

"Uh-huh."

Thunk.

"And not only did you not make any attempt to stop him, you did not even *recognize* him, despite having been given his full name and the make and model of the vehicle he was driving. In fact, when you spoke to the man you had already been warned was planning to assassinate the President of the United States, you…" She checked her notes. "…gave him directions to Washington, D.C."

Both of them were silent.

"Hey," Cassondra finally said, "Albertson was the one who gave him directions. I can't navigate for shit."

"I see," Luna said. "Okay."

She took off her reading glasses, closed her eyes, and pinched the bridge of her nose, taking in a very, very long breath and letting it out very, very slowly.

"Mr. Albertson. Miss Warren," she said. "You have some inkling of the type of life I have lived, and the sort of people I encounter on a regular basis, so you know I do not use these words lightly. But I do truly believe that the pair of you are the two *stupidest* people I have ever had the displeasure of knowing in my entire time on this earth."

"That is a valid assessment, ma'am, yes," Albertson said quietly.

"No argument from me," Cassondra muttered. She threw another pencil up at the ceiling, but it hit a little too hard and caused all the others that were lodged up there to come loose and rain back down onto her head. "Ow! Ouch!

Ow!" Cassondra gasped, raising her hands too late in an attempt to protect her face.

Luna closed her eyes and sighed.

"Cassondra," she said grudgingly. "Are you… okay?"

"What?" Cassondra said, sitting up and rubbing the side of her head. "Yeah, of course. It was just a couple pencils."

"No," Luna said. "I mean after that little, um… *breakdown* at the Presidential rally. Before Mr. LaFuente showed up."

"Oh," Cassondra said. "In that case, no, I am definitely not. But I'm compartmentalizing it for the time being, because I figure I won't really have the time or space to process it until we've dealt with, you know, *the President of the United States being assassinated on live TV.*"

"I mean, he was already dead," Albertson grumbled.

"Yes, but everyone *knows* he's dead now," Luna said. "There were a thousand witnesses, and the news cameras broadcasted it live to every news station and half of the internet. There's no way we can cover it up anymore." Luna's entire posture stiffened and she swallowed hard, trying to fight back the dry heaves. "We have no choice but to inaugurate Patrick Muntz as the next President of the United States."

All four people in the room shuddered in perfect unison.

"So, what?" Albertson said. "This is it? We've lost?"

"Oh, God no," Luna said, standing up from behind the desk. "This is just another temporary setback." She started walking towards the trap door that led down into the catacombs. "But we are going to have to go through the motions until Muntz can be disposed of." She knelt down and pulled the trap door open. "Smile for the cameras and all."

"Uh," Albertson said nervously. "*Disposed of?*"

"First things first," Luna said, beckoning for them to follow her down into the tunnels.

By the time they made their way back to Patrick Muntz's holding cell in the central chamber of the underground tunnel system, there was already a team of doctors down there waiting to meet them. The lead doctor stepped forward to greet Luna as they approached.

"You called for us, ma'am?"

"Yes," Luna said without looking at the doctor as she marched past. "I trust you've seen what's happened on the news?"

"Er, yes, ma'am," the head doctor said, hurrying after her to keep within earshot. "My sincerest condolences regarding your father. I trust that Code Zeta is now in effect?"

"We just need him lucid enough to appear in front of the cameras during the swearing in ceremony." She marched straight up to the bars of Patrick Muntz's cage and folded her arms authoritatively, the head doctor standing next to her while Jacob, Cassondra, and Albertson remained a good fifteen paces back. "Good evening, Mr. Muntz," Luna said coldly.

Vice President Muntz was on his hands and knees, wearing his "Bible Belt" again, drawing patterns on the floor of his cage with his own feces, far too preoccupied to notice anyone else in the room.

"*Patrick!*" Luna said sharply. He stopped what he was doing for a moment and looked up at her, then without any warning threw himself at the side of the cage and tried grabbing at her through the bars. One of the other doctors immediately stepped in and pressed a cattle prod against the cage, causing electricity to arc between the bars as

Muntz's arm darted back in and he scurried to the opposite corner, his eyes still locked on Luna.

"Hey there girlie-girl," he said, his voice low and breathy. "I shouldn't be talking to you while Mommy isn't here. Mommy doesn't like it when I talk to girlies without her permission." He scrunched his eyes shut and shuddered in place for a second, then ripped the Bible off of his crotch and smashed it against his forehead as hard as he could. "I'm being bad!" He shouted, slamming the book against his head again and again, until blood started to trickle from a laceration his temple. "The girlie-girl is talking to me while Mommy isn't here and she's making me have *evil* thoughts."

"Patrick, listen to me!" Luna said. She closed her eyes and took a deep breath, then opened them again, her gaze fixed on the bent, naked figure in the corner of the cage. "Patrick, we're going to let you outside," she said, trying to keep her voice as soothing as possible. "You like outside, right Patrick? Out in the sun?"

"The sun and the moon are God's eyes," Patrick Muntz hissed. "They're how Jesus can see me being *naughty*."

"We're going to let you outside," Luna continued, "but first we need you to calm down, okay?" She gestured to the team of doctors standing behind her. One of them took out a massive syringe and held it up. "We've got some nice, friendly doctors here to give you some calm-down juice, okay Patrick? And then you can go outside, and talk to the nice people."

"But I don't want to talk to the people," Muntz said, still crouched down into a near-sitting position on the floor. "The people are sinners, each and every one of them, and if I let myself interact with them, their sin might contaminate me." He clutched the nearest bars protectively with both hands. "That's why I like it here in my cage, Luna-girl… where I'm *safe*."

“Wait a minute,” Cassondra muttered from the back. “Is he in there… *voluntarily?*”

“I’m not *asking* you, Patrick,” Luna said. She made a hand gesture, and several of the doctors started walking around to the cage door. “I’m telling you what’s going to happen. This will go so much easier for everyone if you don’t fight it.”

“*No!*” Patrick Muntz screeched. “*No no no no no no no no no!*” His entire body started shaking violently as if he were having a seizure, although he appeared to be in complete control of it. One of the doctors reached through the bars with a loop of wire on the end of a long metal pole, the kind dogcatchers use to capture wild animals, and managed to slip it around Patrick Muntz’s neck. With one solid yank, Vice President Muntz was pulled up against the side of the cage—*hard*—and he stood there, struggling against the wire, trying to wedge his fingers under it and pull it off of his neck, while another one of the doctors held the cage door open and the one with the syringe carefully tiptoed inside.

“Okay, Patrick,” the doctor with the syringe cooed. “This is going to be nice and quick. You know we’ve done this before, you’ll hardly feel a thing—”

Patrick Muntz kicked at the doctor with his bare foot, which wouldn’t have normally been strong enough to throw someone off their balance, but with the floor currently slick with shit the doctor quickly lost their footing and crashed to the ground. Muntz reached around a grabbed the pole being used to keep him in place and yanked it back towards himself, giving him just enough slack to pull his head out of the loop of wire, then he was on the ground, digging his teeth into the neck of the doctor with the syringe.

“Oh fuck!” Luna shouted. “Close the door!”

“But—but Doctor Isenberg!” the one holding the door stammered.

"It's too late for him!" Luna screamed. "Just close the—"

Muntz launched himself at the door of the cage with the torn, bloody remains of Dr. Isenberg's jugular vein still dangling from his mouth, hitting it with enough momentum to knock back the doctor trying to keep the door closed and earning his freedom. He spat out the chunk of vein, as well as a mouthful of blood, into the door-doctor's face, temporarily blinding them, then leapt onto them and wrapped his hands around their throat, pressing his thumbs into their trachea until it collapsed under his grip.

"You want me out of this cage so bad?" Patrick Muntz squealed. "Well, here I am!" He leapt off the second doctor, leaving them to wheeze out their last choked, gasping breath on the dirt floor of the catacombs before their world forever went dark. Then, Muntz started stalking towards Luna as she slowly backed away, her three cohorts frozen in place behind her. "I still haven't forgotten about you, boy!" he snarled to Jacob Kirkman over Luna's shoulder. "Those kidneys are calling to me. Sweet and succulent and tender… I can't get my mind off 'em!" Muntz crouched down low to the ground, coiling himself like a spring, then launched himself forward like a jungle cat pouncing on its prey from a hiding place in the tall grass. "*I gotta have 'em—*"

A syringe stabbed into Patrick Muntz's shoulder at the top of his arc and he crashed limply to the floor inches from Luna's feet, twitching. The head doctor—the one Luna had first spoken to when they'd entered the chamber—was standing over Muntz's prone body, breathing heavily, holding the empty syringe at their side, an icy-cold death-glare fixed on Luna.

"I just lost two more good people taking care of this lunatic," they growled. "That brings us to eighteen casualties total." They wiped the sweat off their brow with the back of their sleeve. "This had better be fucking worth it."

"It will be," Luna said. "I promise you that it will be. All the same..." she hesitated for a moment. "...I understand your sacrifice. And I deeply apologize."

"Isenberg had a *kid*," the head doctor snapped. "I mean, the kid didn't like him very much, but *still*." The doctor stared off towards the two bodies lying in and around the cage, and started slowly shaking their head. "I don't know how much longer we can keep doing this. His body has started building a tolerance to the sedatives. They're getting a little less effective every time we use them."

"We won't have to worry about it for much longer," Luna said. She turned back to Albertson and Cassondra. "I trust you've seen everything you need to," she said.

"Wait, what do you mean?" Albertson said. "You brought us down here just to *make us watch this?*"

"Yes," Luna said succinctly, taking a step towards Albertson. "I'd hate to think any of us were *losing our convictions*," she said, then turned her attention to Cassondra. "Or *losing sight of what could happen* if we fail at this."

Albertson and Cassondra exchanged a nervous glance, then both returned their attention to Luna and nodded.

"No," Albertson said. "We understand."

"Yeah," Cassondra breathed quietly.

"Good," Luna said, taking a step back and straightening her shoulders. "Then I think you two should go have a word with the man who just quote-unquote 'assassinated' my father. He's currently being held at a secret detention facility operated by the Secret Service. It's accessible from the catacombs. I'll give you the address, and Jacob will call ahead to let them know you have clearance." She glared back and forth at each of them. "I want you to interrogate this 'Tyler LaFuente' person. Find out *why* he did it, find out *how* he did it, and, if possible, find out if there's any way he can be useful to us in the future."

"Useful?!" Albertson scoffed. "How could that lunatic possibly be useful?"

"I just *said*," Luna hissed, "that's what I want you to find *out*." She abruptly pivoted on her heal and turned to face the surviving doctors, who were tending to the bodies of their fallen comrades. "I apologize once again for your loss," she said. "But we are still on the clock here. I need you to remove the bodies and send someone to hose down the cage before we have to bring him back."

"Fuck you, Luna," one of the doctors grumbled. If Luna heard them, she didn't acknowledge it.

"Come on, now!" she said, clapping her hands. "All of you have your jobs to do! Let's go, go, go!" As everyone else started milling out of the central chamber, towards whatever their next objective was, Luna snapped her fingers and pointed at her husband. "Jacob, you're with me," she said. "Help me drag Muntz's body up to the Oval Office and get him in his suit. It's time to swear him in as President of the United States."

CHAPTER 21

"So what's his *reason* for assassinating Donaldson in the first place, anyway?" Cassondra muttered as they marched through the prison hallways towards the interrogation room where the Secret Service was keeping Tyler LaFuente. Jacob never had actually bothered to call ahead for them, but through a mixture of threats, bribery, and pulling rank on the prison guards (since he *was* still a high-ranking government official), Albertson had managed to secure a couple minutes with LaFuente unguarded and unmonitored. They'd even turned off the room's security cameras. He'd made up some bullshit reason for why they should let Cassondra—a brand new intern with no security clearance—come with him, and the guards had accepted it with a shrug as they counted their money, but the real reason was that Albertson figured Cassondra's spy training would make her a much better interrogator than he was.

"I don't actually know," Albertson stammered. "Why? Does it matter?"

"Oh, it'll just affect how we can interact with him," she said. "You know, is he just a total nutjob in his own little world, or did he actually have a rational reason for assassinating the President?"

Albertson stopped in place and did a double-take.

"What do you mean a *rational* reason for *assassinating the President?!*"

"Oh, there are plenty of rational reasons to assassinate the President," Cassondra said, counting off the reasons on her fingers as she offered them. "He could be trying to prevent the passage of a law that has a direct, negative impact on his community. He could fancy himself some sort of political revolutionary, here to overthrow the corrupt political structures that have been causing very real harm to the world for generations. He could even just want to get his face in the news and the history books so that he always has a legacy. That still 'makes sense,' albeit in a sick, twisted sort of way. I'm not saying we have to *agree* with his logic, I'm just saying that if there is some sort of coherent logical through line to why he did what he did, that'll make it easier for us to talk to him and get what we want."

"Okay, fine," Albertson sputtered. "What would you say is an *irrational* reason to assassinate the President, then?"

"Oh," Cassondra muttered, almost chuckling. "That would be, like, if he did it because his toaster told him to, or something. You can't really 'negotiate' with crazy, so if that's the case, we're all fucked."

Albertson stopped in place and just stared at her, blinking a couple times, dumbfounded.

"Okay, I know we were kind of desperate to hire someone and didn't have a lot of people to choose from," he finally said, "but I reiterate: How the *fuck* did you get through the screening process for this job?!"

Cassondra kept walking as she rolled her eyes.

"My spy trainers taught me how to tell you idiots what you wanted to hear. Like, that was the *first* thing they taught me for this mission. It wasn't even that hard—wrap myself in the flag, drone on about 'honor' and 'duty' and all that bullshit, thump the Bible a little bit, reassure one of the interviewers that the joke he asked me about *totally* wasn't racist, and I was golden."

Albertson was jogging after her to catch back up with her, but as soon as he was beside her again, he gave her the best stern-slash-suspicious expression he could manage without giving away out out-of-breath he was.

"Am I *sure* I can trust you?" he said. "Where exactly *do* your loyalties lie, anyway?"

Cassondra rolled her eyes again, still without stopping. If anything, she even sped up a little.

"Oh, yeah, you got me," she groaned. "I'm totally in it for my Chinese masters. Because adopting a human child with hopes and dreams for the expressed purpose of turning her into a child-soldier *totally* isn't a shitty, unethical thing that I should be resentful about either." She spat on the floor. "Same macho nationalistic bullshit," she grumbled. "Different fucking flag."

Albertson was quiet for a long couple moments.

"Jesus," he finally murmured. "Your spy-parents really should've taken you to Disneyland more often or something."

"They said it was 'capitalist propaganda,'" Cassondra muttered. "Which, I mean, they're not wrong. But, yeah, they wanted me to 'assimilate' for the sake of my mission… but not *that* much."

"Well, whatever kind of a clusterfuck they raised you in, I think the program needs another couple passes," Albertson said. "You don't exactly seem 'indoctrinated' into *their* way of thinking, either."

They had reached the door to the interrogation room, next to the big two-way mirror looking inside. Through the mirror, they could see Tyler's posture was meek and resigned, slumped quietly over the table in front of him with his arms folded loosely in front of his chest. He had no illusions about how this was going to go. He had accepted it.

Cassondra put her hand on the doorknob, but hesitated before pushing it open.

"Let me put it this way," Cassondra said idly. "You ever go to a sex club, Jeff? Like, one of the *really* freaky ones that hold those BDSM group-orgies that look like a cross between *Eyes Wide Shut* and the *Hellraiser* movies?"

"Um," Albertson stammered. "*No?*"

“*A lot* of the people who regularly go to those things used to attend Catholic school when they were kids. Because *that’s* about how much success you can expect when you try to forcibly indoctrinate your kids into your belief system.”

Albertson’s mouth was opening and closing like a fish, like he was trying to stammer but no words were coming out.

“Are you saying *you’ve* been in one of these clubs?”

Cassondra’s hand gracefully glided under her chin, like she was the model showing off one of the prizes on a game show.

“The lube is good for my pores,” she said. For a second, Albertson thought she was going to say something else, but instead she just looked down at her hand still resting on the door handle.

“So,” he said, “you ready to talk to this loony?”

“No,” she said flatly. Then she lowered her head into her free hand and gasped, “Oh, Christ, I really *don’t* know if I can do this.”

“Hey, hey, come on,” Albertson said, putting a hand on her shoulder. “We talked about this. You know what you need to do, how you need to act—”

“Shut up,” she said, closing her eyes. “Just give me a second to get in character.” Her eyes still closed, she took a long, deep breath in, and then let it out slowly through her nose. Her eyes popped back open. “Okay,” she said, then she finally pressed down on the doorknob, and pushed the interrogation room’s door open.

Tyler watched them silently as they both shuffled inside, closed the door gently behind them, and sat down across the table from him. For a small eternity, the three of them just sat there, staring at each other in the calming quiet.

“Good evening, Mr. LaFuente,” Cassondra finally said. Tyler just closed his eyes and held his hand up.

"Save your breath," he grumbled. "I killed the President on live TV. You could give me the best public defender on the planet and it won't matter. The only way this ends is me with a needle in my arm. I came to terms with that from the moment I decided to do this." He leaned back in his chair and glanced off to the side. "Honestly, I'm a little surprised the Secret Service didn't blow me away on stage."

"Yeah, well," Albertson muttered wistfully, "you work with the Secret Service you have, not the Secret Service you wish you had."

Cassondra nudged him with her elbow, hard, and glared at him before returning her attention to Tyler.

"That is… not untrue, Mr. LaFuente," she said, trying to maintain a subdued but courteous smile. "But you and I both know that death sentences aren't immediate, even for crimes such as this. You could be rotting in prison for upwards of twenty years before your day of reckoning finally comes. There are going to be a lot of hard men in prison, Mr. LaFuente, and I can guarantee you that more than a couple of them voted for the man you just murdered. Does spending the next twenty years trapped in a cage with them sound like fun, Mr. LaFuente?"

Tyler just shrugged.

"Frank Donaldson spent his entire campaign feeding off of Americans' xenophobia towards Hispanic people, then as soon as he was President he walled off the border with Mexico and stared locking *children* in *cages*." Tyler stared off at nothing in particular, shaking his head for a second, then glanced back at the two of them without a hint of emotion in his eyes. "For taking his life and removing him from power, the Latin Kings prison gang has already pledged me lifelong protection."

Albertson's jaw went slack.

“When did this happen?!” he said. “You were shuttled straight to this room immediately after you shot Donaldson, and you’ve been locked in here ever since!”

Tyler just shrugged again.

“They got a message to me,” he said. “They’ve got the right channels, I guess.”

Albertson was just staring at Tyler, slowly shaking his head. Cassondra facepalmed.

“Albertson,” she grumbled, “just how shitty *is* the security around here, anyway?”

“I guess it’s even shittier than I thought,” he breathed.

His eyes didn’t change, but Tyler suddenly cracked a half-smile.

“So, what is this, anyway?” he said. “I’ve heard of ‘good cop/bad cop’ before, but ‘good cop/stupid cop’ is a new one on me.”

“Yes,” Cassondra said evenly, looking him directly in the eye. “Good cop/stupid cop. That’s exactly what this is.” Now it was Albertson’s turn to glare and elbow-nudge her.

Tyler leaned back in his chair again and started chuckling lightly, in spite of himself.

“What the fuck do you even want from me?” he said. “You already know I did it. I’m not even denying it. I’m pleading guilty, so there’s not gonna be a trial. I already told the last cops I talked to how I did it all on my own, so there’s no one else you need to track down, no accomplices or nothing.” His eyes narrowed for a second. “Though there was this one guy I ran into out on the road who looked kinda like you. Said he was your cousin or something. And now that I think about it, the girl he was with looked a little bit like—”

“We don’t need to know about them,” Albertson cut in quickly. “In fact, nobody needs to know about those two, so, ha-ha, you might as well just forget they ever existed, right Cass?"

"Shut up, Jeff."

Tyler LaFuente eyed them both carefully for a second longer, then shrugged.

"There's nothing more I can give you, then," he said amiably. "You've already won."

Cassondra's face scrunched up for a second, fuming, then she abruptly turned to face Albertson.

"What do you think?" she said. "Cards on the table time?"

Albertson let out something between a sigh and a groan, then got up out of his chair and turned his back to them.

"Sure, why not!" he said, throwing his hands up in the air. "Blowing enormous national secrets has just been the theme this week! Why not keep the train going?"

"Right," Cassondra said, turning back to Tyler. "We're going to level with you, then. You didn't actually kill the President, Mr. LaFuente."

That got his attention.

"*What?*" he said, suddenly leaning forward and fixing his gaze on them. "But I was there, I saw—"

"A fake," Cassondra said. No need for LaFuente to know *too* many of the disgusting details. "A very, very convincing fake, but not the actual President." She glanced back over her shoulder at Albertson, who still had his back to them. He'd lit another cigarette and was chugging on it furiously. He gave her a quick little hand-wave gesture to continue. "We were using the fake," she continued, turning back to Tyler, "to try and cover up the fact that..." She hesitated. "...that the *real* Frank Donaldson actually died several days ago of natural causes."

Tyler's expression suddenly fell.

"No," he whispered. "You mean... you're saying...?"

Cassondra nodded with a sick smile.

"Frank Donaldson was dead long before you even crossed the city limits," she said. "And would have still been dead, even if you had never pulled the trigger. Your entire crusade was for nothing, Mr. LaFuente."

Tyler's forehead slumped down onto the table surface in front of him with a hollow *thump*.

"But no one knew he was dead," Tyler muttered weakly, his voice high and thin. "So everyone who saw me on TV thinks I actually did it."

Cassondra was nodding slowly, with palpable satisfaction in her expression, giving him all the time he needed for it to sink in.

"Not only were your efforts entirely useless, Mr. LaFuente," she said. "But you have just made yourself the perfect scapegoat. And you're now going to be executed for a crime you didn't even commit."

"*And*," Albertson said, turning around dramatically, "how do you think your little prison gang friends are going to react if word spreads you weren't *actually* responsible for the death of their adversary?"

Tyler just blinked a couple times.

"Um," he muttered, "still have mad respect for me because of all the time and effort I put into *trying* to kill him?"

Albertson's posture fell a little.

"Oh," he said. "Yeah. I guess that makes sense. Um…" Tyler and Cassondra were both staring at him. He abruptly turned his back to them again. "Never mind!" He said. "Carry on!"

Cassondra rolled her eyes, then got up from her chair and walked—slowly—around the table towards where Tyler was sitting.

"At present," she said, "there are only four people on earth who know the truth about the President's demise. And now, because of *your* actions, we don't *have* to tell anyone else if we don't want to. We no longer need to explain *why* or *how* the President is dead, you just gave us the perfect alibi." She leaned over him, so close he could feel her breath on his face, and smiled a wide, toothy grin. "And signed your own death warrant in the process."

She stood back up again and started walking away from him, slowly, leisurely.

"We don't *have* to tell anyone you're innocent," she continued. "In fact, it would benefit us quite a bit if we didn't. It would be *so easy* to just keep quiet and let you take the rap for us, let you rot in prison and die."

"Um, I'm sorry," Albertson said, turning around again. "The way she's wording it, it sounds like *we* were responsible for the President's death. I just wanted to clarify, we *weren't*, we've just been doing a bunch of morally questionable shit in the *aftermath* of—"

"Albertson, *shut up*," Cassondra whined, then she let out a long, beleaguered sigh. This tough-girl act was getting exhausting. "You say you have accepted your inevitable fate, Mr. LaFuente," she continued. "I can even admire that, to a certain degree. But I have a feeling you would not turn down last-minute salvation, if it were offered to you." She smiled at him again, but it was getting harder to maintain that expression. "Especially now that you know the efforts that landed you here were all for naught."

Tyler stared up at her for several long seconds, then finally closed his eyes, lowered his head, and sighed.

"You can really help me beat the rap?" he said. "For *killing the President?*"

"I am confident that we can, yes," Albertson said, walking back over to them and leaning down in front of Tyler, with his hands flat on the table. "Look at me. You know who I am: the Secretary of State. I have the resources and the power necessary to free you from this."

"Yes," Cassondra said, "but only if you cooperate."

Tyler looked up again. He glanced back and forth between one of their faces, then the other, then back again. The longest, most exhausted sigh Cassondra had ever heard in her life echoed out from his throat.

"Okay," he finally said. "What do you need me to do?"

Albertson and Cassondra looked at each other, then back at him.

"We need you to kill the *Vice* President."

CHAPTER 22

"Oh my God, you are such a fuckin' badass!" Albertson said as he and Cassondra marched into the White House, practically giggling to himself with glee. "What you did in that cell was fuckin' amazing!"

Cassondra sighed.

"I'm glad you liked it," she grumbled. "I feel kinda gross about it, though. I hate putting on a fake persona like that, it always feels kinda… I dunno how to describe it… *blerch*."

"You are a spy," Albertson said. "Putting on fake personas is *literally* your job."

"How many times do I have to tell you," she snapped. "I didn't *volunteer* for this shit!" She stopped walking for a second. "And besides, how much of spy work do you think is *actually* fake? I mean, like, the deep cover shit, where you have to live an entirely made-up life. You can't live in a vacuum forever, where the only humans you have regular, honest contact with are other spies and your handlers. I've known guys who stayed in contact with the friends they made adjacent to a mission even after the mission was done, couples who stayed together even though one of them was using an assumed name when they met… I mean, hell, my dad still goes bowling with the league he joined while he was over here on assignment raising me."

"Your dad joined a bowling league just for the hell of it while he was over here trying to infiltrate the government?"

"We're human!" Cassondra said. The words came out a little more loudly than she intended them to. "We still have friends and hobbies, we don't just totally give up on life and dedicate one hundred percent of ourselves to the job. No one could possibly do that and stay sane. Why do you think so many of us defect, or go native, or just get burned out when we *do* try to ignore everything else?"

Albertson gave a nervous half-smile.

"And I suppose it doesn't help that you were still born and raised here, huh? 'Going native' wouldn't be that much further to go for you."

"Oh, no, this country is still totally fucked-up too," she said. "I'm just saying… agh, God, I don't know. Being a spy doesn't mean I'm just some hard-assed automaton, okay? Shit like what I just did in the interrogation room, that takes *a lot* of emotional energy, and I've pretty much been running on empty since the moment I stepped into the White House. And…" She hesitated for a moment. "Acting like that, like this cold, conceited bitch who doesn't give a shit whether someone lives or dies, it makes me feel, well…" Her voice got a little quieter. "It made me feel like Luna Donaldson."

"Ah! God!" Albertson said, dramatically flinching. "Warn a guy before you say that name again! Brrr, I've got goose bumps now."

Cassondra laughed while Albertson mock-shivered and hugged himself, rubbing his biceps like someone caught out in a snowstorm.

"Does your scaly-ass alien skin even get goose bumps?" she said.

"No," he admitted, "but I think the hologram has a setting that would make them appear." He held up his wrist and tapped the face of his watch. "I'd try to turn it on but this thing's still in such bad shape after you smashed it, I'm afraid if I touch it I'll only fuck it up worse."

"Jeez, I said I was sorry!" Cassondra laughed, making a show of how dramatically she was rolling her eyes and slumping forward as she walked. "You break *one* piece of vitally important, irreplaceable alien technology and some people just can't let it go!"

"Nope," Albertson said, turning his nose up at her in mock-indignation. "That's it. Whatever happens from now on, even if you save the world, you're still always going to be the clumsy girl who broke my watch."

Cassondra chuckled to herself for a few seconds, then started to slow down. Her natural walking pace was faster than Albertson's, so he usually winded himself trying to keep up with her, but she came to a stop with so little warning that he had to stumble to keep from shooting past her.

"Hey, whoa," he stammered as he struggled to keep his footing. "What—"

"What are we doing?" Cassondra said, standing frozen in place, not really looking at anything in particular. "I just realized, we don't really have a plan. I mean, we've never had a plan, but up until now it's all been reactive, so we've been able to just roll with whatever's thrown at us, but *now*, we've got to figure out how to assassinate President Muntz ourselves." She glanced back at Albertson with genuine terror in her eyes. "*How the hell are we going to do that?*"

"Hey, hey, don't worry," Albertson said, putting a hand on her shoulder. "Remember, it's not just the two of us anymore. Luna and Jacob are coordinating with us on this, and they've got *way* more experience disposing of political adversaries than we do."

"Yeah, that's not exactly *comforting*."

"Point taken," Albertson muttered. "But as far as I know, all you need to do from now on is just shadow Muntz. Keep an eye on him. He's already in power—he was just sworn in an hour ago—so you need to do whatever you can to prevent him from actually getting anything done. Distract him, keep him busy with other stuff, physically hide and destroy the paperwork if you have to."

"Okay," Cassondra said. "And how am I supposed to get that close to him?"

"Cass, you're a White House intern," Albertson said. "It's literally your job."

"Right," Cassondra muttered. "So, what? I'm just there killing time until someone else can get around to killing *him?*"

"Basically," Albertson said. "Luna said she and Jacob would see to breaking Tyler LaFuente out of his holding cell. Supposedly, they're off doing that as we speak. As soon as he's out, we'll all figure out how to make sure he and Muntz 'coincidentally' converge, and LaFuente's going to do all the actual dirty work, so the rest of us will have plausible deniability." He hesitated for a moment, and looked almost embarrassed. "We'll probably need you to lure Muntz to the rendezvous point yourself, though."

"Great," Cassondra grumbled. "I'll tie a Bible to a string and drag it down the hall, that ought to work." She closed her eyes and shook her head. "Anyway, yeah, I'll figure something out." She opened her eyes again and looked at him. "What about you? What are you going to be doing while we're all performing our jobs?"

Albertson's eyes darted nervously to the side, and he started to sweat again. (Cassondra wasn't sure if he was actually sweating, or if it was just another embellishment of the hologram.)

"I am going to be down in the catacombs looking for Squeally Dan."

"What?!" Cassondra snapped. "Your fucking pig?! While we're up here risking our lives, you're going to be hiding down in the tunnels with your goddamn pig?!"

"He's hasn't shown up yet!" Albertson said defensively. "He's almost never down there for this long. I'm worried about him! He could be wandering around aimlessly down there, just a scared little piggy lost in a big, terrifying world…"

Albertson batted his eyes a couple times, trying to play on Cassondra's sympathies.

She glared back. It wasn't working.

Albertson abruptly straightened up his posture and cleared his throat.

"Besides," he said, "that's most likely where he's hidden Donaldson's head. Donaldson's *real* head, I mean. And we should really try and find that before anyone else does, or else this whole charade could still come crashing down around us."

Cassondra just arched an eyebrow at him skeptically.

"Congratulations," she said. "That 'find the head' thing *almost* sounded like a justifiable explanation." Her eyes narrowed. "Too bad it was the last one you came up with."

Albertson lowered his head and sighed.

"Look, I'm not good with the violent high-octane stuff, okay?" He said. "You already know that. I'm a fucking *space-bureaucrat* for Christ's sake!" He took a step back and slouched down a little bit, making himself look smaller and submissive. "If I were up here running around with the rest of you when the guns started going off, I'd just be getting in everyone else's way."

"You know what, I can't even argue with that," Cassondra grumbled, facepalming. "Fine, go down into the tunnels, I don't care. We'll let you know when all the scary parts are over with."

"Again, I really don't see how 'not wanting to get shot' is a character flaw," Albertson said. His expression got sterner for a second. "And in case you don't recall, I've already had a gun pointed at me once today. It's not really an experience I want to repeat."

"Oh," Cass muttered, her eyes suddenly going wide. "Shit. You're right. I'm sorry, I didn't even think about that."

Albertson shrugged.

"It's fine," he muttered. "You had other stuff on your mind."

"Are you, like, *okay?*"

Albertson shrugged again.

"I don't even remember what 'okay' feels like for me anymore," he said. "Look, I genuinely don't want to leave you and Luna in the lurch for this, so if you *really* need me to stick around, I can."

"No, it's fine, really," she said. "I might as well get a chance to actually *use* all my big, fancy spy training for something, right? Go find your pig. We'll be fine."

Albertson nodded.

"Thank you."

Cassondra acted like she was about to say something, then stopped herself for a moment, then went ahead and said it anyway.

"Okay, question:"

"Shoot."

"You've talked about all the weird ways your translator works," Cassondra said. "How it finds workable analogues for all the alien cultural references and figures of speech we'd be unfamiliar with."

"Yeah."

"So where did your pig's name come from? I mean, really, '*Squeally Dan?*' What's your native language's equivalent for a bad pun based on the name of a classic dad-rock band from the 1970's?"

"Oh, that's not a translation," Albertson said matter-of-factly. "Squeally Dan didn't come along until after I'd been on Earth for a while and started listening to more of the native music. I named him in English."

"So," Cassondra said slowly, "the space alien infiltrating the government intentionally named his pet after the musical group Steely Dan?"

Albertson shrugged.

"They're my favorite Earth band," he said. "What should I have called him instead? Pig Floyd? Hog Dylan? Sow-garden?"

"I don't know," Cassondra said. "I just—"

"Linkin Pork?"

"Yeah, I get it, I was just wondering—"

"Pearl Ham?"

"Please stop."

"Sorry," Albertson muttered, trying to hide his smile.

Cassondra sighed.

"You're a weird person, you know that?"

"I'm an alien," he said. "What's your excuse?"

Cassondra almost laughed, then just shook her head.

"You know what, it doesn't matter. None of this is important right now. There's, like, borderline apocalyptic shit going on in Washington right now. I need to get back to—"

"Electric Light Pork-estra?"

"Yes, very funny, it's just—"

"Swine Inch Nails?"

"All right, smartass," Cassondra snapped. "If those are your favorite Earth bands, what's your favorite non-Earth band?"

"Oh, that's easy. Neep Nerprop and the Hoopie Flobos."

Cassondra just stared at him and blinked a couple times.

"You know," she said, "I'm not even sure what I was expecting when I asked that."

"I'm not either," Albertson said.

Cassondra slowly shook her head.

"Can we get back to the important stuff now?"

"Of course."

"Great. I need to—"

"Ozzy Os-boar."

"We need to keep Muntz from—"

"Depigge Mode."

"*I'm going to the Oval Office now so that we can start—*"

"Notorious P.I.G., also known as Piggie Smalls. I couldn't decide which of those was better—"

"*Will you shut the fuck up and take this shit seriously for once?!*" Cassondra shouted. Albertson went dead silent. Cassondra was breathing so hard she could barely talk. "How can you be so hokey-jokey about everything all the time?" she gasped. "People have *died* because of this man—because of Donaldson—and a lot more are going to die because of Muntz if we don't bring our A-game! We've only got one shot to take this *fucking* crazy, Hannibal Lecter *lunatic* down, and you're acting like it's all this fun little game! You have been since we found out Donaldson was dead, and… and…"

Cassondra abruptly turned on her heel and marched away from him down the hallway, making him run after her.

"Cass, I'm sorry," he stammered as I ran. "I make jokes when I'm stressed out, I deflect, it's the only way I know how to deal with any of this shit!" He caught up to her and put a hand on her shoulder. She stopped. "I had no idea it was having that kind of an effect on you," he said. "I swear, just because I act like an idiot sometimes doesn't mean I'm taking this any less seriously than the rest of you. But if it makes you uncomfortable I can… stop…"

His voice trailed off as soon as he realized she was crying.

She sniffed a couple times, then halfheartedly turned around to glance up at him, tears still clinging to the corners of her red, bloodshot eyes. She slumped his hand off of her shoulder, then turned away from him and quietly shuffled over to one of the plush velvet benches lining the halls and sat down with her face in her hands.

Albertson walked over and stood next to her, but didn't know what to say. Every time it looked like she had stopped sobbing, she let out another pained gasp and resumed dabbing at her eyes with the sleeve of her shirt.

"Do you remember what I said right before the speech?" she finally muttered, without looking up at him. "About how I thought it was tasteless and kind of mean-spirited to keep insulting and making fun of a dead man like that?" She swallowed. "I changed my mind. Frank Donaldson deserves every ounce of piss and vitriol and hate we can possibly dredge up for him."

Her entire body was trembling in place. Her fists were clenched at her sides. Albertson closed his eyes and nodded somberly to himself.

"This is about what the crowd said during the rally."

Cassondra closed her eyes and nodded.

"President Donaldson got off easy," she hissed. "Wanking himself to death was too *good* for him. He deserved to *suffer* for the racist, dehumanizing bullshit he pulled during his presidency." Tears were starting to form at the corners of her eyes again. "I almost wish he had lived long enough to actually *feel* LaFuente's bullet boring its way through his fucking empty head."

"Hey, whoa there," Albertson said, reaching out and putting a hand on her shoulder. "He's dead, Cass. He can't hurt you anymore."

"*Yes he can!*" she screamed, jumping back to her feet so quickly Albertson instinctively scrambled back. "Look at what happened at the rally! He wasn't actually *there!* In fact, you were actively trying to *walk back* his bullshit while impersonating him! And it still didn't matter! Those racist, inbred lunatics who voted for him were still just as ready to whip themselves up into a hate mob in his name! They didn't need any actual direct provocation from him!" She started pacing back and forth in front of Albertson. "That's Donaldson's *true* legacy! It's not that he's an idiot, or he talked funny, or that he just clearly had no idea how to do his actual job! It's that he made racism and bigotry cool again, he made it okay to *hate* people freely and in public, so that now even in his absence these knuckle-dragging flyover-state scumfucks feel empowered to start putting together lynch mobs!" She collapsed back onto the bench, slowly shaking her head as her face rested in her hands. "It's fun to sit around and laugh and joke about how much of a dysfunctional idiot President Donaldson was—and he *was*, don't get me wrong—but the sheer level of actual, destructive *damage* he has done to this country, just by his mere existence…" She wiped her nose on the back of her sleeve and sniffed loudly. "…it's not very funny, I guess is what I'm saying."

Albertson walked back over and stood awkwardly in front of her until she scooted to the side and made room for him to sit down next to her.

"Okay, I'm sorry," he said. "I'm just a tiny bit confused: do you actually like this country or not?" She didn't respond for several seconds, so Albertson finally added, "I mean, I'm not judging you either way. I'm an outsider who came here to fuck things up, just like you. Some of the stuff you say is just starting to sound a little, I don't know… *contradictory?*"

Cassondra sighed.

"It's complicated," she said. "My parents spent my entire damn life force-feeding me all the ways this country was exploitive and economically backwards. But they weren't exactly great parents, so it was inevitable that I was going to fight back and start rebelling against that when I became a teenager. But still, the day-to-day experience of, you know, actually *living* in this country while not being a straight white man kind of reinforced a lot of what they taught me about this country's inherent inequality and oppression. But then I started doing a lot of independent research into China's political system too, and realized that having *them* call out the *United States* on human rights abuses is kind of the pot calling the kettle black on the highest order. And then just as I was starting to really 'go native,' fucking *Frank Donaldson* gets elected President and rips away whatever illusions I did have left about the U.S., and… *sigh*." (She didn't sigh. She actually said the word "*sigh*" out loud.) "The people who raised me aren't the good guys," Cassondra muttered. "And the 'evil enemy' they raised me to destroy certainly aren't the good guys either." She hesitated for a moment. "But… I don't know…"

"What?"

"I've never actually been to China," she said. "The only real connection I ever had to it was hearing my parents' stories about it, which, looking back in retrospect, were probably bullshit. Hell, I've never even traveled outside of the country. America is all I've ever known. It's where all my best memories are. And acting like my *entire* childhood was crap and nothing good ever happened to me would be disingenuous. There were still plenty of really nice times where my friends and I would go to this little hole-in-the wall Mexican restaurant down the street after school and just stay there for hours, talking and bullshitting and putting away plate after plate of taquitos like it was the end of the world. Or when I'd need help with my homework, so I'd go into my dad's personal gym, where he was working out so he could stay in shape for all his spy stuff—"

"And bowling," Albertson said. Cassondra smiled.
"Yes," she said. "And bowling. And as soon as he saw me come in, he'd immediately get out of his elliptical and turn off the music—he always blasted *Bjork* out of the sound system when he exercised, for some reason—and patiently sit there with me until I'd figured out the algebra problem or whatever."

"Bjork…" Albertson said thoughtfully. "Can I turn that into one of my pig puns? '*Pjork?*' Does that work?"

"Shut up," Cassondra chuckled, giving him a light, playful little punch in the arm. "Or when I'd get home from a training session on a cool Autumn afternoon and my mom would have a fresh pot of dumplings waiting for me in the kitchen."

"Dumplings?" Albertson said. "Oh, wait, right. Never mind."

"You know, as strict and regimented as my parents could be," Cassondra muttered, "there were still moments when they could be so genuine and kind… like the longer I was with them, the more I became an actual *daughter* to them, and the more cracks started showing in the cold, distant shell of their spy training. My dad would 'kiss the owie' when I skinned my knee riding my bike or learning how to disarm a KGB agent, my mom would stay up all night talking me through a nasty breakup with my high school boyfriend. It would just be nice if all the good bits had come, you know…"

"*Without* the child abuse of trying to turn you into a soldier?"

"Yeah, that there," Cassondra said. "And, like, national borders are so arbitrary! They're just lines in the sand drawn by rich people that only rich people care about. Most of the actual *people*—the shopkeepers and the single mothers and the teachers and the factory workers—they don't *really* give a shit what country they're in or what economic system it uses. Or they care because they've been told to, but all their country really means to them is a striped piece of fabric and a catchy song and an 'us vs. them' mentality telling them that they're better than other countries. All they really want to do—*really*—is live their lives and keep their families fed, and whatever geopolitical background noise will allow them to comfortably do that suits them just fine." She took a deep breath, and let it out slowly. "I used to tell myself I was fighting for those people. All the spy shit, I wasn't doing it for the sake of governments or borders, I was doing it to protect the everyday ground-level schlubs who were just trying to get by and live their beautiful little lives. But… just…" She was starting to tear up again. "Coming face to face with how many of those same people want to *kill* me… not for any reason, not because of anything I've said or done, but just for the *hell of it…*" She swallowed and looked up at Albertson. "I don't know if I can do it, Jeff. I don't know if I can keep fighting to protect these people." She hesitated. "What if President Patrick Muntz is what these assholes *deserve?*"

"Hey, whoa whoa whoa," Albertson said, with the slightest hint of a nervous laugh. "I wouldn't wish that on my worst enemy, no matter what they'd done."

Cassondra just glared at him evenly.

"Really?" she said. "Have you ever had an entire crowd of people shouting racial slurs at you?"

"Well, no," Albertson muttered. "My planet's culture doesn't really have any conception 'race.' That's kind of just something humans made up as an excuse to be dicks to each other. And my species has four different sexes, so, like, technically speaking, I'm not even male. When I created this identity, I coded myself as a 'white male' because we determined that was the most likely to blend into your planet's power structures—especially in the Donaldson administration—but neither of those signifiers really apply to me, or even have any cultural equivalent on my planet." Cassondra was still just glaring at him. This line of reasoning wasn't getting him as far as he'd hoped. Albertson swallowed nervously. "So, like, we don't really have racism or sexism on my planet," he said. "We just united the entire planet against everyone else. That's how the whole intergalactic empire is able to sustain itself—"

"Good for you," Cassondra said dryly. "But you'll have to excuse me if the whole 'fighting for a world that hates me' angle doesn't quite appeal to me."

"Well don't do it for *them*, then!" Albertson said. "For the people who threatened you, I mean. They're all—what was it?—rich… straight… white people anyway—"

"Do you have *any* idea what you're talking about?" Cassondra said, folding her arms in front of her chest.

"No!" Albertson said. "That's what I'm trying to tell you: I'm an idiot! I never even knew this shit even existed before I came to your planet, and even after I came, I never really had to directly deal with it because I disguised myself as someone on the top of the food chain. Almost everything I knew about Earth culture before I came here was from studying your media and pop culture. *You* tell *me* how accurately your media depicts racism."

Cassondra continued to glare at him with her arms crossed, but her eyebrow arched slightly and her head cocked a fraction of a degree to the side. Albertson figured that was the closest he was going to get to any form of assent in this conversation, and took it as a cue to continue.

"But, like, if you don't want to do it for *them*, fine," he said. "But what about everyone else? The people like you, who are being oppressed, and who would suffer a lot *more* under a Patrick Muntz Presidency than those racist privileged people would in the first place? Will you still fight for *them*, to protect *them* from President Muntz, and even from the other Americans who want to hurt them like the ones out in that crowd did?"

Cassondra lowered her head and closed her eyes.

"God dammit," she muttered. "You stupid fucking alien…"

"What?" Albertson said, his voice starting to sound defensive. "I'm sorry if I'm an idiot. I'm sorry if I'm talking out my ass. What did I say now?"

"One of my friends from high school," Cassondra said, "just married his boyfriend. Cutest fucking couple you've ever seen in your life. They're trying to adopt a child right now, this little baby girl from foster care. Even back in high school, I remember Steven talking about how much he wanted to be a father. If Patrick Muntz gets the chance to run this country, that goes away for him." Her arms unfolded from her chest and went to her sides, her hands clenching into fists. "The guy in the apartment next door to me grows weed. He actually sold me the stash we smoked earlier."

"That was good weed," Albertson muttered idly.

"Uh-huh," Cassondra said. "He also invited me over to Thanksgiving dinner with his family last year, because he knew my family doesn't celebrate it. Believe it or not, that was the first time in my life I ever had home-cooked turkey and mashed potatoes and gravy, and his grandmother, this old Italian lady, actually *sang a traditional blessing* for me when I sat down at the table. I damn near broke into tears right then and there." Cassondra took a deep breath and let it out slowly. "Muntz has already talked about his plans to re-criminalize marijuana in all fifty states and do a massive crackdown on it. If that happens, my neighbor is almost definitely going to jail for a long, long time." Cassondra walked across the hallway and stared up at the portrait of George Washington hanging on the wall. "The nice old lady in my apartment building who brought me soup when I was sick is a first-generation immigrant. Patrick Muntz wants to kick her out of the country. The kid I used to tutor for after school is Muslim. Patrick Muntz wants to kick his entire family out of the country. That kid's sister is transgender. Patrick Muntz wants to legalize fucking conversion therapy." She turned her back to the portrait and faced Albertson with a cold, trembling glare. "I will do everything in my power to prevent Patrick Muntz from serving as President of the United States."

"Glad to hear it," Albertson said. "So are you ready to go down to the Oval Office and get this started?"

Cassondra whipped around and drove her fist through the portrait of Washington, right through his face, then turned back to face Albertson once again, and held her hand up with a fragment of the painted parchment still clinging to it.

"This son of a bitch *owned people*," she said. "The Father of our Country bought and sold human beings like livestock, and forced them to work in his fields and make him rich upon penalty of death, and now we put his face on money and tell schoolchildren he was a fucking superhero. His buddy Jefferson wrote about how 'all men are created equal,' then he went home and raped his fucking slaves. This entire country is built on hypocrisy and exploitation, and it has been from the very beginning. It drones on *ad nauseam* about 'freedom' and 'liberty' that it never had any intention of delivering to anyone who wasn't a rich white guy. All it ever had going for it was a kickass PR department, assuring everyone that it was the 'best country on earth.' Mind you, we don't have the best healthcare, or the best education, or the best employment numbers, or the lowest crime rate, or the highest life expectancy, or the best quality of life, but we still tell everyone we're 'the *best*,' just because we *are*, goddammit! And if you ask why there are so many homeless people in the greatest country on earth, or why so many of its citizens are killed by the law enforcement that's supposed to be there to protect them, shame on you for being unpatriotic! All so no one has to pay too close attention to the crimes against humanity committed by its founders!"

Cassondra finally stopped to take a breath. Her chest was heaving and her breathing sounded hoarse and ragged.

"Okay," Albertson said slowly. "Not *really* what we were talking about, but go ahead, girl, get it out of your system."

Cassondra swallowed hard, then started nodding to herself, not really looking directly at Albertson or anything else in the room. Her mouth started to curl upwards into a menacing, snarling smile.

"*Fuck* America," she growled. "Let's go save some Americans!"

CHAPTER 23

Secretary of State Jeff Albertson wandered through the underground tunnel system hidden beneath the White House, screaming out hog calls at the top of his lungs.

"Sooo-*weeee!*" he shouted into the darkness ahead of him as he walked, cupping his hands around his mouth. "Sooo-*wee-wee-wee-wee!* C'mon, Danny! Are you down here? Come on, boy!"

He had a bag of potato chips with him—the kind that he knew Squeally Dan liked to pilfer whenever one of the White House staffers opened a bag—and he started loudly crinkling it and crushing the chips between his fingers, hoping Squeally Dan would recognize the sound and come running.

There was still no sign of the pig as Albertson crossed into the central chamber housing Patrick Muntz's now-empty cage. It hadn't been that long since they had last been down here, and Albertson wasn't aware of anyone else in the catacombs with him, but apparently someone had been down there in the intervening time, because the cage had already been fully cleaned and sterilized, with nary a trace of the Vice President's shit to be seen.

"*President,*" Albertson corrected himself under his breath. "That monster is the President now. God help us all." The very thought of it sent such a profound shiver up Albertson's spine that, against his better judgment, he pulled out his phone and dialed Luna Donaldson.

"*What?*" her voice came in sharply after the second ring.

"Oh, well, I, um," Albertson stammered. "I was just wondering about a status update. Has, um, has *the package* been—"

"You don't have to use code words," Luna said flatly. "Mr. LaFuente has been released from custody, yes. I spoke with him briefly and informed him of as much of the situation as I believe he is required to know, then told him to hide in the area and lie low until he hears from me again."

"Okay, good," Albertson said. He paused for a second. "Was that awkward at all? Since, like, he did still *intend* to shoot your father?"

"Are you kidding?" Luna said. "I bought the man a beer." She sighed. "Now, I'm almost positive I don't actually want or need the answer to this question," she continued, "but what are you doing right now?"

"Well, um," Albertson muttered sheepishly. "I'm actually looking for my pet pig."

He could feel Luna rolling her eyes, even over the phone.

"Christ, why is it that I'm not even surprised by this shit anymore?" She said it a little more quietly than usual; Albertson wondered if she meant for him to hear it, or if she even cared at this point. "Where are you?" She said. "Your voice sounds weird and your signal keeps breaking up. Are you down in the catacombs or something?"

"Yeah," Albertson said. "That's the last place I saw him, so I figured I should see if I can track him down here."

"Wait," Luna said. "So you're just wandering around aimlessly down there?" Her voice suddenly sounded tense, and almost frightened. "Just turning stones over and poking your nose in everywhere?"

Albertson shrugged, then remembered that she couldn't see it over the phone.

"Yeah, basically," he said. "You ever tried tracking down a pig in this city?"

"I am going to ignore the numerous possibilities for ironic responses to that," Luna said, "and instead offer to send Jacob down there to help you look."

"Wait, really?" Albertson said. "Are you sure you don't need him up there to help with the plan?"

Another one of those eye-rolls he could feel.

"You are severely overestimating my husband's usefulness," she said. "I promise you, we'll be fine. Miss Warren is currently keeping constant tabs on President Muntz and his location, correct?"

"I mean, I hope so," Albertson said. "I haven't really seen her recently, but yeah, the last time I talked to her, she—"

"Please just stop talking so I don't get any further migraines," Luna grumbled into the phone. "I just texted Jacob. He should be meeting you down there shortly to…" She let out a long, grudging sigh. "*…help you find your pig.*"

"Thank you," Albertson said. "Wait a minute, you texted him *while* you were talking to on the phone to me?"

"Yes," Luna said. "I have you on speaker right now."

"You have me on speaker, so anyone can hear me?" Albertson gasped. "While we're talking about *assassinating the President?*"

"Oh, chill out," Luna groaned. "Nobody gives a shit anymore. It's Patrick fucking Muntz, for Christ's sake! Look, I've got a Secret Service agent in the room with me right now: Say hi, Bob."

"Uh… Hi," a deep voice said through the phone.

Albertson just facepalmed and shook his head.

"I'm hanging up now," he muttered wearily. "I'm going to assume everything's going according to plan unless I hear otherwise."

"I've been in constant contact with Mr. LaFuente since he left the holding facility," Luna said. "Cassondra and I will make sure he's in the right place at the right time." He could hear the sneer in her voice as she said, "Just worry about your damn pig." Then she hung up.

Albertson rolled his eyes and slipped the phone back into his pocket, then bellowed out another hog call that went echoing through the maze of tunnels branching out from where he currently stood.

"Sooo-*weeee-wee-wee-wee!*"

He stood in the central chamber and slowly turned his body, staring down each shadowy archway in turn. He had no idea how far out these tunnels spread and where all they went; he'd only even been in about half of them himself. God only knew which one of them Squeally Dan was in, or if he was even down here at all.

Then Albertson had an idea.

"The bunker," he said under his breath. That was the only place down here he'd seen Squeally Dan wander into on his own. And the last time he was in there he had gotten something to eat, so maybe that would be enough to imprint on his piggy little brain and he'd waddle his way back there in the hope of getting another treat. Either way, it was the best lead Albertson had right now, and once he left the central chamber, he was there within a couple minutes.

He wasn't sure if they were still keeping President Donaldson's body in there. No, actually, after a moment's reflection, he decided that they almost definitely weren't. Now that Donaldson's death was public, there was no need to go to the trouble of hiding him. They could just take him to the morgue of a proper hospital.

Except now they'd have to explain why his body was missing a foot. And most of its internal organs. And was probably more beat up and degraded than even having his head blown off could account for. And—

Albertson shook his head. He trusted Luna to have taken care of that *somehow*. Either by arranging for him to be stored in a special morgue only she had access to, or by coming up with a suitably batshit insane excuse when people started asking questions. Either way, it wasn't his problem anymore. He could return his focus to the task at hand.

No sign of Jacob Kirkman yet. He realized Luna had probably intended for him to stay back in the central chamber until they were able to meet up, but he shrugged off the concern. He wasn't really all that excited for Jacob's help, and he was moderately confident he'd find Squeally Dan soon anyway, so he didn't particularly care if Kirkman spent a couple minutes wandering aimlessly through the catacombs on his behalf. The wormy little git looked like he could use the exercise anyway.

The door in front of Albertson was closed, not ajar like the last time Squeally Dan had wandered in, but that didn't necessarily mean anything. It could easily have swing back closed after the pig wandered in, in which case it was even more urgent that Albertson check inside. He quickly punched the code into the keypad and yanked the door open with a smooth hiss.

Albertson didn't immediately see Squeally Dan inside, but there was, in fact, a body lying under a sheet on the examination table.

"Hello?" Albertson said just in case as he quietly took a step in. "Danny? You in here? Hiding under the table or anything?" He held up the bag of chips and crinkled it again. No noise, no motion, nothing. Albertson was just about to turn around and exit the bunker when something just barely caught his attention, something that didn't *quite* fit.

Since there was a sheet covering the body on the examination table, he couldn't immediately see who it was, he had just assumed that it was Frank Donaldson. But even from the body's outline, he could see that this body very clearly still had a head.

Albertson gulped and crept back towards the body on the slab.

"Hello?" he said again, as if there were some chance that the person was really just sleeping, or waiting to jump out at him and shout *Boo.* As soon as he was just barely close enough to touch the figure lying prone on the table in front of him, he reached out and pulled the top of the sheet off the body's head, then immediately let go and stumbled back against the wall. It was Speaker of the House Leo Bronstein. The sheet continued to slide further off Bronstein's body after Albertson dropped the edge, revealing the deep gash running along the man's stomach. He was very clearly dead.

Albertson heard footsteps approaching the bunker and forced himself to stumble back out into the tunnel just in time to see Jacob Kirkman approaching.

"Jacob," Albertson stammered. He gestured loosely towards the door to the bunker as he ran up to the man, quickly closing the distance between them. "In there! You need to see, it's Bronstein, he—"

Albertson said felt a sudden, sharp pain in his shoulder and looked down. Jacob Kirkman had just jabbed him with a syringe, the same sedative they used to knock out Patrick Muntz. Albertson stared dully at it for a moment, then back up at Kirkman's face as darkness already began creeping into the corners of his vision. Albertson was on his knees, even though he didn't remember falling, then he was on the floor. And the last thing Albertson saw was Jacob Kirkman's wicked, cold-blooded grin looming over him as everything went black.

CHAPTER 24

Cassondra burst into the Oval Office to find Patrick Muntz calmly, coolly sitting behind the President's desk, with one of the surviving doctors who had subdued him in the caverns standing beside him. Now that his worst impulses had been curbed by the chemicals they were pumping into his system, and that he was fully clothed for once in a very smart-looking, personally-tailored three-piece suit, Cassondra had to admit that there was something almost regal about Patrick Muntz's appearance and the way he carried himself. He had an air about him that he was just "above it all," and had no concern for the mere mortals surrounding him, nor any reason to. She'd seen brief snippets of Muntz on the news, of course, but just a few seconds of seeing him like this in person was enough to give her a chill.

As the Oval Office doors finally swung shut behind her, Cassondra realized she might have made a little *too* dramatic of an entrance for the current situation.

"Can I *help* you?" Patrick Muntz said, making no attempt to hide the contempt in his voice. Cassondra gulped. She couldn't tell if he remembered her from before, from his time in the cage.

"Um, just reporting for duty, sir," she said quietly. "My name is Cassondra Warren, I just started as a White House intern—"

"Excuse me?" Muntz said, standing up behind his desk. "They assigned one of *your* people to be my assistant? And a *female* one to boot? No no no no no. That will not do at all." He turned around to glance idly out the window, his hands folded neatly behind his back. "Mommy does not allow me to be alone with females. She only barely tolerates it when there *is* someone else in the room."

He gestured for the doctor standing next to his desk. "If it were not for this gentleman's presence, I already would have ordered you removed from my sight. By security, of course. I could never trust one of your kind to carry out such an important task on your own, even one so seemingly simple."

Cassondra took a long, slow breath in, then out.

He's going to be dead soon, she told herself. *Just get through the next couple minutes and then he won't be anyone's problem anymore.*

"Although I am not thrilled that my male company has to be a *doctor*," Muntz continued, the word "doctor" rolling off his tongue as if it were the strongest possible invective. "A man of so-called '*science*.' Anyone who professes to believe in this 'science' denies the power of our Lord and Savior, Jesus Christ, son of the one true God, and they will rightfully burn in Hell for their blasphemy." He turned back towards the doctor and glared at him. The doctor hardly seemed to notice or care. "Just like all of his compatriots down in the tunnels."

Okay, so he *did* remember. That probably wasn't good.

"You mean the ones you killed?" Cassondra said. Muntz's ice-cold eyes flashed up to meet hers for the first time since she'd entered the room.

"As men of science, they were evil men, who deserved to die," Muntz said, without missing a beat. "All of us are sinners, all of us deserve to die and go to Hell. Taking a human being's life, so that they can die and go to Hell as they deserve, is the highest act one can commit in the righteous service of God. With each life I take, I am becoming more and more righteous, holier and holier, purer and purer, until one day I will be able to sit beside God Himself in Heaven, and I will be able to point and laugh at all the evil sinners burning at my feet, just like they deserve, for all of eternity."

Cassondra took a step back without even realizing it. A crazy guy shouting his bullshit to the heavens was one thing, but *this*… someone who was this pants-crappingly insane while still remaining lucid enough to hold a soft-spoken conversation—and lucid enough to realistically *act* on it—she had legitimately never seen anything like this before.

Luna, where are you? She thought to herself, her heart beginning to pound in her chest. *Or Jeff, or Jacob, or Tyler, or anybody?*

With his eyes still locked on hers, Patrick Muntz smiled, and it was the worst thing Cassondra had ever seen. He knew exactly how upset she was. He could smell her fear.

"But, I'm getting ahead of myself," he said, gracefully sitting back down at his desk. "We must learn to run before we can walk, mustn't we? Take things one step at a time." He slid a sheet of paper onto his desk, then pulled a large feather quill out of the pen holder on his desk with a playful flourish. "I know the brain in a creature such as yourself is not well-developed enough to properly appreciate it," Muntz continued, "but you have arrived just in time to witness a truly historic moment for this country. There has been a disease, a sinful plague, that has been allowed to fester in this country for far too long. Not just one plague, dozens of them! The plague of homosexuality, of people daring to change the gender assigned to them by God and living other disgustingly deviant lifestyles. The plague of godlessness, of people worshiping their damnable false idols and trying to remove the omnipresence of Jesus Christ from even a single facet of their lives. And even the plague of people such as yourself, who have been so overwhelmed by the darkness within you that it has become manifest in the color of your skin." Patrick Muntz daintily dipped the quill into the bottle of ink on his desk. "Well, as of today, all of that ends."

"What?" Cassondra said, her entire body trembling, beginning to sweat. "What are you doing?"

"An executive order," Muntz said, staring down gleefully at the paper in front of him. "As soon as my signature is upon this document, all the crimes against God that I have just listed will be illegal, and punishable by death." Still smiling, he straightened out the paper with one hand and began to lower the quill with the other. "And not just those crimes, so many others as well! The crime of miscarriage. The crime of offering assistance to anyone suspected to be a sinner. The crime of education. The crime of taking drugs—not just those that are illegal right now, but *all* medicines. Jesus heals those he wishes to recover. All else is blasphemy." The doctor next to Muntz was quietly fiddling with an app on his phone, nodding slowly as Muntz talked, only barely listening to what was going on. "No trial or charge necessary," Muntz continued, "righteous citizens of this great country will be required to dispose of the human trash themselves, to eliminate anyone even suspected of sinning against God and Jesus Christ, to leave their bodies rotting in the street for all to see. Sure, the courts will challenge this document, maybe even overturn it in time, but then I will just write another one. And think of all the beautiful, glorious cleansing that will be accomplished in the meantime!"

Cassondra vaulted across the room and grabbed Patrick Muntz's wrist, holding it in place as the tip of the quill hovered mere millimeters over the document he intended to sign. Before she knew what was going on, Muntz's other hand balled into a fist and smashed directly into the bridge of her nose, sending her sprawling back.

"You… uppity… *whore!*" Patrick Muntz screamed, throwing the quill aside and climbing up onto his desk. "You *dare* to lay a hand on me?!" He pointed down at her dramatically from the added elevation of the desk while she stayed lying on the floor, trying to regain her bearings. "I, who am so much higher than you, so much purer, so much more righteous! You, who are doomed to burn into the fires of Hell, dare to try and infect me with your touch, you stupid… cunt… whore… bitch… fucking… *fuck… fuck… fuck…*"

"Oh no," the doctor said, frantically looking up as he stuffed his phone back into his pocket. "The sedative's wearing off! We tried to tell them he was building up a tolerance to it, but this is even quicker than we were expecting!" He stood there next to the desk, fumbling madly through his other pockets. "I was supposed to give him his booster when the last shot started to wear off, but I wasn't expecting to need it so quickly, I wasn't ready, I—"

Patrick Muntz grabbed the doctor's head and slammed it into the corner of his desk as hard as he could, sending up a spray of blood.

"All those fuckin' smarty-pants doctor brains!" Muntz cackled. "Ain't no good for thinking, no-siree-Robert! Brains that aren't thinking about Jesus aren't being used for nothing good, and are therefore forfeit! Come to papa!" Muntz opened his mouth as wide as he could and tried to bite into the man's head, but his teeth just ended up grinding against the bone, unable to break through the skull. After a couple more failed attempts at bites, he finally tossed the doctor's limp body aside and focused on Cassondra with a terrifying glint in his eye."

"So, girlie-girlie-girlie-girl," he cooed, kneeling down even though he was still perched on his desk. "Trying to barge in here and stop me from doing God's work. Such a bad little girl, aren't you? Bad little girls need to be *punished*." Still on the floor, Cassondra started to frantically push herself away as Muntz leisurely stepped down from his desk and strolled towards her. "Now, interfering with God's work is just the nastiest, most evil crime imaginable, isn't it?" Muntz said, a long string for drool hanging from his mouth. "So we need to find an extra-special-bad punishment for you, now don't we missy?" He knelt down again over her, his face just inches from hers, his hot breath on her cheek. She closed her eyes and tried to turn away, but there was nothing but floor behind her, nowhere else for her to turn. He grabbed a handful of her hair and pulled her head even closer to his. "When I'm done with you, girlie, you're going to be begging for the relief of when you finally go to Hell."

"N-now that that doctor's dead," Cassondra hissed. "You're alone in this room with me." Her eyes squinted open, and she was breathing heavily through gritted teeth. "*A girl*. Do you think Mommy would approve?"

Patrick Muntz's eyes grew wide, but his pupils were tiny. He immediately let go of her hair and leapt off of her.

"I'm sorry, Mommy!" he stammered to no one in particular, clawing at his temples with his fingernails. "I sinned and I deserve to be punished, Mommy, but the girlie made me so very *angry*, all I'm trying to do is honor and worship Jesus Christ and God, like you told me to, but, but I—but—but—but—"

"*Squee?*"

Muntz and Cassondra's attention both snapped to the source of the noise. Squeally Dan had just poked his head around from behind the couch and was staring at them both quizzically. President Muntz's eyes narrowed.

"*I'm gonna fuck that pig!*" he said with renewed confidence, and started galloping across the room towards the couch. Squeally Dan bolted away just as Muntz collided clumsily with the furniture, knocking it over and landing on the floor next to it in a heap. Dan ran frantically around the room searching for an exit, until he finally let out a surprised yelp as Cassondra scooped him up off the floor.

"Trust me, Danny," she said. "You *don't* want to stay around here."

Patrick Muntz was already almost back to his feet. And even worse, he was standing between her and the door out of the Oval Office. With little more than a moment to think, Cassondra darted to the other side of the room and threw the trap door open with her free hand, taking the spiral staircase down into the catacombs two and three steps at a time, pig still held tightly in her arms, and the approaching figure of Patrick Muntz panting and slavering an indeterminate distance behind her.

CHAPTER 25

Albertson's consciousness came back slowly, and in waves. At first he was just surrounded by darkness, but he was at least aware that it was dark. Then he started hearing a sound, a sort of rhythmic *click... click... click...* repeating over and over again. His vision was blurry, but he could make out a soft, subtle light. Then a humanoid figure standing in the light. He tried to reach up and rub the bleariness out of his eyes, and found that he couldn't move his arms. He began to struggle and strain, but something was holding him down.

He was tied to a chair.

"Oh, look who's finally awake," he heard someone say. *Luna Donaldson.* "How are we feeling, Mr. Albertson?"

"Cig… cig… cigarette," Albertson croaked breathlessly. "Need a… cigarette…"

Albertson's vision had returned just enough for him to see Luna dramatically rolling her eyes.

"Jacob, give the dying man his last request, will you?"

Albertson felt Jacob Kirkman's hand push itself into his jacket and clumsily shuffle around until it found the pocket he kept his cigarettes in. Kirkman himself was little more than a fuzzy grey blob hovering in his peripheral vision, but a moment later he felt the butt of a cigarette poke between his lips and heard the click of his lighter, almost indistinguishable from the same repeated clicking noise that echoed through the background of the room. Albertson could feel the heat, even from the small little flame now smoldering a couple inches from his mouth, and took a long, deep breath.

"Agh, oh God," Albertson gasped. "Thank you—"

A blindingly bright light suddenly flashed into in Albertson's face, and for several seconds, that was all he could see. He blinked a couple times, trying to force his eyes to adjust to the *other* extreme now. Luna Donaldson and Jacob Kirkman were standing in front of him; they seemed to be the only two other people in the room. Luna was playing with a butterfly knife—doing tricks with it, twirling it between her fingers, keeping it in constant motion. That was the source of the weird clicking he'd been hearing since he woke up. And they had just turned a giant floodlight on directly in his face, rendering them little more than distorted silhouettes while they stood in front of it.

Albertson scrunched his eyes shut and tilted his head back as far as it would go. He blinked a couple times. There were bars above him. And above the bars, there was a craggy stone ceiling.

They were down in the catacombs beneath the White House.

And he was tied to a chair in Patrick Muntz's cage.

"What the fuck are you doing?" Albertson wheezed. The smoke was helping to clear his head a little bit, but he was still disoriented. He couldn't even tell if Jacob and Luna were inside the cage with him, or standing on the outside watching their new captive like a zoo animal.

"Well," Luna said casually, with an almost sing-songy tone in her voice, "my father, the President of the United States, is dead. Boo-hoo-hoo, we'll all tell our secretaries to send flowers. So that means the new President of the United States is now…"

"The Vice President," Albertson said. "Patrick Muntz. We've been over this."

"Indeed we have," Luna continued, "and when we did go over this, we all unanimously agreed that Mr. Muntz cannot be allowed to take over his predecessor's position. So, wheels are in motion to get rid of him. Goodbye Patrick

Muntz. That means the next person in the line of succession is…"

"Speaker of the House," Albertson said. "Leo Bronstein." His mind was still hazy, but it only took another second for the memory to flash back to him. "…who is also dead."

"Don't feel *too* bad for him," Luna muttered, without looking up at him. "He was the one running Washington's secret underground pedophile ring."

"Wait," Albertson stammered, "he was doing *what now?*"

"And I'll save you the trouble of asking," Luna continued. "The *next* person in the line of succession—Amelia Lockhart, the President pro tempore of the Senate—was sitting in the exact same seat that you currently inhabit about two hours ago, and after a nice, long chat with me and Jacob, she has graciously decided to resign from her post and spend more time with her family." Luna tossed the butterfly knife into the air, watching as it spun and twirled above her head, then caught it neatly by the handle and flashed Albertson a devilish smile. "Ms. Lockhart cherishes her family very much, you know. She doesn't want anything bad to ever happen to them, especially not her adorable little grandbabies. Which is why she promised me that she would never, ever give another interview, or appear on another news program, or even talk to another human being about a single detail of her political career for the rest of her natural life. And I believe that she won't. Or, at least, I hope she doesn't." Luna idly pressed the tip of her finger against the tip of the knife, testing its sharpness. "I really do hate having to kill children."

"Luna," Albertson stammered. "What the hell are you—?"

"Mr. Albertson," Luna said, somehow maintaining a casual, breezy tone despite cutting him off. "Do you happen to know what cabinet position my husband Jacob currently holds?"

Albertson's eyes flitted back and forth between Luna and Jacob. He cocked his head to the side.

"Wait, Jacob Kirkman has a cabinet position?" he said. "When did that happen?"

Luna rolled her eyes, but retained her bemused smile.

"It was a couple weeks ago, during the last round of disgraced resignations," she said. "He was nominated to replace the *Secretary of Defense*, Mr. Albertson. He currently *is* the Secretary of Defense." She walked over to him, slowly, one step at a time. He could finally tell that Luna and Jacob were, in fact, trapped in the cage with him. Well, probably not "trapped." They wouldn't have done this if they didn't have the key. "You, of all people, should know that," she continued, leaning in close to his face. "Considering *you* signed all the necessary paperwork while you were forging my father's signature."

Albertson's eyes went wide.

"Oh," he said quietly. "Shit…"

Luna Donaldson leaned back away from him. There was nothing sarcastic or condescending about her smile now; she was showing him genuine joy.

It was terrifying to behold.

"So many papers land on my desk—on *his* desk—on both," Albertson stammered. "I lose track sometimes, don't even know what I'm signing, just know it needs to get done to keep the country running—"

"Hey, you don't need to apologize to *us,*" Luna said. "We're *more* than pleased with how things turned out. It does, however, put us in a rather awkward situation." She began to walk in a slow circle around Albertson's chair, her pace leisurely, as if she hadn't a care in the world. "President. VP. Speaker of the House. President pro tempore. All gone. That means that the only person currently standing between my Jacob and the Presidency of the United States…" She swiveled on her heel and playfully pointed at him. "…is *you*, Mr. Albertson. The Secretary of State."

Albertson's entire body was starting to tremble—as much as it could, anyway, with the ropes still binding him down.

"You fucking lunatic!" he stammered. "How long have you been plotting this?!"

Luna closed her eyes and started shaking her head, her smile growing wider and wider until she finally tilted her head back and burst out laughing, the sound echoing off the ceiling and reverberating through the caverns around them. When she finally lowered her head to face him again, tears were streaming down her face.

"That's the thing," she gasped. "I never planned *any* of this!" She took in a couple short, quick breaths; Albertson couldn't tell if they were laughs or sobs. "All I ever *planned* to do was wait out my father's Presidency, get as many kickbacks as I could, *while* I could, and then go live a comfortable, *anonymous* life on some island somewhere after he was out of power! But when he died, I saw all of that crumbling before me, and I started panicking… and then I started *improvising*. And then when we suggested 'taking care' of the Vice President as well… well, my brain just followed the next couple logical steps, and I realized this was the only way to *survive*."

She shook her head, then pressed her face into her shirt sleeve to wipe away the tears. When she looked up at him again, her makeup was smeared and streaking across her face, but she had regained a modicum of composure.

"It's a zero-sum game for us, Mr. Albertson," Luna said. "Jacob and I will either become the most powerful people on earth, so no one will ever be able to hurt us again, or we will be indicted for the *numerous* crimes we have already committed and spend the rest of our lives as prisoners with nothing." She offered him a wan smile. "It really wasn't a difficult choice at all." She clapped a hand on Albertson's shoulder, almost amiably. "I legitimately *am* trying to work with you, here. Calling you a 'dead man' earlier, that was all for dramatic effect. I don't want to kill you—hell, I didn't even *want* to kill Bronstein. I've just known that stubborn old gopher for years, and he was *never* going to give up his seat of power willingly. But Senator Lockhart, she was smart. And now she gets to live out the rest of her years in a happy, fulfilling, well-earned retirement." She made her face level with Albertson's. "You could be smart too, Mr. Albertson. But at this point, it's all up to you."

Albertson stared into her eyes for several long seconds. Neither of them blinked. Finally, he just started to shake his head.

"Why, you *miserable* little *backstabber—*"

Luna lunged forward, jamming the blade of her knife into Albertson's shoulder. He let out an agonized scream as blood oozed slowly out of the wound.

"No, Mr. Albertson," she said playfully, pushing a stray lock of hair out of her face while flashing him just the briefest hint of a smile. "I think you'll find I'm *more* than happy to stab you in the front."

She pulled the knife out of his shoulder, eliciting another yelp of pain, but before she wiped off the blade she stopped to just stare at it. After a moment, she lightly touched her index and middle finger against the fluid covering it, then slowly rubbed it between her fingers and thumb. Albertson's blood was a deep purple color, and had the consistency of maple syrup, as was typical for a member of his species. The holographic disguise was advanced enough to make it look like human blood when it was still on him, but as soon as it lost physical contact with his person, the hologram couldn't cover it anymore and it reverted back to its natural appearance.

"What the hell?" Luna murmured. "Jeff, have you got some kind of weird medical condition or something?" She walked up and put her hand against Albertson's forehead, then immediately pulled it away. "*Holy shit!*" she yelled. Then, tentatively, she reached out and touched his face again. "*Scales…?*"

"I, I, I can explain," Albertson stuttered. "I have, um, eczema! And I, like, cover it up with a lot of makeup, so it's not visible, and—"

"Jacob," Luna snapped. "Check him out. See if there's anything else weird about him."

"Weird?" Albertson said, laughing nervously, "what do you mean *weird*, there's nothing weird about me, you know how it is when you get older, things just start going *ping*, first my skin, then my blood, hell, it'll probably be my knees next—"

He felt a hand close around his wrist. Jacob Kirkman was standing behind him, trying to pry off his watch.

"Hey, no, come on!" Albertson said. "That's just my watch, man! My, um, my *grandfather* gave me that watch, don't make me take it off, I haven't taken it off since he died and I—"

Jacob finally, successfully wrestled the watch off of Albertson's wrist. The change was immediate: Albertson's human visage flickered away like a bad TV signal, and a blue, scaly, dog-faced space alien sat in his place.

Luna immediately stumbled back, almost losing her balance and falling to the floor.

"*Holy fuck!*" she screamed. Jacob just stared at him, mouth hanging open in shocked silence.

"Okay, okay," Albertson said quickly. "I know this *looks* bad, but—"

"*What the hell are you?!*" Luna shouted. Her eyes were wide and she was backing away from him, but she looked more surprised than actually scared. She grabbed

Albertson's watch out of Jacob's hands and held it out in front of her. "And what the hell is *this?*"

"That is a very advanced, very *delicate* piece of technology," Albertson said. "And it's the only one I have, so please be careful with—"

Luna held the watch up to her face and started smacking it against the palm of her other hand, hard, watching it intently.

"And how did you make it do that thing?"

"Aw, no!" Albertson pleaded. Sparks were starting to fly out of the watch, and it was making a small chugging noise that he had never heard it make before. "It's already half broken, don't make it *worse!*"

The glowing, translucent face of a Skreeez soldier suddenly appeared over the face of the watch. It was the same recording he had shown Cassondra. Luna and Jacob both stared at it, enraptured.

"Okay," the face said, just as it had said to Cassondra the last time. "Advance Invasion Scout Theyjey Drizzl, earth designate 'Jeff Albertson,' this is Captain Krelibon Scooch of the Skreeez Imperial Vessel Ackgatackgatack. We've just received your first intel package on the Planet Earth and the American Government. I'm reviewing the info right now as we speak, and... *eeeerrrmmm...*"

With one more loud, electric *pop* and another small shower of sparks, Captain Scooch's face flickered out of view. The rest of the lights built into Albertson's watch dimmed down into nothing, and a thin trail of smoke issued forth from a seam in the casing.

"A fucking alien invasion," Luna whispered, still staring wide-eyed at the dead alien watch. "I don't fucking believe it." She stared at it for several seconds longer, then finally let her arm fall to her side. "Well," she muttered, trying to be as nonchalant as humanly possible given the circumstances. "I think we've heard enough."

"Um, no, actually," Albertson stammered. "Ha-ha, like, I am *dead* serious. The part that got cut off is actually *super* important."

"You're a scout, *huh*?" Luna said, leaning down so that her face was level with Albertson's again. "So does that mean that if you don't report back, or if you die, or if the *next* scout shows up and finds your *severed head* sticking on a *spike* outside the White House, the whole invasion will be called off?"

Albertson's head was lowered. He was starting to laugh deliriously to himself.

"You know what, lady?" he said. "I've got news for you. The invasion already *was* called off. *Months* ago. You know *why?*" He glared up at her. "Cause we decided we don't *want* your stupid fucking planet!" he spat. "You assholes fucked it up with all your greenhouse gasses and fluorocarbons and shit, and then you spent more time and energy killing each other and blowing shit up than trying to save your own fucking lives, and we decided y'all were more trouble than you're worth! Congratulations, humanity! You *suck* so much you aren't even worth conquering!" Albertson's head lowered again, as far as he was able to while trapped in his perpetual sitting position. Quiet, high-pitched sobs began to escape from his throat. "*...oh God I don't want to die...*"

Luna was still staring at him, her hand pensively on her chin, slowly shaking her head.

"And to think," she muttered. "If you had played your cards right, I was *actually* planning on letting you live." She stood back up to full height and clicked her tongue. "Jesus. Talk about close calls." Then she reached down and plucked the cigarette out of Albertson's mouth.

"Hey!" he snapped. "What are you doing?"

"Well, you were *pretty* desperate for this cigarette," she said. "And you sound better since you started smoking it. You seem to be breathing more easily. And even in your human guise, I've never seen you *not* smoking." She took a long pull from the cigarette herself, then blew the smoke out, slowly and leisurely. "And when you exhale, I don't see any of the smoke come back out of your lungs. So I guess I'm putting two and two together, is what I'm doing."

Albertson watched as she snuffed the lit cigarette out in the palm of her own hand, flinching only slightly as the flame sizzled out against her flesh. Then she knelt down in front of him and fixed on him the coldest, iciest, most hate-filled gaze he had ever witnessed on a human face.

"Jacob, start a stopwatch," she called over her shoulder without taking her eyes of Albertson. "When more of these motherfuckers come to invade our planet, I want to know exactly how long it takes them to die."

CHAPTER 26

Albertson was coughing so hard he could barely get the words out.

"*Luna*," he gasped, in between bouts of hacking. "*Please…*"

Luna just stood across from him and continued to stare down impassively, occasionally taking a glance down at her stopwatch. Jacob Kirkman stood behind her, peeking around at Albertson from behind her shoulder.

"Save your breath, alien," she said. "Cause it seems like it's in pretty short supply right now. You're not getting out of this alive." After she'd put out the cigarette that she'd stolen from him, she'd decided it would make an even stronger statement to re-light it and smoke it in front of him while he watched, just barely out of reach. She pulled what was left of the cigarette out of her mouth—almost down to the butt now—leaned down, and leisurely blew the smoke in Albertson's face. "But if you felt like ratting your people out and giving us some details on the coming invasion, so my Jacob has an easier time fighting them off when *he's* President, we might consider extending your life by just a little bit longer."

Albertson's coughs were getting low, hoarse, and wet.

"*No invasion,*" he wheezed. "*Keep telling you—*"

"Oh, *please*," Luna groaned. "How stupid do you think we are? The fact that you're here in the first place proves that that's untrue." She sighed. "Oh, well." The cigarette was now completely spent, so she idly flicked the butt at Albertson, bouncing it off of his nose. "When your people show up, I guess we'll just have to nuke the fuckers into oblivion." She stood back up and playfully tousled her husband's hair. "That works on pretty much everyone, right Jakey?"

Jacob nodded enthusiastically.

"*They're not COMING!*" Albertson wheezed emphatically. All four of his eyes were wide, staring off into nothing. "*I... am... alone...*"

"Ain't that the truth," Luna said, smiling cruelly down at him. "Doesn't look like it's going to be much longer, alien. Your people aren't coming for you." She leaned over again and stared him directly in the eye. "You have no friends, here. No allies. *No one* is going to save you."

And that's when Cassondra ran in from the tunnel that led to the Oval Office, screaming at the top of her lungs and carrying a pig.

"*Aaaaahhhhh!!!!!*"

"*Heh... heh... heh... heh...*"

The second sound, the panting, was coming from Patrick Muntz, who burst into the chamber a moment later, still wearing his fully tailored three-piece suit, galloping after her on all fours. Cassondra started running circles around the cage in the center of the room that held Albertson and his captors, still screaming. Squeally Dan bobbed uncomfortably up and down in her arms as she ran, letting out an occasional annoyed grunt. Patrick Muntz was so close that she could feel his breath on the back of her calves.

"*Piggy piggy piggy gonna fuck the piggy squeal for me you little bitch yeah gonna be my little sex piggy yeah yeah yeah yeah yeah—*" Then, halfway through their third lap around the cage, he abruptly stopped and stared between the bars. "*You!*" he hissed, pointing at Jacob. "*I want your kidneys!*"

He launched himself at the wall of the cage and clung to the side, repeatedly pelvic-thrusting in towards them, forcing the massive erection visible beneath his fancy dress pants in-between the bars. Jacob stumbled back and screamed.

Without a moment's hesitation, Luna whipped out her phone, quickly tapped out a number, and then held it up to her ear.

"LaFuente?" she said. "It's time. Muntz is in the secret catacombs underneath the White House. Central chamber. Get down here *now!*"

As Luna was slipping the phone back into her pocket, she suddenly noticed Cassondra standing at the edge of the chamber, still carrying the pig, just staring at everything that was going on with wide eyes, her mouth hanging open in dumbfounded shock.

"*Hey!*" Luna yelled. "You! Servant girl! Get in here with us before this lunatic tries to eat your face!"

Cassondra just kept on staring back at her, with an expression on her face like her head was about to explode from the sheer weirdness.

"The door's on the opposite side!" Luna said, pointing to the cage wall across from the one Patrick Muntz was clinging to. "We can slip you in without the risk of letting him in too."

Cassondra still didn't respond.

"Come on, you'll be safer in here!" Luna shouted, almost pleadingly. "This cage was built to hold him in! It can sure has hell keep him out!"

Cassondra didn't budge. Her entire body was shaking. She was telling her legs to move, but they weren't obeying. Squeally Dan was starting to squirm and squeal in her arms; she didn't even realize how tightly she was holding onto him. Luna rolled her eyes.

"Oh, for Christ's sake," she said, digging out her ring of keys. "Do I have to do *everything* for you people?"

Jacob glanced away from Muntz for just a moment to see that Luna was unlocking the cage door, and frantically started shaking his head.

"Oh, calm down," Luna said, already sliding out through the door. "I'll only be gone a moment. The door will be locked again before Muntz has stopped humping the bars long enough to notice." Luna walked around the side of the cage with a wide birth so as not to alert Muntz, then ran over to Cassondra. "Listen," she said, "I know you have had a *bastard* of a week. We all have. But this is *not* the time to freeze up on me, girl." Luna grabbed one of Cassondra's arms and yanked her forward, causing her to finally let go of Squeally Dan. The pig jumped out of her grasp and ran, screeching, down one of the other corridors. Fortunately, Patrick Muntz was too distracted by his new target to notice. As Luna dragged Cassondra back towards the cage, she grunted, "We need to get you back where it's *safe*."

"What the hell?!" Cassondra said, yanking her arm out of Luna's grasp. Luna stared at the girl in utter confusion for a moment, then followed her gaze back to the cage. She was staring at Albertson tied to the chair. It was the first chance she'd gotten to notice him. He was still coughing, but the coughs were getting less frequent, interspersed into this constant, low wheeze that didn't sound healthy.

Luna smiled darkly.

"Oh, yes," she said as she pulled the cage door open. "Our pal Secretary Albertson was harboring a secret. It turns out that he—"

"I know!" Cassondra snapped. "Why isn't he smoking?! He told me his people need smoke to survive!"

Luna just stared at incredulously Cassondra for a moment. Then, her eyes slowly narrowed.

"You *knew* he was an alien?" she said, taking a step towards Cassondra. "You were working *with* the alien?"

"Luna, this isn't time to fuck around!" Cassondra said. "If you don't give Albertson a cigarette, he's going to die!"

"*I know!*" Luna shouted. "*That was the idea!*" She closed her eyes and started slowly shaking her head, clicking her tongue in rhythm. "I had such high hopes for you, girl," she muttered. "Sure, you're starting at the bottom, you're going to make mistakes, that is to be expected." Cassondra heard a click as Luna flipped open the butterfly knife. "But betraying your own country for the sake of this alien *creature*… some things are simply inexcusable."

Cassondra stumbled backwards just as Luna lunged forward and slashed at her with the knife. She dodged just quickly enough to avoid any serious injury, but still felt the knife slice along her chest, against her collarbone, just above her breasts. Cassondra screamed. The gash was only skin deep, but it still hurt like a motherfucker. She fell to the ground and clutched at her chest, feeling the blood slowly seep into her clothing.

Luna dove forward for another slash; now that Cassondra was on the ground, Luna's swing was level with her face. Cassondra dodge-rolled out the way—the blade completely missing her this time, but her chest still screaming with pain—and somehow staggered to her feet, despite the blinding agony. Everything felt heavy. She was starting to see spots.

Luna was charging at her, like an animal, blade swinging wildly. The first cut had been a lucky shot; Luna had caught her off guard. She couldn't let the woman land another one on her, and she wouldn't. Now that Cassondra was focused on avoiding Luna's blows, her spy training would kick in… right?

Cassondra slid to the side just as the blade whistled through the air where she'd been standing a moment prior.

"Luna," she said, as calmly and evenly as she could, given the circumstances. "Please, just *listen* to me—"

The knife just *barely* missed slashing open Cassondra's belly, but left a tear in her blouse. She couldn't let it get that close again.

"Albertson is a *threat*," Luna said through gritted teeth. "If you're allied with him, you are a threat too. When my father was in charge, he could protect us from all the threats, but he's not here anymore. It's up to me now." She raised her arm, ready to take another swipe. "And I cannot tolerate *any* threats to my or Jacob's safety."

Cassondra saw the glint of the blade and dodged, but was immediately caught by Luna's other, open hand, which grasped onto her throat.

"Fake out," Luna whispered with a sick smile, and she slammed Cassondra up against one of the underground chamber's stone walls, her fingers digging into the flesh of Cassondra's neck. With her other hand, she pressed the blade of the knife up against Cassondra's chin. If Cassondra budged—if Cassondra *breathed* too hard—she would be slashed open from ear to ear.

For just a moment, Cassondra stared past Luna, at Albertson still tied to the chair. He was fighting against the ropes, desperately struggling for breath. She felt tears starting to well up in her eyes.

"Aw, what's the matter, darling?" Luna cooed. "Did the White House internship turn out to not quite be what you signed up for?"

Cassondra clawed at the hand around her throat, but Luna's grip didn't budge.

"Didn't... sign up... any of this..." Cassondra gurgled. "Parents... made me... Didn't have... choice..."

Luna's grip loosened just a little, allowing Cassondra to breathe, and she lowered the knife away from Cassondra's throat, but still kept it out.

"What was that?" Luna said, staring at Cassondra coldly.

Cassondra hesitated. She'd been telling the truth, but that was the problem. This woman was trying to kill Albertson because she'd discovered his secret. How much of Cassondra's own past could she dare let out?

"I was trained to go into the government," Cassondra gasped, "practically from birth." The words were difficult to get out; while the pressure Luna was putting on her windpipe may not have been lethal, it still wasn't exactly comfortable. "They acted like getting this internship was the only reason they'd had me." Again, not really a lie. "I never really had any choice."

Something recognizably human flickered in Luna's eyes for just a moment, and the hand on Cassondra's neck went completely slack, letting her catch a quick gasp of breath. Then Luna's eyes were steel again, and she slammed Cassondra up against the stone wall of the chamber, and the hand holding the butterfly knife slowly drew back, like a cobra, ready to strike at any moment.

"Well, that's just too damn bad," Luna said. "I can't help it if you're a victim of circumstance. You're here now. That's all that matters."

Cassondra's huddled back, pressing up against the wall behind her, then kicked off of it as hard as she could so that her foot swung up and knocked the knife out of Luna's hand, sending it skittering to the floor.

"What?!" Luna gasped, following the blade's trajectory with her eyes. "You stupid little brat—"

Both of Cassondra's hands shot out and she pressed her thumbs into Luna Donaldson's eyes. The woman immediately screamed and reeled back, letting go of Cassondra's throat. Cassondra started desperately gasping for breath as she slid to the floor. At least one of her old spy tricks had worked. The leverage had sucked, and Luna had reacted too quickly, so Cassondra knew she hadn't permanently blinded the woman—probably gave her nothing more than spots in her eyes for a couple minutes—

but it sure hurt like hell. Cassondra saw the knife on the floor a couple yards away from her. A couple yards in the other direction, Luna was still moaning and rubbing her eyes. Then she lowered her hands, blinked a couple times, saw Cassondra, and followed Cassondra's gaze.

Both of them scrambled towards the knife. Cassondra was still on the floor, crawling towards it, struggling to catch her breath while Luna strode over from the other side of the room. Cassondra was inches from grasping the knife's handle, until a long stiletto heel came crunching down on the back of her hand and she let out a shocked, wailing scream. Luna gave her a sick, twisted smile from above, then reached down to pick up the knife… and wrapped her fingers around the blade instead of the handle. Luna's eyes still weren't quite back yet, Cassondra realized. She had double vision.

Luna screamed and immediately dropped the knife again, her fingers suddenly slippery with blood, and Cassondra caught in midair with her free hand, then slashed at the shin of the leg that was stepping on her. Luna screamed again and stumbled back as Cassondra pushed herself to her feet, breathing heavily, clutching the handle of the knife so hard she felt like she was going to cut off the circulation in her hand. Her chest was in such agony that it had gone numb. Either that, or it was the adrenaline. Cassondra didn't know which, and she didn't care. She could feel the wet bloodstain on her blouse slowly growing in size, especially now that she was exerting herself.

Cassondra glared down. Luna was on the floor, staring back up at her, helpless. Cassondra took a step forward, twirling the stolen butterfly knife between her fingers.

"Payback, bitch," she growled.

"Holy *shit!*" Tyler LaFuente screamed, running into the chamber with a sawed-off shotgun held at the ready. "What the fuck is going on here?!"

"Kill them!" Luna shrieked, scrambling back to her feet. "Kill everyone here who isn't me or Jacob!"

"Uh…" Tyler glanced nervously back and forth between Cassondra and Muntz, who was shaking on the bars so hard that the entire cage was ratting, still seemingly oblivious to anything else that was going on around him.

"*Kidneys,*" Patrick Muntz hissed, pushing his face up against the bars and sticking his tongue as far in as he could.

"*Start with Muntz!*" Luna shouted.

"I don't have a good angle, though," Tyler stammered back. "At this range, I might hit your husband too!"

"Oh, for God's sake—*Jacob!*" Luna said. "The back door's still unlocked! Get out of there!"

Jacob stared at her, wide-eyed, and frantically shook his head. Patrick Muntz, however, suddenly perked up.

"The cage… is *open?*" he whispered.

Luna rolled her eyes harder than Cassondra had ever seen them roll before, and then scrunched them shut.

"Of course he understood *that,*" she groaned, but Patrick Muntz had already hopped off the side of the cage and was scurrying around to the door on the back. Jacob Kirkman grabbed the door and yanked it shut, but he couldn't lock it without Luna's key, and Muntz was on the other side a second later, trying to pull it back open, drooling. For a couple moments the two of them stood there, on opposite sides of the cage door, playing a life-or-death game of tug-of-war, before it became clear that Muntz was by far the stronger of the two as the door started to quickly inch back outwards.

"Let go!" Luna shouted. "Jacob, if you've ever trusted me about anything, trust me now and *let go of the door!*"

Jacob Kirkman followed his wife's advice, and the door immediately swung open without a counterbalance for Muntz's strength, sending the former VP tumbling the ground under his own inertia.

"*Now!*" Luna screamed to Tyler. "Get him *now!*"

But Jacob had seized what he thought was his only opportunity, bolted out of the cage, and run, screaming, down the tunnel that led back to the Oval Office, with Muntz springing back to his feet a moment later and chasing after him.

"*Oh, for fuck's sake,*" Luna groaned, running down the tunnel after Jacob and Muntz. "GET BACK HERE, YOU IDIOT!!!"

While the cacophony of footsteps disappeared into the distance, Cassondra ran into the cage and started cutting off the ropes binding Albertson to the chair with Luna's stolen butterfly knife.

"Holy shit!" Tyler gasped. "Is that an alien?"

"*Shut up!*" Cassondra snapped. Albertson was trying to say something to her, but was wheezing so hard he could barely get the words out. "What are you doing here?!" She shouted to Tyler. "Go after them!"

"What?" he said. "OH! Right!"

Tyler bolted away from them, chasing after the parade of Jacob Kirkman, Patrick Muntz, and Luna Donaldson that they could still hear vaguely in the distance. Cassondra wasn't focused on that. She was still focused on parsing out what Albertson was trying to say to her in between gasps.

"What?" she pleaded, getting down on her knees next to him. "What do you need?!"

Even without the ropes, he stayed seated in the chair, no longer able to stand of his own volition. Cassondra watched helplessly as he doubled over and, with the most ungodly retching and hacking she had ever heard, coughed up something that looked an awful lot like blood.

"Oh, *Gooddd…*" she whined, tears welling up behind her eyes.

"*Cig... a... rette...*" Albertson finally managed to gasp.

"What? OH, GOD, I'M AN IDIOT!" Cassondra said.

It wasn't all her fault, she told herself. The past couple hours—well, the last couple *days*, but the last couple hours in particular—had forced her to deal with so much crazy shit upon crazy shit upon crazy shit that her mind could barely focus on any one thing anymore. Plus, she was starting to get more than a little dizzy from the blood loss. It wasn't all her fault… but that still didn't stop her anxiety-riddled brain from agonizing over whether those extra couple seconds would've made a difference if she'd gotten her shit together just a *little* sooner.

Cassondra's hand dove into Albertson's coat and pulled out the cigarette box, but her fingers were trembling so hard she could barely get one out.

"*Cass… help…*"

"*I'm trying!*" she screamed.

Albertson's voice was a dry, barely-audible wheeze. It sounded like the wind blowing over a cactus.

It did not sound *good*.

Finally, Cassondra managed to fumble one out and stuck it between his lips. Then she reached into his coat for a lighter, but he was struck with another violent bout of coughing that sent the cigarette flying out of his mouth. Cassondra found the lighter—an entire pack of them, because of course he carried extras—and scrambled to her feet, looking frantically around the inside of the cage. Where had the cigarette landed? God, no, why did that even matter, she could just fish another one out of the pack. But would he be able to keep *that* one in, or was he so far gone that he couldn't even smoke properly anymore?

Her eyes fixed on the bucket in the corner. Patrick Muntz's bathroom bucket. It looked relatively clean, but she didn't know how often they changed it out. She scrambled over to it. It was empty and it was dry. *Good enough.*

Cassondra emptied the cigarette box into the metal bucket—there were still about a dozen cigarettes left—and then broke one of the lighters open over it, dousing the entire contents with lighter fluid. Then she lit another one of the lighters and dropped it in. There was a small *whuf!* sound, and smoke immediately started billowing out of the bucket. She picked it up and ran back to Albertson.

He wasn't coughing anymore. He wasn't moving. He was just sitting in the chair, his eyes closed, his head drooped, a thin line of drool trickling out of his mouth.

Tears were streaming down Cassondra's cheeks and as she shoved the bucket into Albertson's face.

"*Here!*" she shouted. "It's here! All the smoke you need! Albertson!" The smoke was pouring out of the bucket and around Albertson's head, enveloping it completely, but he wasn't waking up. His eyes were still closed. His head was still lowered. His chest wasn't moving. "*Jeff!*" Cassondra sobbed, her bosom heaving. "*Breathe!* It's okay, you can breathe now! You just need to breathe!" Between the tears and the smoke, she could barely see anymore. Her legs were quivering beneath her, and she felt like she was going to collapse at any moment. The world was spinning around her. She fell forward, onto Albertson, doing everything she could to keep the pillar of smoke still pointed at his face. "*Why?*" she whimpered, so quietly it came out as little more than a shrill whine. "Why aren't you *breathing?*"

CHAPTER 27

Jacob Kirkman ran through the catacombs as fast as his legs would carry him. He only heard one distinct set of footsteps behind him—those of his wife, Luna—but hovering at some indistinct point between them was *it*: Patrick Muntz, barefoot and galloping on all fours, rendering him almost silent except for that constant sick, wet *panting*, like a rabid dog, like one of the hounds of Hell itself. It was impossible to tell how far that panting was from him; he could've already lost it, or it could be right behind him, just waiting for the smallest little slip up, for him to trip, for him to tire, for him to pause just for a moment to look behind him.

Look behind him…

No.

Better not to risk it.

Best to just keep running.

"*Gonna getcha, boy*," a voice said, either a million miles away or right behind his ear. "*Had my eye on you for a looooong time, boy-oh-boy-oh-boy. Don't worry, though. It'll be worth the wait.*"

Jacob rounded a corner in the hallway, and took the left side of a fork in the path. He was familiar with these passageways; he'd been down here a hundred times before. Maybe that would work to his advantage. Maybe *it* would get lost down here and he would be home free, able to rest for a moment and make his way to the exit at his own pace without the constant sword of Damocles hanging over his—

"*Don't mind the runnin' none, either*," the voice behind him said. "*All those hormones pumpin' through your kidneys. Adrenaline. Sweat. Fear. Just makes the meat that much more...* savory."

Jacob Kirkman closed his eyes. Tears dribbled from the corners of his eyes and were swept away by the constant wind of his own locomotion. His mouth opened, not entirely of his own control, and let out the piercing wail of a wild animal on the Serengeti that knew the lions were upon it, that knew its time was up.

No.

Please, God, no.

He knew these passageways. He knew these corridors. He knew the way out. He was *so close* to the exit. If he could just reach the exit before *it* caught up with him.

The steps were beneath his feet. Jacob Kirkman took them two, three at a time. Winding upwards, spiraling around the central pillar, to the trap door in the floor of the Oval Office. How many steps was it? He had walked this staircase so many times, he ought to be able to count the steps. The exit was near. It *had* to be.

He could feel *its* breath on the back of his neck. Or could he? His lungs were burning. The joints in his legs were screaming. He was sweating more than he thought his body was physically capable of. His entire face felt like it was going to burst open, like a zit. Maybe it was all an illusion. Maybe *it* was lost far behind him, and he was already in the clear.

But he didn't dare stop to look behind him.

It didn't matter, anyway. He already was almost there, regardless. Only a couple more steps…

Jacob Kirkman burst up through the trap door into the Oval Office, and he didn't stop. His legs pounded like pistons, making a bee-line for the door out into the rest of the White House. The door was the only thing that mattered. There were other people out there. Guards, maybe. Secret Service. Someone. They would be able to help. Even if his body immediately gave out on him, even if his legs snapped beneath him like twigs and he was never able to run again, if he could make it out into the open, where the other people could see him, he knew he would still survive. His fingers brushed against the polished bronze knob that adorned his singular portal to salvation, and with just the tiniest suggestion of a smile on his lips, Jacob Kirkman allowed himself one millisecond-brief glance back over his shoulder…

…And felt his ankle twist out from under him as it collided with some unseen obstacle on the floor. In the half-second before Jacob Kirkman's body collided with the ground, the world around him seemed to slow down. It was so unfair, he thought. He had only taken his eyes off the path ahead of him for a moment. Maybe if he'd been watching where he was going, he'd have been able to step over whatever it was that had tripped him.

His eyes darted over to that mysterious something, now that he had an eternal moment to think. He saw what it was, but didn't immediately recognize it. It was round, about the size of a soccer ball, pinkish-white, with a couple odd holes drilled into it. And it was hard to the touch, and heavy, so maybe it was a bowling ball instead of a soccer ball—

It was a skull.

It was Frank Donaldson's skull.

This is where Albertson's pig had brought the head after it had chewed all the flesh off, and somehow no one had noticed it before now.

He was going to die because he had tripped over Frank Donaldson's head.

That was the last semi-coherent thought to cross Jacob Kirkman's mind as he slammed onto the floor of the Oval Office, Patrick Muntz pouncing down on top of him half a moment later like a great jungle cat.

Jacob Kirkman tried to wriggle out from under Patrick Muntz's weight, to kick him off, to struggle, *anything*, but it was no use. He had completely exhausted himself in the chase, just as Muntz knew he would, and even if he hadn't… Patrick Muntz was a force of nature. Patrick Muntz could not be stopped. *Patrick Muntz was God.*

"*Kidneyyyyys!!!*" Patrick screamed as he triumphantly ripped off Jacob Kirkman's shirt, then sunk his teeth into the soft, tender flesh on the side of the man's abdomen.

Jacob Kirkman let out a wailing, squealing shriek, so shrill and high pitched that many would have doubted it had even come from a human. His arms flailed wildly, bluntly pounding Patrick Muntz about the head and shoulders, but the man was latched onto his side like a tick, slowly *chewing*, burrowing himself deeper and deeper into Jacob Kirkman's warm, life-giving body.

Finally, when he *and only he* decided he was ready, Patrick Muntz placed his hands on Jacob Kirkman's body for leverage and pulled his head back, ripping a great strip of flesh from the body of his prey, then immediately spat it out. Patrick Muntz was a proud hunter; he wasn't just content with skin and muscle. No true hunter wanted anything other than the delicious organ meats, still raw and bloody and warm, fresh with the taste of the prey's only-recently-departed precious life force. While his prey still helplessly kicked and screamed and fought against the sad inevitability of its own fate, Patrick Muntz's head drove itself fully into the open wound he had just opened in its side, into where the *real* treasures lay.

"What the fuck is going on up here?!" Luna shouted, throwing the trap door open again and climbing out. "It sounds like someone's torturing a goat!"

Patrick Muntz stood up. And turned. Slowly. His mouth and most of his chest were covered in blood. His eyes were on her now. They were the eyes of a beast. She had his full attention.

The color drained from Luna Donaldson's face.

"Oh… oh my…"

The words couldn't quite come to her. She felt like she should swear, but she knew no words in the English language foul enough to properly condemn the scene she was seeing before her eyes. She had a brief, fleeting impulse to pray, but she was not a religious woman. And even if she had been, she knew not which God she should choose, for surely none of them were listening on this day.

Patrick Muntz took a step towards her. And he *smiled.* The smile of Patrick Muntz was death incarnate, it was the silent screams of those who had died unborn, it was what the vilest demons in the deepest, darkest pits of Hell saw in their most traumatizing nightmares. Patrick Muntz took another step towards her. Luna Donaldson had never been so sure in her entire life that she was about to die.

"Excuse me, Ma'am," Tyler LaFuente said, pushing past her as he climbed out of the trap door. "Did you see where—ah, there we go!" Tyler aimed the barrel of his shotgun so that it was level with Patrick Muntz's chest. "Just one quick—"

Patrick Muntz ducked just as Tyler fired, dodging the majority of the buckshot and scrambling himself towards them on all fours at a sickeningly uncanny speed.

"*Shit!*" Tyler screamed. He lowered the shotgun and pointed at the floor and fired again, blasting Patrick Muntz square in the back. "Jesus," he muttered. "Thank God for double-barrels, am I right—"

"*He's still moving!*" Luna shrieked, pointing down at. Muntz and he dragged himself towards them with the one arm that was still functioning.

"*Heh… heh… heh…*" it was somewhere between a laugh and a pant, made wet and gargled by the blood that was slowly filling up Patrick Muntz's lungs.

"Shit!" Tyler screamed again, scrambling backwards and fumbling with a new cartridge, desperately trying to reload. "Shit shit shit shit shit shit shit shit—"

The gun snapped shut. Tyler fired again.

Now half of Patrick Muntz's face was missing. His arm slumped limply forward and grabbed Luna's pant leg, and he managed to lift his head up just high enough to give her was left of his toothy, blood-soaked grin one last time.

"*Heeee...*"

One more shotgun blast. There was nothing left of Patrick Muntz's upper half except a single arm and a pile of red mush.

Luna Donaldson stood in place, frozen. Her eyes were open and unblinking. Her gaze was locked straight ahead of her. She was not looking at anything.

"Mother of God," Tyler breathed. For a couple seconds he just stood there, panting, gun still held at the ready just in case the man-sized blob of chum that used to be the Vice President somehow got back up for another round. Then, finally, he nodded quietly to himself and knelt down. "Um, here, Ma'am," he said. "Let me get that for you."

"...huh...?" Luna Donaldson said. She looked down. Patrick Muntz's disembodied arm was still clutching her pant leg. She stood perfectly still while Tyler pried the fingers off and tossed the appendage aside.

"Tough little bugger, wasn't he?" Tyler said.

"My... my husband..." Luna said. Her voice was quiet and distant. "Someone call a doctor for my husband."

Tyler arched an eyebrow at her, then marched out into the ransacked, blood-soaked remains of the Oval Office. He was just about to turn around and return to her when he saw something that made even him gasp and have to choke down vomit.

Jacob Kirkman was lying on his back, on the ground, spread eagle. Or, at least, what was *left* of him was. His stomach had been completely torn open and entrails were spilled everywhere, covering the floor, splattering the walls, even something red and wet and solid dangling from the ceiling. His actual abdomen appeared to be all but empty, a gaping red pit with the jagged stumps of a couple stray, shattered rib bones poking out from the edges. There was more of Jacob Kirkman's body covering the various flat surfaces of the room than there was actually *inside* Jacob Kirkman's body.

Still, somehow, through it all, Jacob still looked up at him, his eyes wide and uncomprehending, too shocked even to cry. His eyes were asking a question Tyler did not have the answer to, while his mouth continually opened and closed, and opened and closed, in some profane parody of speech.

"Lady," Tyler said slowly. "There isn't a doctor on earth who can help this." He flipped open the barrel of his shotgun and loaded another round. "The most merciful thing we can do at this point is put him out of his misery."

Luna opened her mouth to speak, but no words came out. Tears came out instead. She closed her mouth and just nodded. Tyler saw her, nodded back, and gave her a military salute. Luna Donaldson turned around, closed her eyes, and covered her ears while Tyler LaFuente pointed the shotgun directly at Jacob Kirkman's face and pulled the trigger.

CHAPTER 28

Luna Donaldson floated through the catacombs like a ghost.

Well, not really. She did still have legs and feet. She just couldn't feel them.

Her path felt aimless and random; she wasn't intentionally telling her body to take her anywhere, just drifting. Finding herself in one cavern, then another, until she finally, somehow ended up back in the central cavern with Patrick Muntz's cage. She wasn't sure how.

Cassondra was still down there, sitting in the same chair where Luna had tied up Albertson, her posture slumped heavily against the back, a dull look in her eyes. She had one arm clutched up against her chest, putting constant pressure on the nasty cut Luna had given her. Cassondra's other hand idly playing with Luna's butterfly knife, spinning it between her fingers and clicking it open and closed. Luna gulped. Cassondra was much more adept with the knife than she would've expected. She wasn't threating Luna with it, though, just keeping it out. Making sure Luna knew she still had it. Just in case.

Albertson's body was lying at Cassondra's feet, surrounded by the slashed-up remains of the rope Luna had used to bind him. Cassondra had rolled him onto his back and crossed his arms over his chest. He was back in his human form, and as Luna stepped up to the doorway of Muntz's cage, she saw that the alien watch was back on his wrist.

Cassondra was glaring at her. Her eyes had been locked on Luna since the moment she entered the chamber. Still, she made no effort to move towards Luna, or even to get up from her chair, as Luna raised her hand and pointed a trembling finger at Albertson's wrist.

"You put that back on him?"

"Yeah," Cassondra said quietly. "It was how I knew him. It seemed, I dunno… respectful."

Luna lowered her hand and swallowed, then returned her gaze to Cassondra.

"Muntz is dead," Luna said. Her voice sounded far away and hollow.

"That's nice," Cassondra muttered. There wasn't a sliver of emotion in her voice. Without breaking eye contact, she continued doing tricks with the butterfly knife.

Luna's nose was running. Still trembling, she raised an arm up to her face and washed the snot off onto her sleeve.

"So… so…" she closed her eyes and started shaking her head. "…so is Jacob."

The sound of the butterfly knife stopped. Luna opened her eyes. Cassondra was just holding the knife still, for the first time since Luna had entered the chamber, and her eyes weren't fixed on Luna anymore. She was just kind of staring off to the side, lost in her own contemplation.

"I'm sorry," Cassondra finally murmured. She folded the knife back up and slipped it into her coat. Luna's arms instinctively crossed over her chest. She closed her eyes again and started nodding.

"Thank you," she whispered. For a couple long seconds, the two of them just stood across from each other in silence. Then, Luna finally knelt down over Albertson's body.

"It's very nice that you want to pay your respects," she said. "But we really shouldn't leave alien technology just floating around." She sniffed. "It's too dangerous if someone else finds it."

Cassondra wasn't looking at her. She just shrugged.

"Yeah, that makes sense," she finally said, her voice so quiet it was barely audible.

Luna started pulling the watch off of Albertson's wrist, but it wasn't easy. Jacob had been able to slip it off of him so easily before; why was she having trouble now? Albertson's wrist couldn't have changed that much since he died. Then she thought of something and paused.

"Wait," Luna said. "How do I know *you're* not an alien too?"

Cassondra moved her arm away from her chest, just for a second. Her blouse was soaked with blood.

"I bleed red," she muttered. Now, it seemed, Cassondra was doing everything in her power to *avoid* eye contact with Luna.

Luna just nodded. Albertson's watch was almost off.

"Okay. Good," she said thinly. "It's just, I was wondering how you got this watch thing to work again. It was damaged pretty badly the last time I saw it."

"Yeah," a terrifyingly familiar voice said behind her. "I was able to fix it."

The watch finally sipped off of "Albertson's" wrist, and his visage flickered away… to reveal *Leo Bronstein's* dead body lying on the ground in its place. Luna felt the blood drain from her face. She looked up. Cassondra was smiling a devilish, "*gotcha*" smile. She scrambled to her feet and whipped herself around just as Albertson's—the *real* Albertson's—hands seemingly came out of nowhere, grabbed her by the shoulders, and *threw* her back to the ground.

The room was spinning. Luna blinked a couple times. She was lying on her back, staring up at the ceiling. Albertson was looming over her in his alien form, a cigarette sticking out of his mouth, his chest heaving. She didn't know if that was because it still hadn't been very long since he'd almost suffocated to death, or just because he was really, *really* pissed. Either one would've made sense. Luna closed her eyes again. She didn't want to get up. She just wanted to lie here forever.

"*Fucking humans!*" Albertson bellowed. "Do you know how *sick* I am of watching you violent little monkeys just going around and *fucking up* everything you touch?!" He leaned down and grabbed the collar of Luna's blouse, hauling her roughly up onto her knees and holding her so that his face was only inches from hers. "I have spent the last couple months of my life trying to *help* you stupid sons of bitches!" He screamed in her face. "Cause you know what, no one *else* in their right mind is going to help you assholes, and you sure as fuck aren't capable of helping yourselves! And what fucking thanks do I get?!" Luna's eyes were scrunched shut as tight as they would go. Tears trickled down the sides of her face in thin streaks. Everything felt numb. "Some power-hungry little sociopath ties me to chair and tries to *fucking torture me to death!*" He threw her back onto the ground, hard. "*Humans!*" he shouted, throwing up his hands as he paced away from her. "*GOD!*"

Luna curled up into a little ball on the ground, hugging her knees close to her chest.

"Don't… don't hurt me," she stammered.

Albertson stopped mid-step, whipped around to face her again, and shouted, "Jesus Christ, you *still* don't get it?! I! Come! In! *PEACE!* I was *never* planning to—"

"Don't hurt me, Daddy," Luna whimpered. "I did what you asked me to, Daddy. Please don't hurt me again."

Albertson abruptly stopped. His eyes went wide. He stared at Cassondra. She stared back, with the same expression.

"I don't like it when the men touch me, Daddy," Luna whispered, rocking back and forth on the floor. "Why do you let the men touch me? I did everything you asked me to."

Cassondra was out of her chair, jogging over. Albertson was backing away from Luna, slowly.

"If this is a trick…?"

"*It's not,*" Cassondra said sharply, kneeling down next to Luna. "I've gone through espionage training. I've seen the best lying that people are capable of. This is real." She slowly lowered her hand onto Luna's shoulder, but immediately lifted it away when the woman flinched. "Hey," she said softly. "Luna?"

Luna turned her head towards Cassondra, but it was clear that she didn't "see" her. Luna's eyes were glazed over, looking at nothing in particular, and all of her movements were slow and loose, like she was underwater. Luna Donaldson had left the building. Her entire body was trembling. Cassondra took off her own jacket and draped it over the woman's shoulders, making sure that she didn't leave the butterfly knife in the pocket, and then softly walked away while Luna gently rocked back and forth in the corner, arms still clutched around her knees, eyes still focused on nothing.

Albertson knelt down to retrieve his watch and slipped it back on, his human disguise instantly flickering back into view.

"Jesus," he muttered, shuffling over to the chair and carefully lowering himself into it, until he was sitting hunched over with his head in his hands. "I just gave someone a trauma flashback. What the fuck is wrong with me?"

"I mean," Cassondra muttered, "she *did* try to kill you."

"Yeah, but can you blame her?" Albertson said. "I mean, for all the horrible things she did *before* that, *yes*, you can absolutely blame her, but when a big ugly space alien suddenly appeared out of nowhere in front of her…" he sighed. "The way she reacted to *that* part in particular, it honestly wasn't the *most* irrational thing she's done."

Cassondra shrugged.

"A big ugly space alien suddenly appeared out of nowhere in front of *me*," he said. "*My* first reaction wasn't to try and kill you."

Albertson let out a dry chuckle, in spite of himself.

"Yes," he said. "Thank you again for that. *All* of that. Everything you've done since you met me. Keeping my secret. Saving my life." He gulped. "Jesus Christ, I was right on the brink there, Cass. If you hadn't figured out to do that thing with the bucket…"

Cassondra idly waved it away as if it were nothing.

"Just imagine what I would've come up with if I weren't a panicky idiot," she said.

"No," Albertson sad evenly. "Don't do that to yourself. Don't sell yourself short. You are one of the most *terrifyingly* capable people I've met since I came to this planet, and you've had to put up with more than a lifetime's worth of bullshit in just the few days since you wandered into my office. *Thank you.*" He hesitated for a moment. "Um, all that other stuff I just said about humans? You know I didn't really mean—"

"You kidding?" Cassondra said, walking over. "At this point, I pretty much *agree* with everything you said." She sat down on the floor next to his chair. "And don't worry about all the help," she said. "You'll make it up to me."

Albertson laughed again, but it was a little more nervous now, a little more on edge.

"Oh, really?" he said. "Why? What did you have in mind?"

"Oh, I dunno," Cassondra muttered. "I'm sure I'll think of something. But you ought to be able to repay me pretty good. After all, you *are* the President now."

Albertson immediately sat bolt-upright in his chair.

"I *what?*"

Cassondra nodded.

"Donaldson's gone. Muntz is gone. Bronstein's gone. Lockhart just tendered her resignation." She glanced up at him. "That means you're next, bucko."

Albertsons hand was on his forehead. His eyes looked like they were going to bug out of his skull.

"Oh fuck," he breathed.

"Yep," Cassondra muttered.

On the other side of the cage, Luna let out a long, low moan. Cassondra and Albertson both snapped their attention towards her and got to their feet.

"It's not that I *didn't* want to follow in my father's footsteps," Luna said quietly. "It's that the question was never even asked. After he lost my brother, I was the only option left for an heir, so I simply *was* going to be his accomplice, full stop, end of story." She swallowed, and looked up at them. "Do you know what I did on my eleventh birthday? I helped my father feed paperwork and receipts from one of his failed business ventures into the fireplace. I was already taking part in international fraud before I'd had my first period." She sniffed. "By the time we were done, my father smiled at me and told me I'd done a good job. I think it was the first time he'd ever said that to me. At the time, it felt like that was my best birthday ever."

She looked away from them again, back into the thousand yard stare. Her body had stopped trembling, and she now sat eerily still.

"Then as I got older, I kept doing it, to make him happy. I married a rich boy with no personality whatsoever, to make him happy. I followed him into politics, to make him happy. There was no point in asking myself whether I liked what I was doing, or agreed with it. I simply *was* going to do it. That's just *how it was*."

They heard more footsteps echoing through the caverns, and all immediately tensed up until Tyler LaFuente finally came strolling through one of the entryways into the central chamber.

"Hey," he said. "There you are. This place is like a fuckin' maze." He stopped and stared at them, cocking his head to the side. "Um, is that Leo Bronstein?"

Cassondra and Albertson both looked down at the corpse at their feet, then back up at Tyler.

"Yeah," they said in unison.

"Jesus," Tyler muttered. "How many more bodies am I going to trip over in this fucking town?" He paused for a moment, still staring at them. "Also, why are you all sitting in a cage?"

Albertson and Cassondra both shot each other questioning glances.

"We probably should get out of this thing," Albertson said.

"Hey," Cassondra muttered, "I was just sticking around here because this is where the only chair was."

"Yeah, but we can move the chair!" Albertson said, walking over and picking it up. "The chair is portable! We don't have to stay in Patrick Muntz's old sex dungeon just to sit in the chair!"

"Fine!" Cassondra said, throwing up her free hand. "Whatever!"

While Albertson carried the chair out, Cassondra walked over, knelt down, and held her hand out to Luna. Luna just stared at it for a second, then took Cassondra's hand and let the girl pull her to her feet and lead her out of the cage.

"So what now?" Tyler said, as the rest of them walked out and formed a semi-circle around him.

"Well, I have the power to officially pardon you now," Albertson said. "So the good news is, I'll be able to honor my side of our bargain."

Tyler's entire posture stiffened.

"Um," he said. "I didn't know there was any *doubt* that you were going to honor our bargain."

"Oh, yeah!" Albertson laughed. "I was *totally* talking out my ass when we sprung you from prison. I mean, I wasn't lying that I *wanted* to clear your name, I just had no idea how we were going to do it." He chuckled a few more times, then put a hand on Tyler's shoulder. "But, I'm the President now, so, yeah. Full pardon. Go on, get out of here. Have a good life."

"Wait," Tyler said. "You're the *what now?*"

Tyler stared at Albertson, his face starting to go pale. For just the briefest fraction of a second, Albertson's holographic disguise flickered, so quickly that someone watching it still couldn't *quite* be sure that it hadn't just been a trick of the light. Albertson smiled warmly. Tyler gulped.

"Er, you *probably* want to keep a low profile, though," Cassondra said. "Pardon or not, people are still going to recognize you as the guy who shot the President on live TV."

"Eh, that shouldn't be a problem," Albertson said. "You're, like, a survivalist mountain man or something, aren't you?"

"*Yeah*," Tyler said, slowly backing away from them. "I got this little shack down south of the border I can go hole up in for a while—"

"*Don't tell us* where your secret hideout is!" Cassondra snapped. "Jesus Christ, don't you know anything about being a dissident terrorist? How have you even stayed alive this long, this is just embarrassing…"

"I, um, I think I'm gonna go now," LaFuente muttered, continuing to back away, still without taking his eyes off Albertson.

"Southeast tunnel leads to a cave in the middle of the woods," Albertson said, gesturing towards one of the caverns branching off from the central chamber. "Probably your best bet." He waved halfheartedly as he turned away from Tyler, who was practically tripping over his own feet in the mad dash towards the tunnel. "Toodles."

"You know," Cassondra said, narrowing her eyes as she watched him disappear into the darkness, "is it *really* a good idea to let the guy with a known history of political assassinations have access to D.C.'s secret underground tunnel network?"

"Oh, God no," Albertson said. "This entire thing has been a disaster waiting to happen. That's why my first act as Commander in Chief is going to be to flood this entire place with concrete and forget it ever existed."

"That's a good idea," Luna murmured, stiffly nodding to herself.

"Oh, shit, you're still here," Albertson said, reflexively flinching back. "Jesus, what are we supposed to do with *you* now?"

"Hey," Cassondra said, putting a hand on Albertson's chest. "Let me handle this one Jeff. Just go drag Bronstein's body back to the bunker, or whatever we're going to do with it, and forget Luna Donaldson ever existed. You're going to have enough on your plate."

Albertson arched an eyebrow skeptically.

"Are you sure?"

"Hey," Cassondra said. "I might be a terrible spy, but I *am* still a spy." Her eyes narrowed. "You know how to make up a fake human identity. I know how to make people who already exist *disappear*."

She flashed him just enough of the butterfly knife in her hand for him to make out the glint of the metal without Luna being able to see. It arguably wasn't even worth the effort of hiding it; Luna was still so dazed that she was only barely even aware of her surroundings.

"Luna Donaldson's going to go live on a *farm* for a while," Cassondra said as she led the woman away by the hand. "Where she'll be happy all the time and can be reunited with her missing brother."

Albertson leaned back, his eyes wide with surprise, and gulped.

"Oh," he muttered. "Well, shit… Remind me never to piss you off."

"Don't worry, *Mr. President*," Cassondra said as she folded the knife back up. She glanced back at him over her shoulder, so that he could make out just the corner of a dark smile. "I'm still the White House intern. I'll be around you every day. You won't *need* the reminder."

CHAPTER 29

Daphne Gould was out working in the field when she saw the big red pickup truck come rumbling up the dirt road, kicking up a cloud of dust behind it. *Again.*

"God dammit," she muttered under her breath. "What is it now?"

She immediately dropped what she was doing and ran up to meet it in the driveway. The truck started slowing down as soon as the driver saw her.

"What do you want?!" Daphne shouted at the truck. "I saw the news! I saw that you already did it! Congratu-*fucking*-lations, you fucking lunatic! What the hell do you want from us now?"

The truck came to a full stop and the driver's-side door swung open. But it wasn't Tyler LaFuente behind the wheel. It was a young African-American woman who Daphne had never seen before, wearing a plaid button-up shirt with the sleeves rolled up and a wide-brimmed straw hat with a thin leather strap wrapped around it as a chinstrap-slash-sweatband.

"Hi," the woman said, stepping out of the truck and slamming the door shut behind her before Daphne could see inside. She offered Daphne her hand. "My name's Cassondra Warren. I take it that you are Miss Daphne Gould?"

"Uh, yeah," Daphne said, taking Cassondra's hand and cautiously shaking it. "Who are you?" She craned her neck to look past Cassondra. "And why are you driving the truck that belonged to the guy who shot the President?"

Cassondra smiled.

"Because there are only a couple people in this country who *know* this truck belonged to the guy who shot the President," Cassondra said, letting go of Daphne's hand. “And I knew—at least in theory—that you were one of them. So I figured it would be a good way to get your attention. And to separate you from the rest of the crowd. If I’d warned you that I was coming ahead of time, or even just cold-called the front door, you might have been less than willing to announce yourself.”

“Oh?” Daphne said. She looked guilty, but was trying to ask like she didn’t. “And why do you think that I would be… less than… um…” She sighed. “Oh, fuck it, you know what I mean.”

“Yes,” Cassondra said. “I do. I figured you would’ve high-tailed it out of here, or at least told someone else in the house to cover for you, when you found out I was here on behalf of the United States government.”

Daphne felt her heart sink in her chest.

“*Oh*,” she said.

“Yeah,” Cassondra muttered. “You thought you were real clever, calling us through a payphone—and you’re right, it *did* make it incrementally harder for us to find you—but the resources we have were still more than capable of tracking you down eventually.”

“*Fucking fascists*,” Daphne hissed. Cassondra just shrugged.

“Well, you apparently don’t have *that* much animosity towards us,” Cassondra said. “Because you were the one who called in to warn us about the threat on President Donaldson’s life.”

“Yeah,” Daphne grumbled, folding her arms in front of her chest. “For all the good it did. You still let the asshole shoot him.”

“That is, admittedly, on us,” Cassondra muttered. “But you’re right in that it still wouldn’t have made *that* much of a difference.” She reached up and lightly pushed the brim of her hat out of her eyes. “It is still kind of *curious* that some anti-government hippie living out in the middle of the desert had the phone number for a classified bunker under the White House."

Daphne's posture stiffened, and she was starting to sweat.

"I, um, one of the other guys who lives here... *a lot* of them, actually, are ex-military, so I just asked if anyone knew how to contact the White House, and—"

"Daphne," Cassondra said, looking here dead in the eye. "I was able to dig up some information on you. It wasn't easy, and I didn't find a lot of it, but I did, for example, find out that your birth name is Frederick..."

Daphne's eyes narrowed.

"Yeah," she snapped. "A lot of trans people change their names when they transition. What about it?"

"...Frederick *Donaldson*."

Daphne just stared at Cassondra for another couple seconds, and then her entire posture just kind of... *fell*. Her head lowered, her back hunched down, and her shoulders slumped inward as she let out a sigh like she'd just been holding her breath for a thousand years.

"When I came out as a teenager," Daphne said, "my dad went ballistic. This was years ago, when he was still an actor, before he even dreamed of becoming President. But he still had connections. He threw me out of the house, out onto the streets, and then burned every scrap of evidence he could that I had ever even existed." A single tear slid down Daphne's face. "It was really hard for a while, but I eventually ended up living in a youth co-op in New York, started building a life for myself completely independent of him. But then, when he started his damnfool bid for the Presidency..." Daphne started shaking her head. "I just had to get away. His face was on every TV, people were arguing about him in every social media outlet... I had to go off the grid for my own sanity. So I came out here." She gestured out to the desert surrounding them, stretching off to the horizon in every direction, then looked up at

Cassondra, her eyes quivering. "He did everything he could to erase me," she hissed through gritted teeth. "And I finished the job for him."

"But when Tyler drifted through," Cassondra said, "with all his big talk about 'assassinating the President…' "

Daphne lowered her head again. That single tear finally relinquished its grip on her face splashed onto the parched desert ground.

"He's still my dad," she said quietly. "And I'm not like him. No matter how many horrible things he did, no matter how much I disagreed with and *despised* what he was doing to the country, the way he was hurting people… I still couldn't help but care about him." She started shaking her head and scrunched her eyes shut. "He was my dad."

Cassondra put a hand on Daphne's shoulder. Daphne leaned in and wrapped her arms around Cassondra, pulling her in for a hug.

"*Agh!*" Cassondra winced. "Ow! Still sore! Still sore!"

Daphne immediately pulled away.

"Oh my God," she said. "I'm sorry! Are you okay?"

Cassondra undid the top two buttons of her shirt and pulled the fabric aside to show a scar running horizontally along her chest, right under her collarbone. Daphne cringed as soon as she saw the wound. It was fresh; it still had the sutures in it.

"Just a flesh wound," Cassondra said, buttoning her shirt back up. "Docs said it'll heal up fine. Still hurts like a motherfucker, though."

"Jesus," Daphne breathed. "How did that happen?"

"A *very* spirited political debate," Cassondra muttered. "Anyway, it's not important. You're probably wondering why I came all the way out here, aren't you?"

Daphne took a half-step back and straightened her posture again, steeling herself for anything.

"Well, my father's dead," she said guardedly. "I'm assuming it has something to do with that?"

"Yes," Cassondra said. "But I wanted you to know that Tyler didn't actually kill him. Your father died of completely natural causes the day before the 'assassination.' What you saw on TV was…" she hesitated, "…*a body-double*."

Daphne exhaled slowly.

"That is good to know, I guess," she said. "It puts my mind just a little bit at ease. Knowing that I don't have to wonder anymore, if there was something more I could've done to stop Tyler."

Cassondra shook her head and pursed her lips.

"Wouldn't have made a difference," she said. "And, all things considered, I think Tyler ended up doing more good than harm once he made his way to Washington."

Daphne just stared at Cassondra like she was crazy for a second, mouth limply hanging open, then abruptly shook her head.

"I don't even… you know what, fine, whatever," Daphne said. "Well, I am glad that you told me all of this, but you could've done it just as easily over the phone. I don't see why you had to drive all the way out here."

Cassondra pointed back at the truck with her thumb.

"Your father," she said. "His body. He's in the back of the truck."

"He *what?*"

Daphne jogged over to the pickup truck and glanced into the bed. Sure enough, there was a black body bag sitting in the back.

"I figured you should have the remains," Cassondra said. "Considering you're family." More hesitation. "Also because you're the only person who even remotely liked him."

Cass wanted to add, "Plus he had so many enemies that his 'official' grave is probably going to be vandalized twice a week," on top of that, but decided it would probably be too much for the girl. Daphne was still just standing next to the truck, staring down at the bag.

"You, um, you might want to take a couple of stuff drinks before you look in the bag," Cassondra muttered.

"You know," Daphne said slowly. "My father was such an *angry* person. It didn't start with my transition, or with his launch into politics. As far back as I can remember, he just always had a bad word for everyone, a special insult he thought was so clever, a reason he thought *this* thing was overrated or why *that* person didn't deserve the reputation they had. I just accepted from a very young age that it was a part of who he was, and tried to love him in spite of it." Her hand lightly brushed a fold out of the fabric of the body bag. "And I know he hurt a lot of people during his life. Especially recently. The laws he made, discriminating against people, deporting people, putting people in *cages*. It is probably what he's going to be remembered for." She looked up at Cassondra, tears welling up in her eyes. "But I know he was not a happy man. Truth be told, he was probably suffering from some pretty mental illness, and was just too proud or too vain or too scared to ever have it diagnosed. He hated himself, he hated his life, and he didn't know what to do other than turn that hate outwards. Even when he was the President of the United States, the most powerful man on earth, that wasn't enough for him. He was never content. He was never happy." She lowered her head back down and closed her eyes. "I like to think that if he hadn't been so miserable, if he hadn't been constantly suffering himself, he might not have been so hateful towards other people. He only wanted to hurt those around him because he was hurting so much himself."

Daphne lightly kissed the tips of her fingers, then laid her hand down onto the bag that held her father's remains. Tears were welling up again.

"I am sad that my father is dead," Daphne choked out between sobs. "But I know that he was suffering when he was alive. And I know that he is not suffering anymore." She took in a deep breath and let it out slowly, broken up by several quick gasps. "And I know that he can no longer hurt anyone else around him, and I can take solace in that."

That's an easier sentiment to maintain when you haven't been to one of his fucking rallies, Cassondra thought, but she didn't say it out loud. Instead, she walked up behind Daphne and put an arm around her shoulders. Daphne glanced over at her nervously.

"Side-hug," Cassondra said. "Won't hurt as much."

Daphne smiled and returned the gesture, putting her arm across Cassondra's shoulders and pulling her close. While they both looked down at the body, Daphne reached up and wiped the tears out of her eyes.

"Heh," she muttered self-consciously. "If you think *I'm* a mess, you should see how much he fucked up my sister."

"Yeah, about that," Cassondra said. "That's the *other* reason I came down here."

Cassondra reached down and rapped three times on the metal side of the truck with her knuckle. There was a shuffling sound from inside the cab of the truck, and then passenger-side door popped open… and Luna Donaldson stepped out into the desert air.

Daphne's arm slid off of Cassondra's shoulders and her jaw hung slack. Luna stood on the other side of the truck, looking back at her, quietly hugging herself. She was wearing a plaid shirt similar to Cassondra's—they'd probably bought them at the same store—with the sleeves just a *little* longer than they needed to be, so her hands were obscured except for the tips of her fingers, and a baseball cap tucked down so that the brim obscured her eyes unless she wanted you to see them. Her natural brunette hair color was starting to show through the blonde dye, and she just looked *different*, somehow. She looked like she'd aged about thirty years in the decade or so since Daphne had last seen her.

Daphne slowly walked around to the side of the truck where her sister was waiting for her. Luna just stood in place, following her with her gaze, until the two of them were standing just a couple inches across from each other.

"Luna?" Daphne said.

Luna's eyes suddenly scrunched shut and she fell into Daphne's arms, sobbing.

"I'm *sorry*," Luna blubbered.

Daphne instinctively started patting her on the back and stroking her hair.

"I know… I know," she whispered. "It's going to be okay."

"I was thinking she could stay here for a while," Cassondra said, walking around the side of the truck to join them. "Work at the commune with you. I think it'd do both of you some good."

Luna pulled away from the hug and glanced back nervously at Cassondra.

"Will I be safe here?" she murmured. "I mean, I have a lot of really powerful enemies," she looked down at the ground sheepishly. "Most of them with *pretty legitimate* reasons to want me behind bars… *or worse*."

"I'm currently the only person on earth who knows that either of you are here," Cassondra said. "And I'm not going to tell anyone if you don't."

"But Albertson…?"

"He didn't ask," Cassondra muttered, "and I didn't tell." She took out Luna's old butterfly knife and idly ran her finger up and down the flat side of the blade. "I'm pretty sure he thinks I took you out into the woods and 'put you down' like a rabid dog, and I see no reason to tell him otherwise. Better that he doesn't worry himself about you anymore, and better that he thinks I'm more of a cold, hard badass than I actually am."

Luna hesitated for a moment, the words balancing just on the tip of her tongue.

"Are you sure we can trust him?" she finally said. "Even though he's, *you know...?*" She held up her index fingers on either side of her head to mimic alien antennae.

"Oh, implicitly," Cassondra said, as she started flipping and twirling the knife between her fingers. "I trust President Albertson with my life, and the lives of everyone around me."

"But how can you be *sure?*"

"Before he became President himself, when he was just forging your father's signature, he signed a couple bills to reduce greenhouse emissions," Cassondra muttered.

Luna almost laughed.

"What?" she said. "So he's a good guy because he cares about the environment?"

"No," Cassondra said. "Well, I mean, *yes*, but not exactly." She glanced up knowingly. "His people breathe smoke, Luna. They *thrive* on pollution. Cleaning up the atmosphere will actively make it *harder* for them to invade." Cassondra smiled. "He hasn't just proven that he's willing to help us... he's willing to help us *at his own people's expense.*"

"Um," Daphne said slowly. "What are you two talking about?"

"It's not important," Cassondra said quickly, holding up her hands and shaking her head. Then she returned her attention to Luna. "But you are right. It would be unwise not to still keep an eye on him. So, *just in case* something goes wrong, I've still got you two. And Tyler left a map leading to his Mexican safe house in the truck—the fucking idiot—so I know where to find him if I ever need a trained assassin for anything. And I should probably track down Senator Lockhart and tell her it's safe to come out of hiding. *And* I know how to fritz Albertson's hologram watch thingy. And, I mean, *absolute* worst case scenario, I know all I need to do to slow him down is to throw a bucket of water in his face." She neatly folded the knife back up with one hand and slipped it back into her pocket. "I sincerely hope that I will never need any of those safeguards. And I genuinely doubt that I will. But, you know... *just in case*."

Luna smiled weakly.

"Ooh, look at you," she said. "You're in business for yourself. I like it."

Cassondra shrugged amiably.

"I just want things to be better," she said. "For people." She started walking back towards the driver-side door of the truck. "Which reminds me," she said, glancing back at Luna, "You can have as much time here as you need to just chill and figure things out. But we know you have good leadership skills. *Great* leadership skills, in fact. If you wanted to get a little more actively involved, you could be invaluable to an organization like this, with all the political outreach they do. Once you've worked your way up to it, of course." She paused for a moment. "You know, *if you wanted to*."

Daphne put her hands on Luna's shoulders and held her out at arm's length, staring at her doubtfully for a moment, then glancing nervously back and forth between her and Cassondra.

"Really?" Daphne said, with palpable skepticism in her voice. "*Her?*"

"Yeah," Cassondra said. "Luna? Tell Daphne what you told me. I think she needs to hear it from you."

Luna nodded and took a step back so that Daphne's hands fell from her shoulders. She lowered her head and took a long, deep breath, then raised her head and straightened her posture, seeming to magically gain three inches of height while Daphne watched. She opened her eyes and gazed into her sister's with a calm and confidence that Daphne finally recognized. And even, to Daphne's shock, a hint of a genuine—albeit nervous—smile.

"Daphne," Luna Donaldson said, her eyes sparkling with their own internal light. "I want to help people."

CHAPTER 30

Albertson's watch had undergone so many repairs, it only barely looked like a watch anymore. There were wires sticking out of it, random pieces cannibalized from portable radios and pocket calculators that he'd grafted onto it as spot-repairs, and more than a little bit of duct tape. But, it was working—better than it had in a long time, actually—and that was all he really cared about.

"This is Advance Invasion Scout Theyjey Drizzl," Albertson said, holding the face of the watch up to his mouth. "Earth designate 'Jeff Albertson,' calling Captain Krelibon Scooch of the Skreeez Imperial Vessel Ackgatackgatack. Or pretty much anyone from the planet Katonk who can pick up on this signal." He tapped lightly on the face of the watch. "Hello? Anybody there?"

No response. Albertson sighed.

"Well, if and when anybody *does* get this message, I just wanted to report that my mission has been going pretty well. Like, *really* well, actually. Um. Okay, so I kind of *ended up* as President of the United States—that's, like, the most powerful leadership position in the most powerful nation-state on the planet. So, um, I'm basically in charge of the entire planet now. Yeah."

He paused again. He wasn't even sure what kind of a response he was waiting for, or if he even expected one at all.

"So, you know, I can just, like, *instantly* declare the planet earth a colony-world of the Skreeez Empire any time I feel like it. You know? Just gotta give me the order and I can carry it out. Just waitin' on the order…"

Silence. President Albertson sighed.

"Well, let me know if you get this message," he said, "and if you ever change your minds and want me to take over earth. I'll be here. Oh, but you gotta do it within the next eight earth-years or so, or else I won't be able to help you anymore. And even that's probably being generous, cause that would mean I got reelected, and I don't know if I'm even going to *run* for another term, and—you know what, that's not important right now. Right now, my mission will remain in standby and I will continue to act as the President of the United States to the best of my ability until I've received further orders. So, um, just let me know. Okay. Bye."

Albertson lowered his arm to his side, leaned back in his chair, and let out another sigh. He was at his desk in the Oval Office—after they'd had a number of different cleaning crews go over it to get all the blood out—with a stack of urgent paperwork in front of him. And, of course, a cigarette in his mouth. Squeally Dan was curled up in a little dog bed next to his desk snoring lightly. He reached down to scratch the pig behind the ear for a couple seconds, then returned his attention to his desk and started reading through the latest budget proposal from the Senate. It wasn't all that different from what he'd been doing as Secretary of State—especially with all the extra duties he'd taken on back then—but it somehow felt higher-stakes now.

"Glad to know I'm not the only one who sucks at leaving voicemails," Cassondra said. She was lying on one of the couches in the Oval Office, typing something into her phone.

"You sent a video of yourself *mooning* the camera to your spymasters in the Chinese government," Albertson said, glancing up from the paper. "I don't think that really counts as a 'voicemail.' "

Cassondra just shrugged.

"If I've officially, well and truly defected," she said, "I just feel a little better having everyone know exactly where I stand."

"I see," Albertson said coolly. "Is that why you asked *me* to moon them too?"

Cassondra smiled.

"Hey, if I'm the only one doing it, they might think it's a prank, or I just got drunk or something," she said. "But flashing my cheeks with the President of their greatest rival country in the room? *That* sends a message."

Albertson just shrugged and returned his attention to his work.

"At least you waited to piss them off until *after* you'd used their espionage network to reunite all the families separated at the border. Did they ever ask you *why* you were using the full information resources of the Chinese government to keep tabs on a bunch of poor migrant families?"

"They did indeed," Cassondra said. "That's about when I sent them the video."

Albertson stifled a chuckle, which morphed into clearing his throat.

"At any rate," he said, "thank you for doing that."

There was a brief pause.

"I didn't do it for you," Cassondra said quietly. "But on that same note, thank *you* for finally closing down those disgraceful fucking camps in the first place."

Albertson got quiet. His face didn't show any visible reaction, but Cassondra could see that his eyes had glazed over a little, and he wasn't really focusing on his paperwork anymore.

"Same thing," he finally said. "I didn't do it for you." He shook his head, seemingly needing a moment to come back down to reality. "So you're not afraid they're going to come after you now?" he said. "The Chinese government, I mean. Now that they know you're not on their side anymore?"

"They'd have to admit that I exist first," Cassondra said. "Even if they were feeling that petty, I'd be dead of old age before my death warrant made it through all the bureaucracy over there. Trust me, I'll be fine." She gestured towards Albertson; more specifically, his watch. "What about your guys? Do you think they're actually gonna get back to you?"

"I don't know," Albertson muttered, returning his attention to his paperwork as he talked. "I was sending out, like, a dozen messages a day when they first stranded me here, and they didn't respond to any of those. I think they might have blocked my number."

Cassondra had to stifle a laugh.

"So the odds of us getting invaded by aliens before your term runs out are…?"

"Laughably small," Albertson grumbled. "Which is honestly probably for the best."

"Yeah, I'd say so," Cassondra said, swinging her legs around and hopping back to her feet. "Speaking as someone who would be one of the poor, subjugated natives if they did show up and start cracking heads."

"You kidding?" Albertson said. "One of Katonk's houses of government is made entirely of representatives from the planets they've conquered. You'd be a shoe-in for the job." He smiled. "You'd probably walk out of an invasion with more political power than me."

"Ha-ha," Cassondra said, walking over to his desk. "I'm starting to think I'd like your home planet."

Albertson shrugged.

"It's remarkably chill for an imperialistic empire," he said. "You'd need a breathing apparatus, though, unless you plan to take up smoking."

"No chance in hell," Cassondra said, waving away the lingering smoky cloud as she leaned over his desk and glanced at his paperwork. "I get more than enough secondhand smoke anyway, just from hanging around you."

Her phone buzzed, and she immediately slipped it out of her pocket again and checked the notification.

"Anything good?" Albertson said.

"Tyler LaFuente just resurfaced again. He made his way to Mexico somehow, and they're refusing to extradite him as kind of a 'fuck you' to the previous administration."

"I have no real problem with that," Albertson muttered. "What's he up to?"

"Well, the good news is, he just went public exposing to the world that you're secretly a space alien."

Albertson immediately sat bolt-upright and grabbed the armrests of his chair.

"*He did what?!*"

"Yeah," Cassondra said, without looking up from her phone. "Apparently he caught enough glimpses of the real you and was able to put two and two together. Just posted a video of himself talking about it on all his social media."

"How is this a *good thing?*" Albertson stammered.

Cassondra slipped her phone back into her pocket.

"Because now that that already-dubious idea has been introduced by the visibly insane man who was responsible for killing the last two Presidents, nobody is ever going to take it seriously again."

"Oh," Albertson muttered, leaning back in his chair and relaxing a little. "Yeah, okay."

"This is honestly the most helpful thing he possibly could've done for us," Cassondra said. "Maybe we should send him a fruit basket or something."

Albertson snorted playfully.

"Thanks for the suggestion, but I don't think that will be necessary."

Cassondra flashed him a mischievous smile.

"What about a basket of *alien* fruit from your home planet?"

Albertson glanced over to her and arched and eyebrow.

"What, you mean just to fuck with him?"

"Yeah," Cassondra said idly. "And so that he'll post another video ranting about it and make himself look even crazier."

"That is fucking evil," Albertson said. "I love it. I've got some seed samples that I smuggled off of Katonk hidden in my apartment. I'll have them to you by Friday."

"Wonderful," Cassondra said. She put her hands flat on his desk and glared at him with the sternest expression she could muster. "I *am* serious, though, about sticking around to keep an eye on you, '*Mr. President*,' " she said. A hint of a smile. "Someone has to."

"Heh. I wouldn't have it any other way," Albertson put down the budget report and started idly shuffling the other documents on his desk into something resembling an order of importance. As Cassondra took her hands off his desk and stood up, he glanced up at her, smiling nervously. "But, I mean, you know I'm on the level, right?" His smile faltered for a second, then forced itself to return. "Like, after everything we've been through, you *know* I'm one of the good guys…*right?*"

Cassondra smiled.

"Of course I do," she said, turning around and walking away from his desk. "That's why I'm tolerating having an alien in the White House in the first place. Because I know it's you." She lay back down on the couch and resumed whatever she was doing on her phone. "A word of advice, though? You may want to go into your holographic disguise thing and lighten your skin tone a couple shades. If people start sniffing around and asking for *your* birth certificate, we're fucked."

EPILOGUE

Kate Phoenix sat on the couch in her living room, arms folded across her chest, with a simmering glare fixed on the woman sitting across from her.

It was the short Black woman who, just a few weeks prior, had shown up at Kate's house at some ungodly hour in the morning to try and pitch her on a role in a science fiction movie. Kate hadn't bothered to remember the woman's name, but she had introduced herself as "Cassondra," which Kate wasn't quite sure was the same name the woman had given the first time she'd visited. *Whatever*. Now "Cassondra" was back, albeit at a much more reasonable hour in the day and, to her credit, wearing a much more embarrassed expression, befitting the reason for her visit.

"You lost the head?" Kate said indignantly.

"Yeah..." Cassondra muttered sheepishly. She couldn't even bring herself to make eye contact with the actress. There was a cloth tote bag sitting limply on the couch next to Cassondra; Kate Phoenix hadn't seen what was inside the bag yet, and at the moment she didn't particularly care.

"*And* the movie deal fell through?" Kate said sharply.

"Er, right," Cassondra muttered. "*Fell through*."

"*Christ*," Kate Phoenix grumbled, standing up from the couch and starting to pace around the room. "I knew letting you walk out of here with that head was a risk when I gave it to you, but I figured it would be worth it if I at least got a paycheck and a career boost out of it. But now I've got nothing!"

"Well," Cassondra said quickly, reaching over and fumbling with her tote bag. "I wouldn't quite say *nothing*."

"Do you know how long it took me to make that papier-mâché head?" Kate Phoenix snapped. "It was one of a kind! I'm never going to have anything like that again!"

"I understand why you're upset," Cassondra said as calmingly as she could while she opened up the bag. "And, okay, yes, I did lose your fake President Donaldson head. And I am deeply sorry for that." She pulled something out of the bag, something round and white and freshly polished. It took Kate Phoenix a moment to realize what it was, but as soon as she did her eyes went wide and a hand rose up to cover her mouth. "But if you'll just hear me out," Cassondra continued, "I think I've got you a pretty sweet consolation prize..."

ABOUT THE AUTHOR

Mallory is a writer and cartoonist based in Los Angeles, California. Their other work includes the novel *But It's for Charity!*, the graphic novel *Egg Behavior*, contributions to the horror anthologies *Monsters, Movies & Mayhem* and *Doors of Darkness*, and a whole mess of short stories published as backmatter in single-issue comic books from Ahoy Comics. Typing out a list of their previous work is always awkward, because half the titles are a full sentence long and contain their own punctuation. Follow them @malloryjustmallory

Made in the USA
Monee, IL
18 March 2025

14009857R00152